Dirty Books

CARLIE & ADAM

THE ONE NIGHT STAND CLUB
BOOK TWO

CARISSA KNIGHT

Prologue

CARLIE

Carlie Taylor doesn't exist—*not tonight.*

Instead, I'm gonna shed her like a skin—leaving behind the woman fraught with self-doubt, obsessed over every curve, and prone to clumsy missteps. Of which there are *many.*

No, *tonight,* I am Zoey Cummings, a veritable *sex goddess,* armed with unshakeable confidence and a voracious appetite for adventure.

Zoey takes what she wants—*from whoever she wants it.*

No burdens to bear. No repercussions.

At least, that's the plan.

Nestled in the familiar sanctuary of my car—just a whisper away from the venue, in fact—I retrieve the invite from my purse.

A shaky breath escapes my lips, and for a fleeting moment, I'm lost in the tactile dance of my fingers over the sumptuous dark paper—a detail I would have lingered on in one of my novels, painting the scene with words.

The gravity of the impending night makes my heart flutter as if I'm on the precipice of my own story's pivotal scene.

I can only wish.

No—no thinking like that. Not tonight.

Shaking my head, I refocus on the invite.

The beautifully handwritten letters spell out *'Zoey Cummings'*—a pseudonym that promises a night of liberation if I can just get my head in the game—*truly.*

This invite is more than just paper and ink—it's a golden ticket to an evening of seduction.

Hell, who am I kidding?

It's a spell to forget, too.

Am I truly ready to be untethered to the past? To my stupid ex?

The wounds from him are still raw, his memory a lingering shadow in my mind and on my heart.

No, I *need* this.

I need to obliterate the ghost of him, even if just for one *ephemeral* night.

Such a great word, ephemeral. It's really not used often enough,

Focus, Carlie—er, Zoey.

Fucksake.

With shakier hands than I care to admit, I turn the envelope over and gently pull out the card. Sparkly silver scrolling glistens on the black silky paper, and I read over the words once more, confirming the details that are already etched in my mind.

"Zoey, it is under the veil of night…" I whisper out loud, then fall into silence as I read on.

> *…that we invite you to an exclusive event, shrouded in mystery and desire within Club Nocté's Upper Tier. The promise of an unforgettable experience fills the air, beckoning you. Can you feel it?*
>
> *Elegance is your armor, a mask your shield. Indulge in fine cocktails and decadent treats, lose yourself to the experience, and let the night unveil who you truly are when the world isn't watching.*
>
> *The stage is set.*
> *The night awaits.*
> *All that's left is to step into the shadows and acquiesce to the adventure.*
> *The night calls.*
> *And your evening awaits.*
>
> *Club Nocté*

I have to admit, the magic and mystery of this invite have done its job well. The copywriter should be paid a hefty bonus, or something.

Nocté wove an alluring spell, captivating the author

in me in a way that hasn't been summoned out for a while. Props and golfers claps, for sure.

When the original notification of my 'exclusive membership' arrived months ago, a mix of emotions swirled within me. More mortification than thrill, to be honest.

To be selected for this secretive club as a consolation for being cheated on was not how I envisioned diving back into the world of dating.

If anything, it felt like a slap in the face.

How Nocté had learned of his indiscretion, I'll never know.

Yet, as I sit here, on the brink of an unknown encounter, the allure of escape and the promise of a mysterious night that I'll never forget is incredibly enticing.

It's been long enough.

Zoey Cummings is ready, even if Carlie Taylor is not.

Tonight, I choose the adventure.

Tonight, I choose to be *Zoey*.

Taking a deep breath, I open the car door, feeling the cool night air gently caress my skin. It's a small, yet poignant, reminder that I'm about to step out of my comfort zone in a big way.

The sounds of Superior at night surround me, a symphony of life that's both daunting and exhilarating.

This city has a reputation for being seedy—or at the very least, the darker one of the Twin Ports. Something about that feels so good. *Right.*

I straighten my dress, a sleek emerald number that

clings to my curves in all the right places—at least, I hope it does.

No, that's a Carlie thought.

I banish it and button my long coat against the breeze.

Throwing my shoulders back, I adjust my mask—a delicate piece of dark green lace that hides just enough to make me feel mysterious. Zoey would wear this with pride and a mischievous glint in her eye.

My heels click against the pavement as I make my way toward the hidden back entrance of Club Nocté, the thumping bass from inside growing louder with each step.

My heart races, not just from the nerves but also from the sheer excitement of what might happen tonight.

As I approach the door, a blond, broad-shouldered bouncer checks my invite, his eyes lingering just a moment too long on the name written in elegant script.

"Enjoy your night, Zoey," he says with a smirk, stepping aside to let me through.

"Thank you," I respond, taking the invite back and slipping it into my purse.

I step past the dimly lit doorway and into a stairwell that leads to an upper level.

Quite literally, *the Upper Tier.*

The transition leading to the seductive ambiance of Club Nocté is momentarily disorienting, but the soft music now piped in through hidden speakers, and the lush foliage strategically placed along the path invites me to proceed.

Now I know why Alice did it ...

This is like being invited into Wonderland.

The air is thick with anticipation by the time I reach the top landing. The soft murmur of conversation is punctuated by occasional laughter in the space beyond.

"May I take your coat?" the hostess asks, halting my progress.

I turn to her and smile. "Thank you, that would be lovely."

Her bright blue eyes survey me and I shrug it off, feeling far more exposed.

"Your mask is beautiful," she offers as she accepts my coat.

My fingertips trace the fabric and a smile floats to my lips. "Thanks, I thought so."

She tips her head before vanishing into the coat room behind her.

I take a moment to steel myself, letting my eyes adjust, as I take in my surroundings.

The club is even more lavish than I imagined—with rich, dark colors and plush velvet. The décor speaks of opulence and decadence, and a fresh thrill runs down my spine.

I'm at a—

"May I offer you a drink?" a server asks, appearing at my side with a tray of champagne flutes.

I nod, accepting a glass. "That would be lovely," I say, my voice steady despite the fluttering in my stomach.

With the glass in hand, I venture further into the club, paying far more attention than I should on walking straight and not spilling the champagne all over some unsuspecting guest.

A little bit of Carlie is still with me, it seems.

The alluring sound of violins playing through the speakers guides me to a large dining area and the crowd grows. The room is a tableau of intrigue—characters in a scene I might have written if I were back home and actually sticking to my deadline.

Laughter and chatter fill the air, every one a protagonist in their own story, hidden behind masks of mystery. Some share knowing glances, like old friends or old rivals —details I'd note as an author to hint at stories untold.

That thought makes my insides flutter again.

I take a sip of the champagne, the bubbles tickling my nose as I let the atmosphere wash over me.

I'm here to forget, to let go, and to embrace the new adventure that awaits.

And who knows? Maybe, *just maybe,* I'll find something—*or someone*—that will make the night unforgettable.

With that thought in mind, I lift my chin, square my shoulders, and walk into the room.

"Miss Cummings?" another hostess inside asks when I enter the space.

"How'd—?" I ask, turning to her with my eyebrows drawn.

She smiles sweetly. "We've been given specific orders to know each of our guests so we can tailor the experience for you. Now, if you'll follow me, I'll bring you to your assigned seat."

A hushed anticipation settles over the room as the lights dim, casting long, dancing shadows across the patterned walls. The flicker of candles becomes the heartbeat of the space, their warm glow softening the edges of masked faces and creating an intimate cocoon of secrecy and allure.

The transformation is swift but profound, and I feel the persona of Zoey enveloping me more fully, as if the dim light is a curtain, drawing closed and leaving Carlie firmly behind in the shadows.

The hostess, a vision of poise, really—guides me with a gentle hand on my elbow. She points to an open seat at a small, intimate table and I slide into it.

"Ladies and gentlemen, if I may have your attention, please," she begins, her gaze sweeping across the room, ensuring she has captured the attention of every attendee. Her voice carries a weight of authority that commands attention, even as it remains soft and melodic. "Tonight, you are embarking on a journey of connection and discovery. In the spirit of trust and intimacy, you will spend the evening with the person—or in some cases, persons—at your individual tables. We have taken great care in choosing your companions for the evening, seeking to create connections that extend beyond the superficial."

A murmur of curiosity ripples through the room, and I feel a prickling of excitement—*or is it apprehension?*—at the base of my spine.

What if they chose poorly?

"As we serve the first course, we invite you to share an experience of vulnerability and care with your companions. You are not to feed yourselves, but instead, nourish the person beside you. Speak of your desires, your fears, your dreams—let the masks you wear be the only barriers between you tonight."

The room falls into a hushed silence, the gravity of her words settling over us. A man slides into the seat opposite me and I can feel the intensity in his gaze as I turn, offering a small, tentative smile.

I don't dare look too closely as I try to quell the butterflies in my stomach.

The hostess gives a nod as if to say 'begin,' and the servers move gracefully through the room, placing plates of exquisite food in front of us.

There are chocolate-covered strawberries, watermelon, and other finger foods I have no name for. The aroma is tantalizing, a symphony of flavors waiting to be explored.

The entire room breaks out into a hum of conversation as we each turn to our prospective companions and partners for the evening.

If I were writing this as a story, I'd make sure the man beside me was the exact opposite of the real me. He'd be gorgeous, fit, and adventurous in every way.

But this is no story ...

My gaze drifts to him—a stranger cloaked in the anonymity of the night.

Who is he?

What stories lie behind those eyes of his?

Was the deceit that brought him here as difficult to overcome as it was for me?

The mystery entices me, and Zoey's boldness surges, eager to uncover the secrets hidden by his mask.

I pick up a large strawberry, its chocolate coating melting into my fingertips.

"Well," I start, my voice steady even though my heart has galloped away, "I suppose we should dive in."

His eyes, a stormy gray, meet mine, and I sense a flicker of curiosity in their depths. The corner of his lips tilts upward in a half-smirk as if he's both amused and intrigued by the situation as well.

Before he can speak, I extend my arm, the strawberry held between my fingers, and I can't help but notice the slight quiver in my hand—a betrayal of my inner turmoil.

I swallow hard, my heart thrumming wildly with the vulnerability of this sensual act.

The strawberry hovers before his lips, and for a brief moment, time stands still. There's a silent question in his gaze, an invitation to share more than just the sweetness of the fruit.

I take a deep breath, steadying myself, and gently press the strawberry to his lips.

He accepts it, his teeth grazing my fingers ever so lightly, sending a shiver down my spine. His eyes never leave mine, and in them, I see a spark of something indefinable.

Is it curiosity?

Interest?

I can't be sure, but it draws me in, compelling me to know more.

"So," I begin, my voice barely above a whisper, "tell me something real about yourself. Something you've never told a stranger before."

His pause lingers, and the weight of the unspoken stretches between us, taut as the violin strings being strummed in the background music.

"I've mastered the art of guarding secrets," he offers, his voice a hushed murmur that sends shivers down my spine. "But for you, tonight, I might be willing to share one." He leans closer, so close that the edges of our masks nearly touch. The scent of his cologne—a tantalizing blend of cedar and citrus—fills my senses. "Only if," he continues, the challenge evident in his stormy eyes, "you reciprocate with a truth of your own."

A torrent of emotions whirls inside me—curiosity, apprehension, excitement. His words are a dare, a high-stakes game of trust and revelation. But the night's theme revolves around vulnerability, doesn't it?

If I were writing this scene, my protagonist would face an internal dilemma—torn between self-preservation and the lure of the unknown.

Tonight, reality most certainly mirrors fiction.

My pulse races and the weight of my decision bears down on me.

Of course, I'm going to say yes.

After a heartbeat that feels like an eternity, I muster a sly smile, matching his challenge with bravado of my own. "All right," I whisper, my voice shaking with a blend of excitement and nerves. "Shall we trade truths, then?"

His lips twitch in response, a hint of satisfaction flashing behind his mask. But before he can answer, the lights dim even further, and a captivating melody fills the room, momentarily distracting us.

The game of truth—now hanging precariously in the air—promises a night that will either expose or ensnare.

It's a gamble—and the stakes have never felt higher.

Adam

"Okay, Adam, spill it. Who was she?" Dylan presses, his keen eyes cutting through my façade with unsettling ease.

Honestly, I don't know how he even does it. It's unnerving.

I take a swig of my beer, the chill of the liquid in stark contrast to the warmth spreading across my face. "Who?"

I play dumb, my gaze flitting across *Jaded Brews'* dimly lit interior. Couples are coupled up and those who are single cast hopeful glances at anyone who moves through the space solo.

Yet, my seemingly casual search is anything but. This weird desperation underlies each sweep of my eyes as I hunt for a flash of vibrant red in the crowd.

I shake my head. I shouldn't be looking—*shouldn't even be hoping.*

"Don't bullshit me," my best friend insists, leaning in with one of those tones that demands honesty.

I force a shrug, feigning indifference while my trai-torous heart races in rhythm with the music thumping from the jukebox. "I have no idea what you're talking about, man."

But who am I kidding? She's all I've thought about for the past two freaking days.

The mysterious redhead who turned a simple one-night stand at Club Nocté's masquerade event into something ... *inexplicable*.

I went seeking a night of forgettable fun, only to be left haunted by the memory of her.

"Adam," Dylan says, softer now, his spectacled gaze filled with concern as he snaps his fingers in front of my face. "Yep, focus. Right here—eyes on me. You've never been like this after a hook-up. What's going on with you?"

I shake my head. "I wish I knew, man. I wish I knew."

"Come on, you gotta give me *something*," he sighs, tapping the bar top with the bottom of his pint glass.

My older brother, Brian—also known as tonight's bartender and owner, flips him the bird in return. Then, he turns back to a sassy-looking blond at the other end of the bar.

Dylan chuckles under his breath before turning back to me with an expectant gaze. When I don't say anything, he snorts, "Just please tell me it wasn't Jillian again."

My beer nearly goes down the wrong pipe, and I cough, eyes watering. "What? *No.* God, no."

Again, he levels me with that knowing, x-ray stare. "You sure?"

"No way, man," I repeat, shaking my head. "That's—no, we're *completely* done. She made sure of that."

He narrows his eyes momentarily but nods. "Good. She's a bitch." Then, he jabs me in the chest with his index finger. "And you deserve better."

Fuck, he's not wrong.

Sighing to myself, I scan the room again, my heart holding onto this foolish hope that I might catch a glimpse of those red waves.

But it's like searching for a needle in a haystack, and I know it.

The city is too big—and besides, our tryst happened in Superior, Wisconsin. Not Duluth, Minnesota.

While the distance isn't profound—there's only a short bridge ride separating us—the distinction could be enough to ensure I never see her again.

Especially since the majority of my life happens in Duluth. It's part of the reason I went for it—that night with a stranger to get Jillian fully, and completely off my damn mind.

Well, it worked.

My stupid brain wanders back to Friday night at Nocté, and I'm flooded with memories of my mystery woman. She was different—adventurous in a way that I've never encountered before.

And sexy as hell ...

I've been with plenty of women, but for the most

part, they've all been the same. Attractive, confident, and *demanding*.

Despite their preening and high maintenance—*of course, I need to get my nails done again*—bullshit, I never really gave much thought to the fact that there were other types of women out there.

Women like her…

She was so different from the women I'd been choosing for myself. Shorter, definitely curvier …

I guess that was the point, too.

But the way she looked at me … Her green eyes were filled with mischief and promise, and it made something inside me ignite.

I became a different person with her.

Someone confident, vulnerable, but ready. *So ready.*

She was flirty, provocative, and she knew exactly what she wanted.

My neck heats as I think about all the positions—the commands she'd let slip past those gorgeous lips.

Again, I shift in my seat, but this time, to give my crotch more room.

And she wasn't afraid to let me explore, either. We pushed each other's boundaries, and it was … *exhilarating*.

I've never been with someone who was so uninhibited.

But it wasn't even that—it was the way she gave me everything. It was almost as if she knew the perfect places to touch, to kiss, to flick that tongue of hers … The way to edge me out and leave me desperately wanting more.

My pleasure was hers and vice versa.

Hands down, it was the hottest night of my life.

Now, all I can think about is whether or not I should go back to Nocté. Not for another fleeting one-night stand, but to find *her*. To get her name or her number—something, *anything*, more concrete than just a memory.

It makes me wonder if this is why the rules for Nocté's Upper Tier exist. Someone, somewhere, knows that for people like us—*like me*—it's hard to detangle the heart from physical pleasure. But sometimes, one night is all you need.

One night that will never be more.

I take another sip of my beer, trying to drown out the thoughts. But they're persistent, nagging at the back of my mind.

I want to see her again, *rules be damned.*

Dylan nudges me, pulling me out of my thoughts. "This isn't you, bro. You've been out of it all night and I need a wingman—or hell, a conversation will do at this point."

I force a smile, not wanting to dive into it right now. "Yeah, just ... *thinking.*"

He raises a quizzical eyebrow. "About her?"

I shrug. "Maybe."

Dylan shakes his head, chuckling. "Shit, she really did a number on you, huh?"

I laugh, but it's forced. "You have no idea."

Dylan takes one look at my face and shakes his head, pushing his thick-framed glasses up the bridge of his nose. "Alright, we need a change of subject. You're getting that faraway, sappy look again."

I roll my eyes, despite being grateful for the distraction. "I don't have a *'sappy look.'*"

"Yes, you fuckin' do," he counters, a grin playing on his lips. "It's the same one you had when you were crushing on Tamara back in high school. Remember? It was when you went through your vegan phase and you found out she was one, too."

I burst out laughing at the memory, shaking my head. "Okay, okay, maybe you have a point."

Dylan's grin widens, and he leans back on his bar stool, looking entirely too pleased with himself. "So, speaking of vegan disasters, do you remember Melissa?"

"The yoga instructor who tried to cleanse your aura with a bundle of sage?" I snicker into my beer bottle.

"That's the one!" he exclaims, his dark eyes lighting up. "Well, she came into the coffee shop yesterday."

"Oh, yeah?" I quirk an eyebrow, my lips sliding into a smirk.

He nods. "She brought her pet ferret. *On a leash.*"

I stare at him. "She has a pet ferret? And she brought it into the coffee shop?"

Dylan nods, his curly hair bouncing with the movement. "Yup. And you know what she named it?"

I shake my head, not sure I want to know.

"Chakra," he says, matter-of-factly.

"Of course she did," I say between laughs. "Only you, Dylan. Only you could attract someone like that."

He grins, shrugging nonchalantly. "What can I say? I'm a magnet for the wild ones."

I take another sip of my beer, the laughter fading as I look at my best friend. "Hey, Dyl ... You ever think about settling down? You know, finding someone ... *normal?*"

Dylan raises an eyebrow, his gaze turning thoughtful. "Normal's overrated. But yeah, I think about it sometimes. Not even *I* can have epic, mind-melding hook-ups *every* day."

"Have you ever?" I roll my eyes, but I can feel the smirk tugging at my lips.

He nods vigorously. "Oh, yeah. All the time."

"Shut up," I fire back, shaking my head.

He chuckles, raising the new beer Brian slid across the bar to him in a toast. "To the wild ones and the sappy looks they give us."

I can't help but laugh, clinking my bottle against his glass. "To the wild ones."

As we drink, the weight on my chest lightens, and the image of the redhead fades to the back of my mind.

For now, at least.

I take out my phone, quickly glancing at my schedule for tomorrow.

"Really? Checking your phone now? I'm hurt," Dylan teases, pretending to stab himself through the heart.

I snicker under my breath, locking the phone and putting it back in my pocket. "Just checking to see what time I need to head into work."

Dylan snickers. "You've been here drinking with me

for the past couple of hours and you just think to check that now?"

I shrug. "Didn't occur until just now. Normally, my times are pretty consistent, but I start training a new client tomorrow. My schedule is already so packed—and now they add this. I don't know why they didn't give them to Jillian."

Dylan laughs, shaking his head in mock sympathy. "Yes, it's truly shocking."

"What's that supposed to mean?"

"Seriously, dude?" He makes a pointed WTF face.

I stare at him.

He sighs heavily. "It's because you're the big-deal Instagram star. People actually want to train with *you*, not whore Barbie."

I huff a laugh at the colorful nickname for my ex, not really in the mood to dive into the intricacies of my social media status. "Yeah, yeah. In reality, it just means I have to wake up an hour earlier."

Dylan gives me a slap on the back, smirking. "Come on, man. Who knows? Maybe this new client will be a breath of fresh air. Something to shake up your routine. You need that right now."

I raise an eyebrow, the idea intriguing, yet unlikely. "Maybe. But I'm not holding my breath."

I glance at my phone one more time, the name of the new client is just another line in a sea of appointments. Unremarkable and unknown.

And yet, as I slip the device back into my pocket,

there's a strange flutter in my stomach—an inexplicable sense of anticipation that I can't quite shake off.

Probably the beer and Dylan's prediction, come to think of it.

I need to forget that night and focus on the here and now.

"Let's hit the road," I say, pushing back from the bar. "We've both got early mornings."

Dylan groans. "Don't remind me."

I slap him on the back. "You're the one who wanted to run a coffee shop, man. You have no one to blame but yourself."

He nods. "Don't I know it."

We throw down our cash to cover the tab and tip and I wave at Brian. He's busy talking to another patron, but he tips his chin in goodbye. Then, Dylan and I head out into the cool night air.

I can't shake this strange feeling. Like I'm on the cusp of finally breaking free from Jillian's shadow.

I throw a casual arm around Dylan's shoulders. "To new beginnings, eh?"

He chuckles, wrapping his arm around my waist. "And the mysterious women who make them happen."

Carlie

The shrill cry of my alarm wrenches me from sleep —a rude intrusion if you ask me.

Why did I do this to myself?

I bat at the clock with my eyes closed, miss it, and nearly tumble out of bed. With a little more vigor, and eyes semi-open, I reach out, silencing it with a loud slap.

It's too early in the morning—or maybe I was too late to bed. Last night's writing session stretched into the wee hours as I chased a muse that was as elusive as sleep is now.

Shaking my head, I force myself to sit on the edge of my bed. The darkness of my room seems to lean in close, whispering its doubts about this *new chapter* of my life.

The borderline excitement from signing up for a personal trainer to help me get back into shape is a distant echo now. Instead, it's been replaced by the groggy dread of reality.

Yeah, this might very well be a bad idea.

But there's only one way to find out for sure.

I manage a quick shower—just something to wake me up. The water is nothing more than a cascade of tepid motivation.

When I step out and towel off, I'm no more alert than I was before. Thank goodness for my coffee date with Lily before the madness begins.

Swaddled in a towel, my reflection in the foggy mirror is a bleary-eyed stranger.

If I were writing this day into a novel, the protagonist would be facing her moment of comedic doubt, teetering on the brink of a decision that could change everything —or have her crawling back to bed.

Bed seems the better option. Not gonna lie.

Instead, I go through the motions, hoping I find my motivation hidden in the actions. Or at least at the bottom of a *really* strong cup of coffee.

Clothed in optimism—also known as new workout attire —I find myself outside of my favorite coffee shop *'Bean There, Done That.'*

It's a cozy little establishment I sometimes like to write at and the place Lily and I agreed to meet up at this morning since it's on the way to the gym. The windows are fogged with the warmth of fresh coffee and early morning chatter.

Taking a deep breath, I hoist the strap of my gym bag higher on my shoulder and make my way to the door.

When I walk in, Dylan, the owner, is offering up small talk to patrons with the ease of someone who's found their niche in the early hours among the caffeine-deprived zombies of the world.

That wasn't too bad of a description.

Good job, Carlie.

I mentally pat myself on the back for that one.

"Rough morning?" Dylan asks, his tone light as I walk up to the counter to place my order.

"Something like that," I reply. I want to tell him that I'm about to meet my maker thanks to a personal trainer named Ada, but my mouth can't seem to form the words without yawning.

I spy Lily near the window, her posture as straight as her peppiness is unwavering. She's a morning person, bright and chipper like the first pages of a well-loved book—*comforting and familiar.*

Her smile beams back at me when our eyes meet and she has that *mind-blowing sex glow* about her. Oh, boy.

My mind instantly goes back to Friday night …

I pause at the memory, an unbidden smile flirting with the corners of my lips. Friday night was … *an adventure.*

A story I might write someday, if I dared. But for now, I carry that evening close like a secret.

The feelings it evokes are a jumbled script of sensation and emotion—scenes that played out under cover of darkness, leaving my reality tinged with a dreamlike quality.

If I were to put it into words, they'd be all metaphor

and innuendo—shadows dancing just beyond the reach of morning light.

"Carlie? Earth to Carlie—" Lily's voice snags me from my reverie, pulling me back to the here and now.

I tuck the memories and descriptions away, like pressing a treasured flower between the pages of a book. "Sorry, I was just ... thinking about a plot twist," I mumble, which isn't entirely a lie.

Lily's knowing smile tells me she doesn't buy it, but she lets it slide.

For the next half hour, we chat about trivial things, about her job and my writing, carefully skirting around the edges of Friday night. There's an unspoken agreement, it seems, that some chapters are left unshared, even between friends.

Though, I'm nearly certain she knows ...

She knows where I was headed on Friday night and perhaps even why. I haven't had the courage to ask her.

The coffee I sip is strong and grounding, a much-needed anchor for the day ahead. It doesn't erase the images that flicker at the edges of my consciousness, but it dulls them and brings me back to my purpose today.

My workout attire seems like a costume now—like it's nothing more than props for a role I've committed to playing. Much like the one I donned for the event at Nocté, if I'm honest.

While that was the role of a sexy, confident woman, the persona I'm trying on today is the healthier, stronger version of me I want to write into existence.

It's all about taking control of the narrative, isn't it?

Michael might have cheated on me because my weight was—

I stop that thought in its tracks, not willing to give it the power of voice, even in my head. I've given it enough airtime over the past few months and I'm stronger now.

Lily interrupts my thoughts with a light touch on my hand. "You know, I'm really proud of you, Carlie," she says earnestly, bringing me back to the moment. "This step—it's a big deal. I don't know that I could do it."

I nod, the corners of my mouth lifting in a grateful smile. "Thanks. I was super nervous to sign up, but thankfully, I managed to get paired with a woman named Ada. Should be less intimidating. Less ... I don't know, *judgy?*"

The word feels awkward, but it's the best I can do to describe the relief I felt when I realized I could be training with someone who might understand the struggle and not some beefed up guy who likes to add protein powder to his coffee.

"I get it." Lily nods. "And who knows, she might become a new friend. Or at least a cheerleader for the new Carlie."

A laugh escapes me, short and slightly hysterical. "Hopefully, the *new Carlie* isn't just a figment of my overactive imagination."

Lily gives my hand another squeeze. "She's real. She's *you*. Just waiting for her cue to enter stage right."

I mull over her words, turning them over in my mind like I would a particularly powerful line in one of my novels. My characters often surprise me, taking paths I hadn't plotted, and developing in ways I hadn't anticipated.

Perhaps I could do the same. Life imitating art and all that.

But first, I have to face Ada.

"Well, speaking of the new Carlie, it's time to make her first appearance." I stand, slinging my gym bag over my shoulder, a modern-day warrior armed with nothing but spandex and hope. "I'll text you after," I promise, my voice steady, though my knees feel like they're penned in italics—shaky and uncertain.

"Go get 'em," Lily cheers, shaking her hands in mock excitement.

I smile, feigning my own enthusiasm.

Here goes nothing—or maybe, here goes everything.

Lily waves, then shoos me to go.

With that, I'm moving to the door, heading towards what I expect to be a battle with dumbbells and discipline.

I exit the coffee shop with the same determined stride one might reserve for approaching the gallows—or in my case, a gym full of potential humiliation and sweaty butt cracks.

I shudder that thought away.

Truthfully, the idea of physical exertion before noon seems more criminal than motivational, but here I am, trying to prove to myself that I can be one of those gym people—the kind who say things like, *"I love the burn!"* and *"No pain, no gain!"* without a trace of irony.

Seems unlikely, but I'm gonna roll with it.

I stroll into St. Mary's Hospital—the VIP entrance to my very own workout apocalypse.

After a short elevator ride, the hospital's gym looms ahead, a modern-day Colosseum where the gladiators are replaced with treadmills, and the lions are … well, probably still lions if my imagination about personal trainers is accurate.

As I near the entrance, I can't help but notice the variety of people going in and out. There's a man with biceps the size of my head, and he's drinking from a gallon jug of water. *A gallon!*

I wonder how many times he pees a day?

Is he part human, part camel?

Camel shifter. Yeah, I could go with that.

Maybe I should switch genres and write a story about a gym that's actually a front for a shifter training facility. It would explain a lot.

The idea amuses me, and I almost miss the sight of a woman walking past with leggings so bright they could probably be seen from space.

Fashion at the gym is a whole new world—one where neon and spandex reign supreme. I look down at my own outfit, which is a less vibrant, more *'didn't want to scare myself in the mirror'* shade of black.

I snicker to myself.

It's a wonder they let me in wearing such tame apparel.

Once inside, I'm greeted by the unmistakable scent of determination and disinfectant. I make my way to the front desk to check in, where a chirpy attendant with a name tag reading 'Skye' meets my gaze.

"First day?" she asks, her voice filled with the kind of pep that suggests she's never faced the cruel betrayal of a snooze button.

"Is it that obvious?" I ask, attempting to smile, but it probably looks more like a grimace.

Skye just laughs—a sound so cheerful it practically bounces. "Don't worry. You're going to do great. You're in good hands."

"Oh, good."

I hope Skye's optimism is infectious because I need all the help I can get.

She hands me a schedule, and my eyes skim the bonus classes being offered.

'Aqua Zumba.'

'Kettlebell Khaos.'

And 'Yoga for the Soul.'

They sound like a list of bands that would play at an extremely niche music festival.

With a few minutes to spare before my meeting with certain death—*I mean, Ada*—I venture further into the facility. Each area reveals new devices of torture.

There's the weight area, which I promptly nickname '*The Iron Jungle*'. The cardio section is '*Treadmill Territory*,' and I decide the less said about the free weights area, the better. I'm pretty sure the grunting noises from that quadrant are a form of communication I'm not advanced enough to understand.

There's an aerobics class in progress, and through the

window, I catch a glimpse of synchronized suffering. I entertain the thought of joining, but then I remember my coordination is on par with a newborn giraffe's.

Instead, I find a corner to stake out—somewhere between a row of stationary bikes and a rack of dumbbells.

Here, I can observe, and possibly blend in with the surroundings. If I stand still enough, maybe I can pass as an out-of-place piece of equipment.

I check my phone, pretending to look busy as I wait for Ada to come find me, but really I'm drafting a mental will.

- *To Lily, I bequeath my coffee maker. May it fuel your mornings.*
- *To my unwritten novels, find someone worthy to tell your tales.*

A man locks eyes with me, and I brace myself, only for him to ask if I'm using the dumbbells I'm leaning on. I shake my head, resisting the urge to apologize for giving the impression that I could actually lift them.

I'm about to hunt for a water fountain—hydration is key to survival, after all—when I see her.

Ada.

Or at least, I think it's Ada. She strides confidently across the gym, a beacon of health and athleticism. She has that personal trainer glow, the kind that says, *'I eat burpees for breakfast and have more protein shakers than friends.'*

I watch as she nears, her gaze locked onto me with a serious intensity. Her physique is nothing short of intimidating, muscles defined under the skin-tight fabric of her gym attire that hugs her like a second skin.

Jealousy flares inside me.

She's the embodiment of every fitness magazine cover that's ever made me think twice about reaching for a slice of cake. I can't help but compare the definition in her arms to the softness of my own, the tautness of her abs to the comfort of my belly.

My stomach knots with nerves, and I practice the smile I've been rehearsing—the one that's meant to say *'I'm friendly and totally ready for this,'* but probably screams *'I'm terrified and considering bolting for the nearest exit.'*

I wipe my palms on my not-so-spandexy spandex, hoping the sweat doesn't betray my cool exterior.

This woman is everything I'm not, everything I aspire to be in those secret, vulnerable moments before sleep when the day strips bare my confidence.

My heart rate picks up, not from exercise, but from the sheer panic of having to match her stride for stride. I can almost feel the weight of her expectations bearing down on me, threatening to squash my newly found resolve like a bug.

Why did I think a woman trainer would be better again?

I'm honestly at a loss.

Thankfully, she veers off, heading over to *'Treadmill Territory'* instead.

I exhale a little too loudly.

Dodged a bullet there.

Before I can breathe a full sigh of relief, my thoughts scatter as a man enters the room and stares right at me.

He's tall, his build athletic but not imposing—instead, it's the kind of fit that speaks of strength without intimidation. His hair is a sandy blonde, slightly tousled, as if he's run his hands through it a few times.

But it's his expression that catches me off guard—a look of shock or maybe confusion?

In a few fluid steps, he's standing in front of me.

"Carlie?" he asks tentatively, his voice drawing me in like a seductive embrace. There's something in his tone, a familiarity that shouldn't be there, considering we've never met.

"That's me," I manage to say, feeling a little breathless and more than a little lost.

"I'm Adam," he extends his hand, which I take, finding his grip firm and warm. "Your trainer."

My brain stutters to a halt.

Adam?

He seems to read the confusion on my face. "I hope you weren't expecting a woman. I noticed there was a typo in the schedule," he explains with a chuckle that doesn't quite reach his eyes, which are still studying me with that same perplexed intensity. "Unless you'd like to work with Jillian," he points to the fit goddess across the room, "you're stuck with me."

I blink at him, trying to process this new information but my brain has completely malfunctioned.

Can you say plot twist?

CHAPTER 3

Adam

My heart hammers a frenzied beat against my ribs. *It couldn't be her.*

The odds would be laughable—*astronomical*, even.

Dylan would laugh himself silly if I told him my heart nearly stopped beating. He'd tell me I was insane—and maybe I am.

But as the woman with the fiery crown of hair tied up in a knot of controlled chaos stands in front of me, I can't quite put the thought to rest.

Despite myself, my gaze drifts over her collarbone, but the birthmark—the distinct heart shape that I'd all but memorized as I kissed it that night—would be hidden under her high-necked workout shirt.

That is, if it's even there.

In fact, with the way she's staring at me—with a vivid clash of disarray and determination, her green eyes wide, I'm not entirely certain.

Carlie's eyes dart to Jillian and back to me as she

decides her fate. It doesn't appear she's all too thrilled with the prospect of switching to Jillian.

Good.

"What'll it be?" I clear my throat and shoot her a reserved smile, the one I give to new clients who seem like they'd bolt at any hint of intimidation. "Ready to jump into the fire with me?"

Her eyes round, the whites embracing her green irises all the way as she nods.

"Yeah, fire. Jumping—*great.* Love fire." She pulls up short, raising a hand to her cheek. "I mean, not *actual fire,* it might ruin my outfit. Not that it's a great outfit, but it's the only one I really like at the moment. So ... just, you know, the metaphoric—*workout*—kind of fire," she stammers, a mess of words and wide-eyed glances that somehow amplify her charm. "Good, god. Someone stop me."

I can't help but grin and exhale. While there's a hit of disappointment, it's pretty clear this woman isn't the one from Nocté.

"Right, metaphoric fire it is, then." I gesture toward the mats. "How about we start with some warm-up stretches?"

She nods, enthusiasm waning slightly at the prospect of actual exercise, it seems. It makes me wonder why she's motivated to be here.

Something to ask her when she's more comfortable.

As she follows me to the mats, her movements are a dance of awkward angles and misplaced steps. To be honest, it's endearing in its rarity in this place.

"Take a seat and just watch what I do. Then, you do the same. Think you can handle that?" I ask dropping down onto the mat.

She nods tentatively, a small squeak escaping her lips as she sits down opposite me.

I roll through toe touches, figure fours, and even some knee and hip mobility stretches, since it looks like her joints could benefit from a little strengthening. Her hamstrings are awfully tight.

However, watching her attempt to mirror my stretches is like observing a fawn on ice—there's a willingness, but the execution is wildly imprecise. It's almost comical, the way she fumbles, with each slip or overreach.

"Good. Feel warmed up?" I ask when we've made it through the full warm-up routine.

Her eyes meet mine and despite the crimson in her cheeks, she nods. "The metaphorical fire is stoked and ready."

I chuckle, gesturing to a large, inflated balance ball. "Good. That's what we want. I'll focus today on core and upper body, with a little bit of cardio thrown in for good measure. Sound good?"

"Whatever you say, boss," she says, standing up and brushing off her backside.

The gleaming blue balance ball sits in the corner of the room like a challenge made manifest. Perhaps it's pushing my luck a bit, considering her initial awkwardness, but we gotta start somewhere. Right?

Carlie approaches the ball as if it's a wild animal that might spook.

"This is pretty basic, so don't let it freak you out. Here's what I want you to do ... Just sit down gently, like this, feet flat on the floor. Then, we'll have you do a few crunches and back extensions." I model the position I want her to get into and stand back up. "I'll walk you through everything. You've got this."

"Okay." She nods, then exhales loudly. Her hands lightly skimming the rubbery surface before she turns around and commits her full weight to it.

The ball accepts her with a gentle give, and for a moment, it seems like she might master this precarious throne with perfection.

Her smile beams at me as she glances up and declares, "I am the queen of the— *Whoa!*"

In an instant, her victory crumbles as the ball skids away, sending her toppling sideways. Her arms windmill, but without much to grab onto, it's the gym schedules and an advertisement for green juice she takes down with her. She lands with a soft thud, covered in a sea of fluttering paper.

"Are you okay?" I ask, rushing over to her.

Her face peeks out, sheepish and flushed.

Before I can reach a hand out to help her, she's back on her feet, batting away the paper with a tight laugh.

"I always wanted to make a dramatic entrance. Consider that a rehearsal," she quips, though her eyes have taken on a wild, maybe even crazy edge.

"That ball can be tricky," I say, hoping to inject a bit of levity back into the session as I bend down and pick up the papers. "It gets the best of us. I can't tell you how many times I've ended up on the mat."

Carlie narrows her eyes as if she's not buying it for one second.

"In case you haven't noticed, I'm basically a walking infomercial for *how not to gym.*" She offers a smile, thin and fragile. "You might want to think twice about training me. And if you are, I don't blame you."

"You're not that bad." I chuckle, shaking my head as I guide her over to the resistance bands. Somehow, they seem like a safer bet. Nothing heavy to drop on a toe or a foot.

Grabbing a band for myself and one for her, I go back into teacher mode.

"Here's what I want you to do. Hold the band with one hand to the center of your chest, like this," I demonstrate the movement I want her to test—clutching the band to my torso, then I slip my right hand into the other end of the loop. "Place your palm inside the loop and press down. Like this."

"What's the point of that?" she asks, watching me go through the motions, all curiosity and no snark.

I grin. "It's a tricep extension."

"Oh." She squares her shoulders and mimics my stance. Then, she stretches the band as I showed her.

There's a look of fierce concentration etched onto her features as she presses down. A grin floats to her face, as she does it a couple more times.

"This is easier than I thought," she admits with a bit of triumph laced in her words. But then, in a slip of focus, the band snaps from her palm. It zings through the air, smacking against my forearm with a sharp sting.

"Oh my god, Adam, I'm so sorry," Carlie gasps, her hands flying to her lips.

"You know, they usually work better if you don't weaponize them," I tease, rubbing at my arm and picking the band up from the floor.

Her face is the color of ripe beets but she quips back, "Go me. Guess I'm just preparing for the gym apocalypse —one snapped band at a time."

I huff a laugh. The things that come out of her mouth.

"Are you sure you're okay?" she asks as she steps closer with concern flooding her features.

"It's fine, really." I smile, hoping to ease her embarrassment, but as she reaches out, her fingers brush the reddening skin.

The touch is light, fleeting, yet it sears me more profoundly than the snap of the band.

Her eyes meet mine, wide and apologetic, and in that split second, I'm transported back to a feather-light touch just like that.

But it can't be.

The woman from Nocté was confident, and coordinated, and so sure of herself.

"Really, I'm okay," I reaffirm, trying to shake away my conflicting thoughts.

We move on, and I decide to steer clear of equipment for a while.

"Let's try something a bit less ... *adventurous*," I suggest.

Her eyes dart to mine as if something I said caught her off guard.

Shooting her a lopsided grin, I continue, "How about a break to regroup?"

We walk over to the lounge area and I hand her a St. Mary's branded water bottle from one of the mini-fridges. Pretty hard to weaponize that unless she plans on throwing it at my head.

"Thanks," she says, tentatively taking the bottle from me and indulging in a long swig.

My eyes are drawn to the movement, but I shake it away, grabbing one for myself and taking a sip.

"So, tell me, what are your fitness goals, Carlie?" I ask, shifting gears and trying to lighten the mood.

Based on her intake sheet, I already know she wants to lose weight and get toned up. But it's always nice to connect about goals one-on-one. It helps me understand what truly motivates them and comes in handy on those days when the going gets tough.

She shrugs. "To be able to sprint to the fridge during chapter breaks without losing breath."

I shoot her a confused look.

She grins sheepishly. "Priorities, am I right?"

I'm about to ask her what she means by *chapter breaks* when she takes another big gulp. But as she does so, her gaze catches on something over my shoulder.

Distracted, water dribbles down her chin, soaking

into the collar of her shirt, and she sputters, coughing as she tries to stem the flow with the back of her hand.

"Good god, I'm just ... *I'm a mess,*" she says, her voice raw and vulnerable as she looks up at me.

"No, it's ... *refreshing,*" I reply before I can censor myself.

"Not as refreshing as I feel right now, let me assure you," she fires back, tugging on her shirt to pull it away from her skin. She shakes her head and drops her gaze to the floor.

We stand there for a heartbeat, the noise of the gym fading into a backdrop, and I'm aware of nothing but her. For some reason, I really want her to feel better—to not be so self-conscious.

"You're doing great," I start, hoping like hell it hits as truth. "Getting used to this place, the movements ... Hell, everything, really. It's all part of the process. Give yourself a little grace as you get used to it."

"Grace—pretty sure that's a foreign concept in my world." She wipes her face with the neckline of her shirt, and as she does, the fabric lifts ever so slightly. My eyes betray me, darting down, searching for that birthmark, but the fabric falls back too quickly.

I check my watch. "Okay, we still have a little time left. How do you feel about treadmills?" I ask, hoping it's a safer bet and one I can give her a solid win on.

"I feel like they don't usually fight back, so ... *better chances?*" Her laugh, bright and unguarded, fills the space between us.

"To better chances it is," I echo, feeling a smile tug at my lips.

As we walk out of the weight room and approach the wall of treadmills, I show her the basic controls, my hand hovering over the buttons as I explain how to use it.

"Start slow," I advise, glancing in her direction. "We'll gradually increase the pace. I want to see where you are now so we can gauge your progress."

She nods, and I can't help but notice the way her hair has started to escape her knot, framing her face with errant strands that beg to be brushed back. For some insane reason, it's a challenge to keep my hand from tucking them behind her ear.

"All right, let's walk." I set the machine to a gentle pace, and she steps on, albeit a little hesitant at first.

I watch her find her rhythm, the initial awkwardness melting away as she moves. There's a grace in her steps now, a natural flow that hints at hidden depths and core strength.

"This is a lot easier when there aren't things in your way to trip over," she says over her shoulder. Pride filters into her tone and I can't help but feel a bit of that pride myself.

With each step she takes, I find myself taken aback by the simple motion, the roll from heel to toe that seems both innocent and intoxicating in the gym's fluorescent lighting.

Her curves are more pronounced than many of the women in here, just like the woman I'm searching for—and my eyes want to take in the way her hips sway.

To distract myself, I ramble on about maintaining a steady pace and proper form, but my words feel hollow—secondary to the thrumming pulse of curiosity and draw I feel towards this woman.

Maybe the woman from the club was just a kick in the pants—one I needed to break out of my comfort zone and date women who aren't my typical style?

God knows, I now seem to have a thing for redheads.

Carlie looks over, catching me mid-ramble about incline, and her smile shifts. It's almost as if it becomes something more knowing—like she sees through the façade of the fitness trainer to the man beneath who's reeling from some internal revelations.

"Do you go out much?" The question slips out, a poorly veiled attempt at nonchalance.

She slows her pace slightly.

"Not a whole lot," she replies softly. "I guess I'm more of a homebody. I'd rather sit on the couch with a good book. You know?" She scrunches her nose. "Thus the need for you."

The confirmation shouldn't come as a relief, but it does. It simplifies everything, and strips away the complexities.

"Same," I whisper, unsure where to go after that. "I mean, I like staying home, too. Good book and all."

We fall into a comfortable silence, the only sound is the rhythmic beat of her footsteps on the treadmill. I find myself studying her profile, the way her eyelashes cast long shadows down her cheeks, the slight parting of her lips as she breathes.

Then, without warning, the treadmill jolts, a sudden malfunction that has nothing to do with her at all. Yet, her footing stumbles.

I lunge forward, instincts taking over, and my arms wrap around her waist to steady her as she hops off. For a moment, we're locked in an unintended embrace, her body pressed against mine, and the room's remaining sounds fall away.

"Holy shit," she breathes out, her voice a husky whisper that grazes my senses.

"Are you okay?" I manage to say, even as I gently step back, aware that the heat I feel isn't solely from the proximity of our bodies. "Equipment can be unpredictable. That was totally not your fault."

"Unpredictable," she laughs, shaky but recovering. "That seems to be a recurring theme for today."

I take another step back, physically putting more space between us.

"Let's call it a day," I suggest. "I think we've had a good start. Don't you?"

Her agreement is soft as she nods.

At first, it seems like she plans to move around me, but she pauses, her gaze lifting to mine. There's a question in her eyes—something she wants to say and I inhale sharply, waiting for it.

"Thanks, Adam," she finally says with a ghost of a smile. "I appreciate you getting me through this mortifying day. If there's a gym blooper reel, I'm pretty sure I just filled up the annual quota. So, uh, enjoy."

Before I can say anything to that, she stalks off, leaving me standing there, surrounded by the hum of cooling treadmills and the echo of my racing thoughts.

45

CHAPTER 4

Carlie

I rush out of St. Mary's, desperate to escape the humiliation still clinging to me like the sweat running down my back.

The warmth in my muscles is a testament to Adam's training session, but it's the warmth in my cheeks that quickens my strides.

God, I'm such a mess. What Adam must think of me …

Sunlight glares down on me, a stark contrast to the gym's bright indoor lights. I slip on my sunglasses and hike my gym bag up further.

My phone vibrates in the hip pocket of my leggings.

I bet it's Lily, wondering if I've survived my first day with Ada.

I snicker under my breath.

She'll be in for as much of a shock as I was when I fill her in that I was paired with a personal trainer who looks like he stepped right out of one of my steamy scenes.

At least he wasn't one of those muscle-bound, brain-addled alphaholes.

In fact, he was way too sweet—*and hot*—to be anything but dreamy.

I decide not to check my message just yet. If I do, I'll likely walk into a lamp post or something and I need my wits about me if I'm gonna make this new version of Carlie come to fruition.

As I stride down the sidewalk, I try to shake off the embarrassing first day—the trip on the treadmill, the unfortunate incident with the water bottle, and the way my voice cracked when I first said hello to Adam—*not Ada*.

If clumsiness is an art, I'm the friggin' Picasso of it. Or would that be the Polluck of it?

Yeah, Jackson Polluck's more my jam.

But it's not just the mishaps that keep replaying in my head—*it's him*.

The way his shirt stretched over his muscles, how his lips twitched into a lopsided smile that looked like it was just for me—even when I was making a complete fool of myself.

He's like that guy from Club Nocté, only ... tangible, real, and able to make me blush without even trying.

Especially when I think of my idiocy on full display.

I mean, all the mishaps aside, my attempt at *hello* came out more like a haunted house soundtrack—part creaky door, part startled cat.

I was soooo not expecting an Adam.

While he looked like he'd been photoshopped in real

life, my brain, *ever so helpful,* supplied nothing but elevator music.

I run my hand over my face.

As I reach the corner, a breeze picks up, and I get a whiff of the lake—fresh and cool and somehow full of possibilities. I never thought I'd feel that way again.

Not after ...

Shaking my head, I drop that line of thought.

Instead, the past few days have made me think more about my novels—of the wild, adventurous romances I pen down for my readers.

Only now, the line between my fictional escapades and my real-life choices seems to blur a bit. Between that one incredibly sexy night to—hell, even to this day with Adam, I feel like something is stirring.

Is it the sunshine or is it him making me feel like the heroine in my own story?

Ridiculous.

My stomach growls, a rude interruption to my daydreaming. I haven't eaten anything today—unless you count swallowing my pride. There was plenty of that.

Maybe a stop at my favorite bakery will cure the blush that I can't seem to shake—or at the very least, provide a sugar-laced consolation.

I pull up short.

No, Carlie. For crying out loud, that's what got you into this mess. Go to the fancy protein shake place. It's time to act like you love the taste of green powder.

Adjusting my direction, I'm almost to the protein place when my foot decides to tango with the other, and like the most awkward dance partners, they step on each other's toes.

My arms flail in a desperate attempt to find balance, of which I have none. And just like that, I'm wrapped up in the leafy arms of a hydrangea bush outside one of the downtown businesses. The blossoms whisper what I imagine to be floral expletives in my ear.

"Looks like you could use a hand," comes a voice, wreathed in the kind of mirth that suggests its owner has seen a thing or two.

I look up, ready to find a bemused bystander with a phone out, capturing my downfall for internet immortality.

Instead, it's a lady my grandma's age, her eyes twinkling with undisguised amusement. She extends a hand, her grip surprisingly firm. Her bracelets jangle like a medieval court jester's bells—a sound that seems to underline the absurdity of my situation.

"I suppose hydrangeas are in this season," I quip, as she helps me to my feet.

"Oh, darling," she chuckles, her voice a melody of past laughter and wisdom, "you're just ahead of the trend. Next week, everyone will be wearing them."

I smile, grateful for her good humor, as I dust myself off.

"Do you think they go well with embarrassment?" I ask, plucking a rebellious petal from my hair.

"Better than pearls with pajamas," she says with a wink that suggests she's no stranger to either.

The elderly woman pats my hand, her own crinkled

with the maps of a life well-lived. "You remind me of myself when I was your age. Always rushing, always tumbling. Took me a few years to learn the art of walking without making the flora fear for their lives."

I can't help but laugh. "Any tips on mastering that art?"

"Darling, the key is confidence. Walk like you've got nowhere to go, and everything's waiting for you," she advises.

I thank her, promising to practice the art of nonchalant walking, to which she responds with a sage nod. "Don't make the hydrangeas dread your approach. Reserve that for your exes."

As she walks away, I realize that her steps are measured and sure—a balletic grace that contradicts her years. I take a deep breath, square my shoulders, and try to emulate her poise, managing a whole three steps before nearly tripping over a crack in the sidewalk.

Where's that sloth treadmill when I need it? Well, before it tried to buck me off, anyway …

"Well," I mutter to myself, "Rome wasn't built in a day, and my poise won't be either."

Reinvigorated by the woman's kind gesture and her light-hearted laugh, I continue on my path to the shake place.

It's one of those trendy spots with smoothies named after Greek gods and goddesses—though whether or not any of the patrons knows that is beyond me.

As I get close, I can't help but feel out of place among the sea of fitness enthusiasts entering the establishment.

None of them look like they've tripped over air in their life.

"Suck it up, Carlie," I mutter under my breath and reach for the door handle.

The bell jingles as I step inside *Olympian Blends*.

A gust of air conditioning hits me, chilling the sweat on my back and providing immediate relief from the heat that's starting to build outside.

I scan the menu, pretending to contemplate the choices before settling on *Hera's Harvest*—a mix of kale, spinach, green apple, and a hint of lemon—all with added protein powder proclaimed to be the best in the area.

If it's good enough for the queen of the gods, I guess it's good enough for me.

While waiting for my shake, I finally give in and check my phone.

There are two messages from Lily, both checking in to see how it's going. I quickly type out a response assuring her I'm alive and haven't yet succumbed to the perils of gym life.

But as I hit send, a message from an unknown number catches my eye.

I open it, half-expecting it to be a spam message promising a fortune left by a distant relative who was an eccentric millionaire with an affection for adopting random people as kin.

But no, it's not a promise of unclaimed riches.

> Hey Carlie, it's Adam from St. Mary's.
> Got your number from your intake
> form. Hope that's cool. Just wanted to
> check in and make sure you're doing
> okay after this morning's ...
> adventures. Also, you left your water
> bottle. They're highly coveted around
> here. Wouldn't want you to miss out.
> ;-)

My heart does a peculiar flip.

Adam.

Texted me.

This can't be right.

My brain kicks into overdrive, ricocheting between possible explanations. Maybe this is one of those bizarre social experiments, and somewhere someone is watching to see if I'll respond.

I glance around conspiratorially.

Or perhaps Adam lost a bet with the beefy Jillian chick, and the dare was to text the most grace-challenged person at the gym because I'm sure she noticed. She was watching me as much as I was stealing glances at her in the hopes she didn't witness my demise.

I can almost picture the other trainers drawing straws, and Adam, with his luck just slightly better than mine, drawing the short one.

Or maybe, in a plot twist worthy of my novels, he's actually an undercover prince forced to work in a gym to escape the paparazzi, and I am the unwitting civilian who's stumbled into his story.

Right, and next, I'll be fleeing from villainous henchmen in a high-speed Vespa chase through the city.

The blush that I'd managed to tamp down flares up again with the force of a supernova. There's something seriously wrong with my brain.

I type out a response with fingers that suddenly feel like they belong to someone else—a parallel universe version of me who can actually talk to men without turning into a walking cautionary tale.

Hi Adam, all good here. Just a typical day in the life of a human disaster. Thanks for checking in, and I'll retrieve the water bottle tomorrow, if that's okay. Embarrassment should be less lethal by then. Hold it for me?

I hit send before I can concoct another wild scenario —like Adam being a secret agent who mistook my water bottle for a gadget-filled counterpart.

The thought makes me chuckle.

As if anyone would trust me with gadgetry more complicated than a pen. I'd probably accidentally activate a laser in the middle of a crowded street or something.

The woman behind the shake counter calls my name, and I collect my goddess drink that looks like irradiated sludge.

One sip and my taste buds immediately regret the decision not to go to the bakery. The tang of the lemon does little to mask the taste of liquefied lawn, despite half-expecting to sprout a peacock feather or throw a lightning bolt once I've swallowed.

The girl behind the counter eyes me expectantly as if waiting for me to transform into an Olympian deity right before her eyes.

I force a smile. "Mmmm, so good."

Apparently appeased, she nods and turns to make the next drink.

I find a seat near the window, pulling out my notebook from my gym bag. It's time to process everything—the good, the bad, *and the Adam.*

My pen hovers over the paper as I contemplate where to start.

Rather than focusing on the disaster that was my gym experience, my mind drifts back to Friday night. The next-level sexiness and seduction that had played between me and the mystery man from Nocté.

I flip to a new page and begin to write a new scene, one where my heroine meets her hero in a sexy nightclub. The words flow from my pen like they've been waiting for just this moment.

It's strange how life works—I leave the gym thinking my day can't get any worse, and then a series of stumbles lead me to the perfect scene. Maybe it's the universe's way of telling me to keep at it, no matter how many bushes I end up making out with.

As if on cue, a hydrangea petal flutters from my hair and lands on the notebook. I shake my head, and brush it aside.

An hour passes before I lift my gaze to see the sun casting its golden glow across the city streets. Gone are the early morning shadows.

On the upside, I've filled pages with witty banter and heart-racing moments, and for the first time in a long time, I feel like I'm exactly where I'm supposed to be. At least, with my current work in progress.

Life, now that's another story. *Literally.*

My phone buzzes with a new message, snapping me back to reality.

It's from Adam.

> I thought you should know, your courage today was inspiring. Not everyone would get back up after that many falls. Looking forward to our next session. And don't worry, your water bottle is safe with me.

I read it once, twice, then a third time, letting his words sink in.

Inspiring? *Me?*

Part of me wants to hardcore scoff. However, there's an undeniable warmth that spreads through my chest, too.

I grin like an insane person, and pack up my things, ready to face whatever comes next.

CHAPTER 5

Adam

I take up my usual spot at my brother's bar, the day's weight finally lifting as I settle onto the stool.

It's been a hell of a day—starting with the blare of my alarm clock dragging me into the gym earlier than usual. But the real twist came with Carlie barging into my usual morning routine, bringing with her an unexpected jolt—like the first hit of caffeine that I didn't know I needed.

As I take a sip of Brian's newest craft beer, the sharpness of the hops doesn't quite cut through my rumination.

I nod to the regulars who take up residence in the stools beside me as I try to shake off the ghost of the day and the crazy redhead it brought in with it.

A part of me can't help but draw parallels between the woman from Friday night and Carlie.

The way Carlie looked at me today, there was a flicker of something—something I can't quite put my finger on

—or perhaps it was just my imagination fueled by wishful thinking.

Hell, that's probably it.

I push the thought aside.

Carlie is *Carlie*—a client who's somehow become an intriguing part of my new routine.

And the woman from Nocté ...

Well, she's just a phantom now—a hauntingly beautiful *'what if'* that slipped through my fingers like smoke.

I sigh.

Now I'm here, trying to drown out the day's second act—Jillian flaunting her new guy like he's the latest shiny equipment at St. Mary's.

It wouldn't be so bad if he wasn't the guy she cheated on me with.

How he's still able to walk is a testament to my character—at least, I'd like to think so. Because I seriously considered breaking both kneecaps.

My brother glances over at me and I can tell by the look in his eyes he's about to wander over and start in with some sage brother advice.

I groan inwardly.

"You look like someone stole your Peloton, man. What's up?" Brian asks, his voice rough with concern.

Rolling my eyes, I itch at the side of my forehead.

I don't really want to get into it, but without Dylan here as a buffer, I know I'm only delaying the inevitable.

"It's Jillian," I admit, hating how her name still sours my mood. "She's all over the new guy at work, and I have to stand there, spotting him like I'm not phased by it."

Brian's expression hardens and he swipes my pint glass to refill it. "You know, if you left St. Mary's—*started Foxx Fitness*—you wouldn't have to deal with that shit."

The idea of starting my own gym flickers in my mind and a burgeoning hope blooms like always. It's a dream I've nursed quietly, but doubts are stubborn. They cling like the calluses on my palms.

I don't want to fail and if I do, it would be an Instagram sensation and everyone would be watching.

"Yeah, but what if it's a flop?" I ask, even though part of me knows it's the fear talking.

Besides, as much as I'd love to own my own place, I don't want to give my boss the idea that I'm not grateful. St. Mary's took a risk on me when I was just a punk kid who liked to lift weights.

"Dude, you've got a goldmine of followers, Adam. People would *kill* for that kind of free advertising," he counters, the certainty in his voice is both enviable and intimidating. "Hell, *I* would kill for that kind of advertising. Do you know how hard it's been to get the bar to where it is now?"

I shoot him a sympathetic look and roll the pint glass between my hands, the coolness a sharp contrast to my warm skin.

If I close my eyes, I can picture it—my own space, my rules, my brand.

It's definitely tempting, but the risk ...

"Look, you won't know unless you try. No guarantee or magic fairy'll grant your wishes. It's about taking a leap and hoping for the best. That's what I did with this place," he says, gesturing around the brewery that's become a local favorite. "You think I knew it'd be the inevitable hit and hotspot it is now?"

"But what if I'm just … good at working for someone else? I know how to train people. But run a business?"

Brian leans in, his eyes locking onto mine. "You're selling yourself short. And since when do you settle for *just good?*"

He's got a point. I've never been one to settle. Not with girlfriends who cheat or, hell, even my own fitness.

And in fitness, failure is a good thing. It means you're making gains.

"Think about it," he says, pulling back and giving me space to process. "I've seen you in action. You're a natural leader, Adam. You inspire people. That's a gift. It's wasted at St. Mary's."

I take a long drink, letting the beer wash over my tongue, buying myself a moment.

"I just … I don't know if I'm ready," I confess.

Brian levels me with one of his brotherly stares. "That's the thing about leaps of faith—you're never *really* ready. Are you? You just have to decide it's worth the risk."

His words resonate with a truth I can't ignore. Maybe I am holding back, clinging to the safety of the familiar.

It's something to chew on, along with the salted peanuts Brian slides my way. I pop a small handful into my mouth. Their crunch is a mundane distraction, but it's a welcome one. It gives my brain a break from the bigger issues—like my career, and yes, even my tangled mess of a love life.

"So, speaking of jumps," Brian says, breaking the silence that had settled between us, "have you thought about getting back out there? You know, *dating?*"

I nearly choke on a peanut. The question comes out of left field, but it's Brian's way. He's not one to tiptoe around the tulips.

Either that, or he read my mind. Wouldn't be the first time.

"Out there?" I scoff, chasing the nuts with a sip of beer. "In case you haven't noticed, *'out there'* is a dumpster fire."

Brian chuckles, the sound rich with the kind of amusement only a sibling can muster. "Can't be any worse than having to spot *Mr. Boned-Your-Girl* every day."

The mention of Jillian's new lay stirs the embers of annoyance, but I force a shrug. "I've had my own distractions."

A flash of red hair burns through the recesses of my mind as quickly as it fades.

"Oh?" Brian perks up. *"Do tell."*

I shake my head, a smirk playing on my lips despite the annoyance. "Can't."

His eyebrow arches in a silent challenge.

"It was a one-time thing," I offer, feeling the heat rise in my cheeks. I hadn't planned on telling Brian about that night, but here we are.

"Like a one-night stand?" Brian presses, leaning in closer. "Or like, you don't know if it will be more yet?"

I shrug, but I have no doubt he'll read between the lines of my shitty grin.

"Holy hell—why is this the first fuckin' time I'm hearing of this?" he practically bellows.

"Christ, keep it down," I mutter, glancing around the bar. Thankfully, no one is really paying us any attention.

"What was it like? What was *she* like?" Brian asks, his mouth gaping open.

I huff a laugh. "It was hot, okay? She was ..." I blow out a slow breath, remembering the way that night went down. "Some sort of sex goddess or something."

Brian whistles, a teasing glint in his eyes. "A sex goddess, huh? Sounds like someone wants a round two. Maybe you need to hunt her down for another romp—could help you get the rest of Jillian out of your system."

"I wish I could, but I can't."

An image of Carlie flashes in my mind, her intelligent eyes and the curve of her smile.

"Funny thing is," I start, hesitating as I try to connect the dots myself, "I met a new client today—Carlie. She reminds me of her ... but she's so *different*."

"Carlie, eh?" Brian leans against the bar, his expression thoughtful. "Thinking you might ask her out?"

I think on that a moment, then shake my head. "Nah, man. I've learned my lesson on mixing business and pleasure. Besides, you're one to talk about the whole dating circus," I say, raising an eyebrow at him. "Last I checked, you weren't exactly jumping back on the love wagon."

He pauses, the levity draining from his face as the topic of his own love life—or lack thereof—surfaces.

"Love's a gamble, and I've already lost enough at that table," he admits, his eyes briefly clouding over with a mixture of regret and resignation.

I lean back, eyeing him. "You've been pretty quiet about all that," I say cautiously. "You doing okay with everything?"

He pours himself a beer, the golden liquid cascading into the glass with a familiar hiss.

"Divorce has a way of teaching you things you never wanted to learn," he admits quietly.

I nod, unsure of what to say. It's a side of Brian I've rarely seen—vulnerable, stripped of the easygoing demeanor he wears as effortlessly as the apron around his waist.

"Honestly, man, I thought Jillian was your forever. Five years is a long time to suddenly ..." Brian trails off, not finishing the sentence, but the weight of it hangs in the air between us.

I shrug, trying to shake off the heaviness. "I thought so too. But turns out, I was just a stepping stone for her, you know? Onward to bigger and better things. Or so I was told. Repeatedly."

"Yeah," he says, his voice dropping an octave. "I know exactly what you mean. After my divorce, I realized some stones are best left unturned. I'm happy here, with the bar—the regulars. It's uncomplicated. Women?

They're welcome as customers, not as heartbreakers. Not for me."

There's a bitterness in his laugh, a sharpness that makes me realize just how deep his wounds are. He's not just out of the game—he's boarded up the field.

"But you," Brian says, pointing a finger at me. "You're not me. You've got that ... *thing about you.* People are drawn to you. Don't let Jillian's mistake turn you into a cynical old bastard like me."

I ponder over his words. "I'm not cynical, just ... *cautious.* I've seen what love can do to a person. What it did to us."

"Cautious, huh?" Brian's eyes hold mine, a silent understanding passing through them. "Just remember, not every risk ends with a crash and burn. Some might actually be worth the jump. Like the one to start Foxx Fitness. Get on that, man. I'm telling you, it's your calling."

The conversation shifts, then, to lighter topics—sports, the latest beer he's brewing, the regulars with their quirks and stories. But his words about risks and jumps linger with me, a nagging thought that maybe I've been standing still for too long, trying to avoid a fall that's already happened.

Brian might be pessimistic about love, but when it comes to taking chances on dreams, he's a damn believer.

He makes me think that maybe, *just maybe,* it's time I become one too.

CHAPTER 6

Carlie

Once again, I stumble through the entrance of St. Mary's gym, still burning from yesterday's humiliation.

And I'm not just talking about the low-grade muscle burn from my training session, either. Because, *oh yeah,* that's there.

Who knew making a fool of myself with something as basic as drinking water could rival a walk of shame?

But here I am, back at the scene of the crime, ready to face Adam—the unfairly attractive trainer with eyes that see right through my gym-intimidated soul.

"Morning, Carlie," he greets me with that half-smirk of his, and I swear my heart does an involuntary cardio session.

Note to self: *falling for your trainer is the new falling off the treadmill*—embarrassing and likely to result in injury.

Don't do it.

I muster a smile, one that I hope says, *'I'm a confident, put-together woman,'* and not, *'I cataloged every muscle in your arm when you helped me up yesterday.'*

For research purposes. *Obviously.*

"Morning, Adam. Ready for front-row seats to my next workout comedy special?"

Adam's laugh is a low, easy sound that fills the space between the clanking of weights and the rhythmic whirring of treadmills. He extends the water bottle I left yesterday.

"Thanks. I'll try to remember it this time," I say, raising it in cheers.

"I have a feeling today is going to go better than yesterday. You got all of the first-day jitters out," he says, gesturing toward a row of machines with a grace that suggests he's more at home here than anywhere else. "Let's start with a basic warm-up on the elliptical machines today."

I nod, trying to hide my skepticism. "Okay."

I follow him into a small room I hadn't noticed before, filled with wall-to-wall elliptical machines. He points to one that's open and I step up to it to place my water bottle in its holster.

I'm determined to look like I know what I'm doing today.

Adam leans against the machine next to me and his proximity is a little disconcerting, but not unwelcome. He's close enough that I catch the clean, sharp scent of his aftershave mixed with a hint of something—citrus, maybe?

Tucking that thought into the recess of my mind, I hop on the elliptical machine with the grace and ease of a cat.

At least, that's what I'm telling myself.

No one died and the machine didn't inadvertently start on its own. *Win.*

I start pedaling, and Adam's gaze fixes on the digital display, but not before I notice a quick sweep over my form. Professional, sure, but it lingers just a heartbeat too long on my mouth before he shifts his gaze.

And then, for just a fraction of a moment, his eyes drop to my neckline. The intensity of his look, fleeting as it is, makes me self-consciously tug at the collar of my shirt, pulling it up slightly.

Despite the warmth in the gym, a shiver runs down my spine as I ponder why he'd glance there.

Does he notice something off about my outfit? Or is he noticing the extra *me* I carry around—my love handles and double chin that could seriously rival a bakery's best croissants?

Or maybe he's thinking about how the elliptical under my less-than-svelte frame is getting a workout of its own.

I force the thoughts away, reminding myself that I'm here to work on me, not audition for the role of *'Girl Who Can't Take a Compliment or a Trainer's Glance.'*

But the tiny gremlin of doubt doesn't quite leave, settling instead in the pit of my stomach, doing its best impression of a lead weight. I suck in a sharp breath and try to force it back down.

"Keep the pace steady. The goal is to warm up the muscles and stretch them out a bit," he advises, his voice firm but encouraging. "You're doing great."

I want to seriously snicker at the 'doing great' part—my thighs are already protesting, and I've barely begun—but I bite back the sarcasm. Instead, I focus on the burn in my muscles, the steady beat of my heart, and the man who somehow makes me want to push myself harder than I have in a long time.

Throughout the warm-up, Adam stays by my side, his attention occasionally drifting over the other gym-goers but always snapping back to me like a magnet. Each time his eyes meet mine, I feel a little jolt—like there's something he wants to say.

"Okay, I think that's enough. Your muscles should be fairly warm. Let's add a little more resistance," he says after a few minutes.

When I fumble with the settings, his hand brushes mine as he helps me adjust the resistance. His fingers are warm—the touch fleeting but electric.

I look up at him, and our eyes lock—again, a silent conversation in a glance. Adam's attention seems split between my elliptical settings and something less tangible, something that's not spelled out on the digital dashboard in front of us.

"So, Carlie," he says, and I can't decide if my name sounds better or just different when he says it. "Tell me something about yourself. What do you do when you're not braving the gym?"

I nearly miss a step, and it's not the added resistance

that catches me—it's the question I always dread when I meet new people who have no idea I write dirty books for a living.

What do I say?

Well, Adam, I weave steamy love stories from the comfort of my couch, complete with rugged heroes and bold heroines who enjoy a good shag.

"I'm a writer," I blurt, which is true enough. "Fiction, mostly."

The word 'erotic' sits at the tip of my tongue, but I wrestle it back.

Not yet. *Not ever.*

"Fiction, huh?" He sounds genuinely interested, the question mark at the end of his sentence inviting more than just a polite nod. "Anything I might have read?"

This time, I snicker far too loudly to be ladylike.

Unless his bedtime reading includes shirtless men on the cover and a heat level that could melt steel, *doubtful.*

"Not likely," I say instead, with a laugh that I hope doesn't carry all my nerves in it. "It's a bit niche."

Adam smiles, and it's not a half-smirk this time but a full-on grin that reaches his eyes. "I like niche."

And just like that, I'm not just a woman on an elliptical anymore—*I'm niche.* There's something in the way he says it that makes me feel special about that.

"What motivates you?" he asks next, shifting smoothly from my professional life to my personal ambitions.

It feels intimate without crossing a line, and I'm caught off-guard by how much I want to answer.

"Other than not making a fool of myself?" I retort, but then I get serious. "I guess I want to be someone who can be proud of what she's accomplished, you know? Not just in writing, but in life. In ... *this.*" I gesture to the gym around us.

Adam nods, and there's a respect in his eyes that makes my heart expand. "I get that. We're all here to be better versions of ourselves."

I take that in, thinking about all of the people in here working their asses off simply to be better versions of themselves, too.

"I guess, I never thought of it that way," I say with a soft smile. "I always assumed the people who frequent gyms are kind of born that way."

He shakes his head. "Not even a little. Okay, maybe a few. But for the most part, we have to earn it."

I blink at that. "Hmmm."

We settle into a contemplative silence as I continue to push myself on the elliptical.

"You ever watch a horror film where you can predict who's going to trip over nothing while running from the monster?" I ask, the memory of last night's movie combined with my hydrangea bush escapade sparking a laugh between breaths.

Adam chuckles, nodding. "I have. Makes you wonder if they've ever heard of track practice in horror movie land."

"And yet, I can't stop watching them. It's like, they're so bad, they circle back to being good," I admit. "Besides, it makes me feel better about myself at the end of the day.

At least my two left feet haven't resulted in a horrific and bloody death. *Yet.*"

"Definitely something to be proud of," he fires back. "And I totally agree about the so-bad-they're-good horror movies. Ever watch Nosferatu?"

I shake my head.

"Oh, definitely one to add to your list, then. My brother Brian and I watched it one night, and because it's a silent film, we made up all the dialogue. I've never laughed so hard in my life," he says, his eyes sparkling with the memory. "Fair warning, though. Beers *may* have had something to do with the hilarity."

A completely dorky giggle escapes my lips. "I'll have to check it out."

"You'll love it. Just make sure you have someone with you so you can throw dialogue back and forth."

I swipe a hand in the air and almost miss a step. "Eh, I'm awesome at coming up with witty banter. It's a hazard of the job."

"Ah, that's right. Well, enjoy. Though, I still think it's more fun with someone else," he says, laughing. "It's more unpredictable that way."

"True." I nod.

His laughter encourages me, and I watch, fascinated, as his professional demeanor gives way to a more relaxed charm. He doesn't just laugh—*he gets it,* and that's more than I expected from Mr. Perfect Form and Function next to me.

Before I can stop myself from prying, I ask, "What

about you? When you're not making gym miracles happen—what do you do for fun?"

The question seems to take him by surprise because there's a flicker of hesitation before he answers. "Believe it or not, I like to cook," he confesses, and there's a humility in his tone that makes me smile. "There's something about the process, the ... *precision* and creativity of it."

I raise my eyebrows, pedaling in time with my growing intrigue. "Cook, as in *chef* cook?"

"Yeah," he laughs, pressing a button on my console, and increasing the pace slightly. The sweat trickling between my boobs protests, however. "Sometimes after a long day, I'll make risotto from scratch. Or a soufflé. It's sort of meditative."

My rhythm stutters as I imagine Adam, not in gym shorts and a tank top, but an apron, wielding a wooden spoon like a wand.

"Risotto, really? That's impressive. I can barely manage mac and cheese without burning the pot." I wipe the sweat from my forehead with the back of my hand.

Adam's chuckle is rich and warm. "Well, everybody starts somewhere. I could give you some pointers if you're interested."

The offer hangs in the air, heavy like the gravity around planets, pulling me into an orbit I never anticipated when I signed up for personal training.

Cooking lessons with Adam—the idea is both terrifying and tantalizing.

The elliptical suddenly feels less like a torture device

and more like a bridge, bringing me toward new territories, and new connections.

"Maybe I'll take you up on that," I reply, the words more breathless than I intend. But maybe that's the cardio going on here. "Though, I should warn you now, it could end tragically."

His expression turns thoughtful. "Everyone can cook, Carlie. It's like following a story—you have the plot—*the ingredients*—you just need to put it all together."

I glance at him, his analogy striking a chord with me. "If that's the case, consider me perpetually stuck in the messy middle."

He glances over to me, his eyes crinkling. "Maybe you just need a good editor."

And just like that, we've slipped into a place where our conversation has depth, shared secrets between breaths and beats, creating a layer of something that feels an awful lot like the beginning of a friendship. Not just a trainer—trainee sorta thing.

By the time we're done, my muscles are singing hymns of both protest and praise, and something in my chest feels lighter.

I step off the machine, and for the first time, it's not my potential embarrassment that's at the forefront of my mind—it's the surprising connection forming between me and Adam.

"Looks like you survived the elliptical without any mishaps," Adam notes, a touch of pride in his voice.

"Yeah, no comedy show today," I beam back. "Guess I'm full of surprises."

He mirrors my smile, and I can't help but think, so is he.

Adam hands me a towel, his fingers grazing the back of my hand. It's a casual gesture, but it sends my pulse into a frenzy. I dab at my forehead, trying to appear nonchalant, but my cheeks are hot, and I'm not entirely sure it's all from the workout.

As we stand there, the comfortable silence stretches between us again, filled only by the sounds of the gym winding down from the morning rush.

Just when I think he's about to say goodbye and move on to his next client, he leans in slightly, as if compelled by a thought he can't hold back.

"You know, Carlie," Adam begins, his voice lower, almost conspiratorial, "there's a little-known gym secret I haven't shared with you yet."

I tilt my head, intrigued despite myself. "Oh? And what's that?"

He hesitates, a playful yet somehow meaningful tension building in his pause. "I usually save it for the second week, but I have a feeling you might appreciate it earlier. But I warn you, it's a bit ... *unconventional.*"

I can feel my heartbeat pick up, my curiosity piqued, for sure.

"I'm no stranger to unconventional," I reply with a lightness that has my memory flash through the past weekend's escapades and the scenes it's inspired me to write.

Adam's smirk reappears, a hint of mischief lighting his eyes. "Good. Because it's not just about the physical training around here. There's something else, something that might just change the way you see everything in this place."

Despite myself, a mixture of excitement and apprehension courses through me.

What could possibly make such a difference?

He leans in even closer, his breath a warm whisper against my ear. "It's a special class," he murmurs. "One that requires a certain ... *openness*. A willingness to embrace the unexpected."

A shiver races through me like a lightning bolt sent from Zeus himself.

"And when is this mysterious class?" I ask, unable to hide my smirk.

"Tonight," he says, pulling back just enough to search my face for a reaction. "Meet me here at six. Wear loose, comfortable clothes. I promise it'll be worth your while."

With that, he steps back, the spell of his closeness broken, leaving me with a heart racing and a mind whirling with possibilities.

Was he asking me out on a date? Was that his veiled way of getting me to agree?

"See you tonight, Carlie," he offers with a wink.

Dumbfounded, I watch him walk away, pondering over how he made a wink look so sexy.

CHAPTER 7

Adam

6:00 p.m. sharp, and I'm pacing outside the gym, trying to play it cool.

I told Carlie to meet me here so I could bring her to this class. All the while, reminding myself to stay professional.

But she's late, and I'm starting to think I might be waiting for no one.

Maybe I should have been clearer about what I planned.

Vagueness can be off-putting, right?

Maybe she's not the adventurous type?

However, just when I consider calling it a day, the doors burst open.

She's not in anything I'd call workout attire. Instead, she's sporting a casual turtleneck tank and a skirt that outlines her curves with an accuracy that screams *'tailor-made.'* And those sandals, flaunting teal-painted toenails, look more suited for a dance floor than a yoga mat.

Holy hell.

It takes a moment to get my brain to snap back to trainer mode.

This isn't a date.

"Hey," she says, walking up with a sheepish grin that suggests she's fully aware of her apparel mishap. "I might have misunderstood the invite? And dress code, come to think of it."

I laugh, unable to help it because she's just so damned cute when she's flustered. "No worries, you look ... *nice*. Really nice." I catch myself before I can go too far. "But what I have planned might challenge the integrity of that skirt."

Her cheeks flush with a warm rose glow and I wish I could read her thoughts.

She clears her throat gently. "With all that chat about classes, I hoped we'd be sitting cross-legged, omming our way to enlightenment—or engaging in a high-stakes staring contest."

"I'd pay to see that," I chuckle, enjoying the lightness between us. "But tonight's agenda is a bit more ... *interactive.*"

Her eyes widen just a touch, curiosity sparkling there. "Interactive?"

"Yeah, trust me, it'll be fun," I say, leading her inside, my brain scrambling for solutions before she decides her outfit won't work.

The gym is quiet in the current evening lull and her class at the back is a tranquil space that will seem like worlds away from the clanking of weights and the hum of treadmills.

Curiosity dances across her features. "And what is it we're doing?"

"Yoga," I say, hoping she'll be game. "It helps a ton with the muscle soreness and flexibility. There's also a lot of functional strength training."

She nods softly, contemplating as we continue towards the studio.

I'd planned this to be simple—she'd be in the yoga class, I'd be on the sidelines, offering tips. However, when I open the door, it's clear fate has a sense of humor.

Instead of solo participants, partners are intertwined in synchronized poses as they begin their pre-yoga stretches.

My gut twists with an unexpected jolt.

Partner yoga.

"Uh, we might have to improvise a bit," I say, turning to her and rubbing a hand across the back of my neck.

Carlie peers through the glass, her eyes now wide green orbs. "Are those couples buddying it up together in there?"

"Seems like it." Caught off guard, I nod—all the while, my brain is a whir of sirens. I should let her go home. Tell her we'll try again. Instead, I hear myself say, "Since I'm the one who dragged you here, looks like you have me as a partner."

"It's okay. I mean, I don't exactly have yoga clothes with me ..." She sweeps her hands over her body.

"There's a shop just around the corner. They'll have

everything you need." I offer, knowing I can charge it to my work tab. "My treat, since I sprung this on you."

We stand there for a moment, a strange buzz of unexpected excitement hanging between us.

Then, in the absence of a rebuttal, I gesture for her to follow me. "Let's get you geared up so we're not too late."

She nods, allowing me to lead the way.

As we head towards the shop, I can't shake the feeling that tonight might just stretch both of us in more ways than one.

Twenty minutes later, we're facing each other on adjacent mats. We were a few minutes late, but welcomed in like we were the long lost Dalai Lama.

Now that we sit here, I realize Carlie's hastily chosen yoga gear fits her a bit too well for my peace of mind. Keeping it cool pushes itself to paramount in my alarm-sounding brain.

The instructor, a serene woman with a voice as smooth as silk, starts the class with a simple meditation, guiding us to connect with our partners through synchronized breathing.

I have to smile a bit, remembering what Carlie first said before we entered this space. Yet, even despite her teasing, she's taking the meditation in stride, settling right into it like she's done it her whole life.

Her eyes are closed, long dark lashes casting shadows over her cheeks, as I watch her chest rise and fall with each breath. Oddly enough, there's nothing relaxing about watching it. If anything, it makes my insides jumble.

"Now, open your eyes and maintain the connection," the instructor murmurs in her sing-song voice.

Carlie opens her eyes and our gazes lock. It feels like a silent conversation happens—one I'm all too keen to continue.

"Ready?" I whisper, half teasing, half challenging.

She nods, her lips curving into a smile. "As I'll ever be."

"First pose," the instructor announces, "the Double Tree. Balance on one foot, and press the sole of your other foot to the inside of your thigh. Then, reach out, holding your partner's hands to find your center."

Getting up, we move slowly, mirroring each other's movements. Carlie wobbles a bit, her foot slipping.

"Oops," she giggles, gripping my forearm for support. "I'd love to lie and say I'm usually more grounded than this, but you already know better."

I chuckle, steadying her with a gentle touch. "Nothing wrong with a little wobble. It's all part of finding your balance—in *yoga* and I guess in … other things too."

She laughs, a sound that seems to fit perfectly in the quiet studio, and finally finds her footing. "Okay, Mr. Philosopher, let's see how well you do when we move on to the next pose."

"No pressure," I say, trying to maintain my own pose. Turns out, my hamstrings are tight and staying upright is more of a challenge than anticipated.

As we secure our balance in Double Tree, Carlie's concentration is palpable. She's determined not to let her initial wobble define the session.

"Nice recovery," I compliment her, and her responding grin is nothing short of triumphant.

"Thanks to my human crutch," she fires back, her dimples digging into her cheeks.

"Not at all. You've got this," I say, releasing my hold just a bit to show her.

She whimpers at the loss of contact, but remains upright, as predicted.

We move on to the next sequence of poses, and I can't help but notice the seamless ebb and flow of motions between the other pairs in the room. Their ease with one another speaks of shared spaces and intimacies far beyond what Carlie and I have—*or should have.*

Each touch, no matter how innocuous, carries a ripple of something more between the other participants and it does strange things to my head.

"Next, we'll be doing the Seated Forward Bend with a twist," the instructor announces.

Carlie and I sit facing each other, legs extended, our feet barely touching.

"You'll lean forward and reach for your partner's hands," the instructor guides.

As we fold towards each other, our fingers awkwardly lace together, and I can feel the hesitant pressure of her palms against mine. They're in contrast to the confident clasps around us.

"Now, look into each other's eyes, and synchronize your breathing again," the instructor continues.

I look into Carlie's eyes, and feel a jolt of something I have no right to be feeling, but I can't seem to help it. We breathe in, and as we exhale, I catch the faint scent of vanilla and something wild—like the night air mixed with adrenaline.

We move on to a Cat-Cow stretch, hands and knees grounded, moving our spines with the breath. I sneak a glance as Carlie arches her back, her hair cascading forward, and for a moment, the room around us fades.

Her hair sweeps past her shoulder and drifts like a red feather across my arm. The brief contact is like a live wire to my senses and my body goes rigid.

"Remember to keep your movements fluid," the instructor says, placing a guiding hand on my shoulder and giving it a pat.

Oh, if she only knew.

I nod, trying to relax into the pose and ignoring the sudden rush of blood down south.

Thankfully, by the time we transition into the Revolved Chair pose, things have settled back to normal. *Thank fuck.*

However, this whole session is an odd mix of control and vulnerability—a push and pull that somehow feels like the very definition of our blurring relationship.

At one point, our hands are supposed to mirror the other, but instead, my fingers graze Carlie's as I twist, causing a momentary break in her concentration.

She looks at me, eyes wide, and there's that current again—stronger now.

"Sorry, looks like I've got butterfingers today," I say, though the touch was more electric than slippery and I'd do it all over again.

"It's okay," Carlie responds, her voice just above a whisper, "I don't mind a little ... *butter.*"

Her words are laced with innuendo, whether intentional or not. Especially with where my traitorous mind keeps pulling me to.

We continue through the poses, and with each one, I find myself admiring her more—not just for her physical grace, but for her ability to laugh at herself when that grace slips.

As we end the session with Corpse pose, lying flat on our backs, the distance between us is now pronounced. I close my eyes, and the afterimage of red hair fluttering against my skin lingers.

It blurs the lines between past and present.

Between what's real and what's simply a ghost.

Is that why I feel so connected to her? Because I want to see in her what I felt with the woman at Nocté?

The chime signaling the end of class pulls me back to reality, but I remain on the mat a moment longer, caught in the throes of a memory that feels both too close and too far away to grasp.

By the time we roll up our mats, I find myself actually disappointed it's over. Not because of the similarities to another redhead, but because of *her*.

In fact, I wouldn't mind coming back for another

session—another chance to discover more about the woman who's crashed into my life. *Literally.*

"I didn't make a complete fool of myself, did I?" Carlie asks, breaking into my thoughts.

"Far from it," I assure her, my words sincere. "You were ... *impressive.*"

As we walk out of the yoga studio, a shared silence enveloping us, I can't help but steal glances at Carlie like I'm seeing her for the first time.

She's unaware, caught up in her own thoughts—perhaps mulling over the evening's unforeseen closeness, too. But then, she turns to me, a question in her eyes that she hesitates to voice. Instead, she shakes her head and we continue on our way.

Just as we reach the street, my phone vibrates in my pocket.

A flicker of irritation crosses my mind—now isn't the time I want to be pulled away from this moment. Yet, reflexively, I pull it out and glance at the screen.

It's a text, but not just any message—it's from an unknown number— and what it says chills the post-yoga warmth right out of my bones.

> Crossing some lines, don't you think?

I stare at the message, the words a jolt of cold water down my spine. It's too pointed—too *intimate* to be a coincidence.

My gaze lifts to scan the parking lot's dim light as a niggle of paranoia creeps into my mind. However, there's nothing out of place—just the gentle hum of the city at night.

"Everything okay?" Carlie's voice cuts through my thoughts.

"Yeah, all good." I lock my phone and slip it back into my pocket, offering her a reassuring smile that feels like a lie. "Just an odd message from a wrong number, I guess."

Her eyes hold mine, a flicker of doubt there, but she doesn't press. Instead, she offers a tired chuckle, "Well, if it's someone telling you that you've won a million dollars, just remember who sweated through an embarrassing round of yoga with you tonight."

I laugh, the sound, unfortunately, feeling forced. "You'll be the first to know, promise."

We walk together, both lost in our thoughts until we reach her car.

The evening feels like it's reached its end. But the text's echo lingers with me. It's a nagging whisper that tells me sleep will be elusive tonight—chased away by the shadows of unanswered questions and the silhouette of a woman who's quickly becoming more than just a client.

CHAPTER 8

Carlie

I flop onto my couch with all the grace of a fainting goat—which, coincidentally, is also how I'd describe my current yoga skill level.

The session with Adam left me feeling like a pretzel —a slightly overheated, *very confused* pretzel—who can't figure out if it wants to be in a bakery or doing naked downward dog with my personal trainer.

My body's still buzzing from the surprise yoga session with Adam. Not to mention the memory of his hands guiding my hips, and his breath warm on my neck as he adjusted my posture.

Whatever it is about him, it's more than physical. There's a stirring inside me that I can't quite name. And to be quite frank, I'm a little scared to.

As I lay there, contemplating my life and whether I might need to hire a crane to hoist me up later, I can't help but be amazed by Adam.

He's like the hero from one of my steamier scenes,

except he wears sexy tank tops that showcase his incredible arm muscles and doesn't solely exist on a page.

And let's be honest, no man in my books has ever made me feel like I need a safe word for stretching.

I chortle to myself at that thought but still don't make a move to leave the warm embrace of my couch cushions.

I need to work—*to write*—but I'm not sure I've got it in me tonight. There's a frantic energy—something building that needs release.

Staring at the ceiling, I huff a laugh.

Being hot and bothered is part of the job description. It's how some of my steamiest scenes have become literary art.

So, begrudgingly, I stand up and walk over to my writing nook. I open my laptop, but the blank document stares back at me like the final round of a staring contest I'm about to lose.

Instead of typing, my mind does a backbend right into the memory of Club Nocté. The dim lights, the scent of mystery, and possibly too much cologne in the air—*it's all there.*

I close my eyes, surrendering to the daydream.

It's less of writing a scene and more of mentally choreographing one. And, boy, do the characters move in ways that would make tonight's yoga instructor blush— or who knows, maybe she'd give me a high-five for imaginative flexibility.

The daydream spins out of control, and I'm caught

in a whirlwind of 'what-ifs' that leave me wishing I had a way to bring it to life again.

The man at Nocté was so incredibly attentive. Sexy in a way I've never experienced and certainly built in a way that only Greek gods have been known to be. His muscles had muscles.

Never in a million years should I have been having sex with a man like him—and yet, that's what we did.

All.

Night.

Long.

Like we were a couple of sex-deprived rabbits ready to repopulate the earth.

Every surface, every angle …

Lord, I did things that would make my characters clutch their pearls.

But the best part …

Not once did he make me feel out of place or too fat to fuck.

No, he made me feel like I was the air he desperately needed to breathe and every touch was something that could bring him to his knees.

He was sexy in a way I didn't *even know* existed. And that's saying something since I make a living dreaming up new ways for my characters to cop a feel.

In his eyes, that night I felt so sexy. So beautiful and intriguing. And I've never, *ever* seen myself that way—but always wished I had.

I guess that's all thanks to my Zoey persona.

I embraced all she is and stands for and definitely

seized the moment—amongst other things. Large, *girthy* things.

An involuntary shudder skitters down my spine as I think about the rest of his physique hidden below the belt. His long, hard length in my hand, my mouth—hell, *everywhere.*

Whew, that night...

I fan myself, my core tightening and nipples hardening just at the thought.

The tension has to go somewhere, and let's just say, the shower head and I have become better acquainted as of late.

Right now, I definitely hear its siren song.

Slowly lifting from the cushy fabric of my desk chair, I make my way to the bathroom with a purpose that screams *release.*

Release from my new workout shirt.

From my yoga pants.

My hairband.

From *everything.*

When the water has warmed up, I step into the stream, allowing it to consume me. The warmth rushes across my neck and back, cascading slowly over my swollen breasts and stomach.

Closing my eyes, I trace the soft curve of my breasts, letting my fingernails gently brush across my nipples. I hiss from the contact, wishing I was back in Nocté— wishing it was his hands running across my chest again.

Visions of him flutter behind my eyelids—his sandy brown hair that stood up, messy and tousled thanks to my fingers. His dark mask firmly in place the whole night.

I'd never be able to spot him in public—even though I've been looking.

Truthfully, the only thing that would give him away is the small tribal tattoo in the space beneath his belly button and just above his happy trail.

It's unlikely I'll ever witness him running around the lakewalk with that part of himself exposed.

I shiver again at the memory and drop my fingertips to circle the bundle of nerves that desperately need release.

The image shifts as I let my fingertips roam my wet skin. Instead of the man from Nocté, it's Adam's hands touching.

Pulling.

Playing.

His strong arms, the stability that comes so easily from him.

What would his kisses feel like?

Would he be able to help me forget my experience at Nocté? Or will that mystery man haunt me for the rest of my life?

My lips curve into a smile as I ponder *both* of their hands on me.

That's enough to send me tipping over the edge.

My orgasm rips through me and it's a struggle to stay upright as my legs quake and my gasps echo against the shower walls.

For the longest time, I stand there, letting the after-shocks roll through me.

Last Friday has ruined me for vanilla sex.

But Nocté isn't the only reason I'm restless for more.

I make a mental note to maybe, *possibly,* thank Adam for the unintentional inspiration—or bill him for the water usage.

Morning greets me with the tenderness of a jackhammer, despite falling into sleep's embrace swiftly after my aquatic bliss.

Not only does my head throb, but every muscle in my body sings a chorus of aches in a key I can't quite place—but am pretty sure could be classified as *torture.*

The gym is a no-go today unless Adam's got a session called *'Gentle Weeping on a Mat'* hidden in his back pocket.

I'm as likely to lift weights as I am to fly to the moon.

Instead, the highlight of my day is going to be choreographing a one-woman show titled *'The Perils of Sitting Down'* every time I need the bathroom.

Because, yeah, *that's* gonna suck.

I trudge my way to the bathroom, cursing my existence.

Why can't women be the ones with dicks?

Sore muscles, you say?

Whip it out, and pee standing up.

No problem-o.

Instead, because I'm a woman, I'm in a tragicomedy that deserves a standing ovation—primarily because sitting is not an option.

It's in the midst of this performance that I hear a key slide in my back door—a sound that's as out of place in my locked-down fortress of solitude as a snowman in a sauna.

My grandma wouldn't bother with the key. She'd call and demand I come downstairs to see her.

Cursing life, the universe, and my angry muscles, I pull my sweats up and hobble to the back door with a plunger in hand as my weapon of choice.

The door creaks open, and in waltzes Michael, *my fucking ex,* as if he's just popping by for a cup of sugar and not like he's the human equivalent of expired milk.

"What in the home invasion handbook are you doing here?" I gasp, leaning against the doorframe in a way that does little to support my dignity.

Where the hell is Grandma and her freakishly keen eyesight? She should have warned me here.

"I, uh—still have my key," Michael says, holding it up like it's the golden ticket to the kingdom.

With great effort, I push off the wall and snatch it from his hand. "Check-out time was when you decided to play 'hide the salami' with Sasha," I retort, feeling a spark of the old fire that I usually reserve for sassy dialogue in my books.

Michael stands awkwardly in the doorway, the very antithesis of Adam's confident posture.

Where Adam is all muscular certainty, Michael is

leaner, his frame lacking the same intentionality. His hair, once my fingers' favorite labyrinth, now just seems unkempt. And those dark eyes that used to twinkle for me, now just look ... well, *dim*.

"I came to apologize," he says, looking like a dog caught raiding the trash.

Just as I'm about to deliver a biting retort, my ringtone—a maddeningly catchy pop tune that will be stuck in my goddamn head all day—cuts through the tension.

Holding the plunger like a scepter for the domestically challenged, I fish out my phone from my sagging sweats pocket, nearly dropping it in my limberness-lacking stupor. "Hello?"

"Carlie, it's Adam. You were supposed to be here ten minutes ago. Everything okay?" His voice is warm, concerned, and it triggers a blush that creeps up my neck as memories of last night's mental escapades flood back.

"Oh, yeah, just ..." I manage, my eyes darting to Michael who seems to shrink under the scrutiny, "dealing with some unexpected housework."

There's a soft chuckle from Adam, and I can almost picture his half-smile. "Housework, huh? Well, don't overdo it. Remember, rest is just as important as the workout."

I'm smiling now, the image of Adam's teasing grin making my heart do odd little flips. "Thanks, I'll ... keep that in mind."

"Tomorrow?" he prompts and I swear, I hear a hint of hopefulness in his tone.

I nod, smiling to myself. "Tomorrow."

"See ya, Carlie," he says, the soft beep of the phone call ending echoing in my ear.

Michael's still hovering, an apology half-formed on his lips.

With my phone clutched at my side, I cut him off with a gesture to the plunger in my other hand. "You see this? It means I'm cleaning house, Michael. Starting with taking out the trash."

How a plunger has anything to do with trash is beyond me—but it made sense at the time.

Thankfully, though, he gets the hint, *finally*, mumbling something about leaving as he backs away.

When he's on the other side, I close the door with a soft click, leaning against it for a moment to collect myself.

I can't help the giggle that escapes me.

Adam's casual check-in, the absurdity of the situation with Michael, my insanely sore body—it's all too much. I'm not sure what's more laughable—the fact that my ex thought he could waltz back into my life for God knows what reason, or that the man I fantasized about last night is the one who saved me from the whole ordeal.

Shaking my head, I text Adam a quick thank you for his concern and assure him I'll be back on the mat in no time.

As I hit send, I realize that my interactions with men lately are more fraught with comedy than the romance I write about.

But that's life, isn't it?

One big romantic comedy, minus the romance but with an extra helping of comedy. At least, in my world.

I chuck the plunger under the sink—my symbol of victory.

Today, I've fended off past mistakes and embraced my present—a present that might just include a too-caring personal trainer and a showerhead that's seen way too much.

CHAPTER 9

Adam

The gym feels emptier than usual this morning.

Maybe it's the absence of Carlie's laugh, which, despite our brief acquaintance, has become a sound I've found myself actually looking forward to.

I keep glancing at the clock, half-expecting her to walk in, apologizing for being late, but I know better.

After our conversation, it was pretty clear she had no intention of making her session today. For some reason, it disappointed me more than it should.

I get blown off all the time.

But after last night, I had hoped to continue whatever it is we seem to be building.

I don't want to push it though.

If she's sore or has other things going on, the last thing I want is to scare her off. I've seen clients bolt for less, and the thought of Carlie not coming back feels like it would hit different.

With an unexpected gap in my morning schedule, I head over to Dylan's coffee shop for a caffeine fix and some light-hearted banter to lift my spirits.

The bell above the door announces my arrival, and Dylan looks up from behind the counter, his trademark shitty grin locked in place.

"Look who's graced us with his presence," Dylan calls out, already reaching for a large cup. "The usual?"

"Yeah, thanks," I reply, sliding onto a stool at the counter. "And maybe some of that banana bread if it's fresh."

"You're in luck. Stacy made a batch this morning. So, how's life in the land of spandex and sweat?" he teases, slicing a generous piece of banana bread.

I shouldn't even be eating the stuff—*too many carbs*—but I can't seem to help it. It's *sooo* damn good.

I chuckle, accepting the coffee and treat as he hands it over the counter. "Not bad. Had a no-show today, though."

Internally, I cringe at the nonchalance in my words because I know Carlie's already so much more than that.

"This the new client you were talking about on Sunday?" Dylan asks, leaning in with a raised eyebrow.

"Yeah, actually," I nod. "I think she's sore but just doesn't want to say it. But who knows? She said something about unexpected housework."

"Women. They're unpredictable, man," he scoffs, sliding his glasses up his nose. "Speaking of unpredictable women ... Any new hookups I should be aware of?"

I roll my eyes, taking a sip of the hot coffee. "Still on that, huh?"

"Always." He flashes me a wide grin. "After last time, I figure I need to be proactive from here on out. So, who's the new client? Anyone I should hunt down after work and ask out?"

I pause, coffee halfway to my lips, the steam tickling at my nose.

"Nah, she's ... *different*," I find myself saying, the words feeling both protective and foreign. "Definitely not your type."

I try to laugh it off, but a knot forms in my gut.

Dylan's eyebrows shoot up in mock surprise. "*Different*, huh? That sounds to me like Adam Foxx, the man who's seen it all, might be intrigued. What's her name?"

I swallow my coffee, the sting of it burns all the way down. "Carlie."

"Huh, that name's familiar." His eyes go distant for a moment. "I swear there's a Carlie that comes in here once in a while."

"I'm sure there's more than one Carlie in the whole of Duluth, Dyl," I say, matter-of-factly.

He shrugs it off with a laugh. "Yeah, suppose you're right. Regardless ..."

"How's business?" I interject, with the hope of deflecting the conversation away from anything too personal.

Dylan shrugs, slicing another piece of banana bread for the display case. "Good, good. You know, the usual crowd. Your brother swung by yesterday and said you're still moping about Jillian. Tell me that's not true."

"What?" I sputter. "No. *Hell* no."

"Not what Brian says," Dylan presses, a mischievous glint in his eyes. "He thinks you're not over her."

I shake my head, a potent mix of sibling annoyance and general amusement bubbling up inside me. "Brian's got a big mouth. And as for Jillian, she's the past. It's just … I'm so sick of her flaunting her new relationship around the gym. Besides, whatever Brian said—our conversation wasn't even really about that. He thinks I need to put more energy into Foxx Fitness."

"He's not wrong," Dylan says, giving me one of his knowing, *'I've been around the block as a barista,'* looks. "Maybe channeling your energy into something positive or brand new is just what you need. But back to this Carlie …"

I groan. *Loudly.*

"Are you sure there's nothing there? Seems like she's got you thinking differently," he continues, giving zero fucks that I'm obviously not into this line of questioning.

I open my mouth to deny it, but the chime of the doorbell interrupts me. We both turn to see the door swing open, and in walks Jillian, as if summoned by our conversation about complicated women.

Her eyes lock onto me, a storm brewing in their depths. She strides over, her heels—*definitely not work-out-ready*—click against the tiled floor like a metronome ticking down to an inevitable confrontation.

Her latest boyfriend, a guy who's more brawn than brains, trails behind her like a shadow.

"Adam," she announces, loud enough for half the coffee shop to hear. "We need to talk."

Dylan raises his eyebrows, looking from me to Jillian and back again—his unspoken question hanging in the air.

I set my coffee down, bracing myself.

"And what exactly would you like to talk about?" I say, keeping my tone even—almost bored. I know how much she *loves* that.

She clicks her tongue. "We need to talk about how *unprofessional* your little yoga session with the gym's new client was. Partner yoga? *Really?*"

I stare at her dumbfounded.

"First of all, what I do after my shift is none of your goddamn business. Second of all, how'd you—" I begin.

She waves her hand like she's waving away the world's most inane question. "It's all over the gym and someone posted about it on Instagram."

I narrow my gaze, totally confused.

Who the hell would post about me and Carlie on Instagram?

Dylan stands up straight and crosses his arms. "Jillian, this isn't the place for—"

"I'll decide what's *appropriate*, Dylan," she snaps, then turns her focus back to me. "I can't believe you'd be so reckless. What if people start talking and it impacts the quality of the gym? You're supposed to be a professional, Adam."

Her words hang between us, and I can feel Dylan's heavy gaze boring a hole into the back of my head.

I take a deep breath, trying to keep the situation from escalating right here in his coffee shop. This was supposed to be a quick stop to chill with my best friend, not a stage for Jillian's drama.

I glance over my shoulder at Dylan, who wisely decides to busy himself with cleaning the espresso machine, and giving us the illusion of privacy.

Jillian's presence, and her accusations, however—they're the last things I need right now. Especially with thoughts of Carlie already occupying too much of my headspace.

I feel my jaw tighten. "Like I said, what I do with my clients is none of your damn business. And last I checked, you're not exactly the authority on professionalism."

My eyes dart to the guy beside her.

She balks, her face flushing a deep red, and for a moment, I think she's going to cause a scene for that one. Because let's face it, at least I'm not cheating on anyone.

But Dylan steps in, his voice calm and firm. "Jillian, you need to get coffee somewhere else today."

She huffs, muttering something under her breath before storming out, her new boyfriend following without a word.

Real stand-up guy, that one.

I let out a sigh, feeling the weight of her words and the uncertainty they bring.

When the door has closed behind them, Dylan lets

out a low whistle. "Exes, huh? Can't live with them, can't avoid them in a town this size."

"Yeah, especially when you work with them," I mutter, running my palm over my face.

"Truth. I thought for sure, I was gonna have to bust out my authoritative, business owner voice," Dylan chuckles, but his tone quickly changes to one of concern. "You okay, man? Jillian really knows how to push down all of your buttons at the same time."

I shrug, trying to shake off the lingering frustration. "Yeah, I'm fine. It's just typical Jillian bullshit. Nothing I haven't dealt with before."

He nods, pouring himself a cup of coffee. "Still, the whole Instagram thing is weird. You sure there wasn't some crazy fan at the gym who could've posted about whatever the two of you were doing? Which I'm gonna need more details on, by the way."

I frown, pondering over it. Truthfully, I was so engrossed with Carlie that I didn't even notice anything outside our bubble.

Sidestepping his last sentence, I say, "I don't know. It was just a yoga session. Carlie's new to working out, so I thought it would help. I mean, sure, it was a bit close, because we ended up being in partner yoga, but it was all professional." The image of Carlie, the way we moved together during the session, flashes in my mind, causing a stir of something I can't quite define.

"Sounds like it was more than just 'professional' for someone to make such a fuss about it," Dylan observes, a teasing glint in his eyes.

My expression deadpans.

He clears his throat, taking another sip of his coffee. "So, Mr. Yoga now, huh? Weren't we just talking about Melissa? Was she your instructor?"

Thankfully, our yoga session was *not* taught by the enigmatic instructor with a pet ferret.

"No, it wasn't Melissa. And the session *was* strictly professional," I insist, but even to my ears, it sounds like I'm trying to convince myself more than Dylan.

"Sure, Adam. Okay," he chides, his tone playful yet a little too knowing for my liking. "But you don't have to convince me. What you do with your dick is your business. I just want to know if whatever transpired was any good." He wiggles his eyebrows, but his tone turns serious. "But just remember, if you ever need to talk about anything—professional or not—I'm here for you, bro."

I nod, appreciating his offer and ignoring the slight innuendo there. "Thanks, Dylan. I'll keep that in mind."

"Anytime," he says with more eyebrow wiggles. "Now go show those weights who's boss. And maybe think about setting some boundaries with Jillian. For your sanity, man."

I chuckle, though the thought lingers uncomfortably in my mind. "Yeah, I think you're right there."

The question is how?

As I stand to leave, my phone buzzes in my pocket.

Pulling it out, I see a notification for a new Instagram post tagged at the gym.

Curiosity piqued, I open the app. And as luck would

have it, it's a picture of Carlie and me in a yoga pose. Our bodies are pressed far closer than I remembered.

The caption reads: *"New training methods at St. Mary's? Where do I sign up?"* with a couple of suggestive emojis behind it.

I don't know the account, or who posted it, and by the looks of it, they're not exactly a gym rat.

My heart sinks.

"Something up?" Dylan asks, noticing the change in my demeanor.

I show him the post. "This is what Jillian was talking about. I was just tagged."

Dylan whistles. "That looks ... *intimate*, man. Can see why Jillian flipped out. Who posted it?"

I lock my phone, my mood soured. "No idea. But I need to sort this out before it blows up."

"Good luck, man. And remember, keep it professional," Dylan says with a teasing smile, but his eyes are sympathetic.

"Always do," I reply, though my thoughts are already racing.

How am I going to explain this to Carlie? What if she sees this and thinks I crossed a line last night? Is that why she's not here today?

Stepping out of the coffee shop, I decide to head back to the gym.

I need to track down whoever posted this and clear the air.

Then, I need to talk to Carlie. I need to make sure she knows that whatever that photo suggests, it wasn't my intention to make her uncomfortable—or a target for the gossip mill.

This isn't just about the gym's reputation—though I'm sure Jillian will try to make it that way to ease the scrutiny on her.

No, this is about Carlie, and how much I don't want this to change her perception of the gym—*or me.*

CHAPTER 10

Carlie

I stumble into Dirty Books, Tasia's unique bookstore, and the unofficial sanctuary for my kind—bookworms with a penchant for pinot and smut.

Clutching a couple of bottles of wine to my chest like a lifeline, because my legs are still screaming bloody murder, I'm fashionably late to the Dirty B's book club —or as I like to call it, my weekly reality check with a side of sarcasm.

I make my way to our alcove, a place now likened to a haven of literary chaos. Tasia smiles broadly, sitting in a brand new dark burgundy wingback chair—one of three, by the looks of it.

Excellent, no more horrifying metallic fold-out chairs to contend with. I don't think my ass could take it—definitely not while it already feels like it's being shredded apart from my ill attempts at getting fit.

"Oh, look. Carlie's here. *With wine,*" Anna drawls without even looking up.

How she knows that is beyond me, since her face is still plastered to her phone. She extends a hand to Vivian, who slaps money in it.

When Vivian catches my gaze, she smiles sheepishly. "Anna said you'd remember."

"Ah." I nod once.

Translation: *she didn't.*

When I glance at Tasia and Lily, they're both shaking their heads, but have big grins on their faces. I have to admit, their smiles are contagious, and I can't help but grin back, even as I gingerly lower myself into one of the new wingback chairs, grateful for its plush embrace.

"Of course, I remembered the wine. After the week I've been having, it's a necessity at this point," I mutter, all the while the dietary drill sergeant in the back of my head says, *'But is it, though?'*

Curse you, drill sergeant.

Lily looks up from her tablet, her eyes twinkling with mischief. "So, what's been going on, Carlie? Besides plotting world domination one romance novel at a time," she adds with a wink.

"More like surviving my own personal boot camp," I sigh, setting the wine on the table and massaging my aching thighs. "My new trainer is on a mission to reacquaint me with muscles I forgot existed."

Tasia reaches out, opening one of the bottles and pouring wine into each glass. Her eyebrows are raised in amusement.

However, it's Lily who cuts in again, "And how has Ada been? Is she nice?"

"Uh," I hedge.

Looks like I forgot to fill her in that *Ada* is actually *Adam*. Whoopsie.

I take a deep sip from my glass, feeling the wine's warmth spread through me. Truthfully, it's a welcome contrast to the soreness that's become my constant companion.

I bite the side of my lip and fiddle with the fabric across my thighs. "Well, about Ada ... turns out there was a tiny misunderstanding."

Lily's eyes widen. "What do you mean?"

Vivian's eyes also narrow on me and I flinch slightly under their scrutiny.

"Turns out, Ada isn't Ada after all. My trainer is Adam." I shake my head. "As in, a very much *male* Adam."

Anna's head slowly rises and her eyes leave her phone. "Hold up. You've been getting trained by a guy this whole time and you didn't know his name?"

I shift uncomfortably in my seat, feeling all of their eyes on me. "In my defense, the email from the gym had a typo. It said 'Ada.' I just assumed they knew how to spell their trainer's names ..."

Vivian leans forward in her chair and bursts into laughter, nearly spilling her wine in the process. "So, you were mentally prepared to meet Ada, and in walks this Adam? I would've loved to see your face."

My cheeks flush at the memory. "Let's just say I was *... a bit surprised.*"

"So, what's he like?" Lily takes a sip of her wine, her

eyes dancing with curiosity. "Is he the gruff, silent type, or more of a chiseled Adonis?"

I can't help but laugh at the thought. We've only known each other a few months, but she already knows my adjectives so well. "He's certainly ... *fit*. And maybe a little too enthusiastic about squats and lunges for my liking. He's the reason I hobbled in here like my eighty-year-old grandma."

Vivian's grin is feline. "Enthusiastic about squats, huh? That paints a picture."

Anna turns to Vivian with a sardonic eyebrow raised. "Did your mind just take a detour into the gutter?"

"When doesn't it?" Tasia fires back, a huge smile spreading across her lips before she takes a sip from her glass.

Lily nods in agreement. "So, how have the workouts been? I assume he's good, since you haven't swapped him out for a female trainer."

A soft smile floats to my lips as I think back to our yoga session. "He's ... *surprising*. Challenging, but in a good way, I guess."

Vivian bites her lip, her eyes glinting with mischief. "Does this 'good way' involve appreciating his sexy form while he demonstrates those squats?"

I feel my cheeks heating up. "I'm trying to focus on the exercises, not ... *that.*"

"But you're not denying it," Vivian interjects, her tone teasing. "Come on, Carlie, we're all friends here. You can admit if he's hot."

I take a deep breath, the wine emboldening me.

"Okay, fine. He's definitely attractive. There, I said it. Happy?"

The group bursts into laughter and teasing remarks, but Anna remains quietly focused on her phone, her fingers moving with a purpose. After a moment, she looks up, her deadpan expression hiding a glint of something I can only assume is amusement. It's hard to tell with her.

"So, this Adam ... is he Adam Foxx by any chance?" Anna asks looking like a cat who caught a canary.

I pause, blinking in surprise. "How did you know his last name?"

Anna holds up her phone, displaying an Instagram profile. "Because Adam Foxx, your mystery trainer from St. Mary's, happens to be somewhat of an Instagram celebrity."

The group leans in, peering at Anna's phone.

There he is—Adam—in various shots showing off his perfectly toned physique, engaging in workouts, and even some behind-the-scenes glimpses of his personal life.

I practically fall out of my chair.

His follower count reads in *the millions.*

Vivian whistles, her eyes wide. "Holy ... Carlie, you've been training with an Instagram sensation?"

My mouth feels like I've been sucking on a desert dune. "I ... I had no idea. He never mentioned anything about this."

Anna's smirk widens. "Seems like you've got more than just a trainer. He's a whole brand."

Lily's voice drops low as she says, "And here we were, thinking you were just getting *regular* gym sessions."

"Bet that makes those squats and lunges a bit more interesting now, doesn't it?" Vivian chimes in, nodding in my direction.

My cheeks feel like they've burst into flames as I pat them down.

The Adam in these photos seems worlds apart from the Adam who teases me about forgotten water bottles and pushes me to my limits at the gym. It's like seeing a completely different side of him, one that's polished, public, and ... *intimidating.*

Oh, god ... What he must think of me.

"Wow, Carlie. Training with a celebrity and you didn't even brag about it," Tasia jokes, reaching across her chair to nudge my shoulder gently.

I manage a weak smile in her direction but my mind is racing. This new revelation about Adam adds a whole layer of complexity to my already confusing feelings.

"Yeah, I guess I'm just humble like that." I force a laugh. "Or clueless. *Probably* clueless."

Anna, still scrolling through Adam's Instagram, says, "Look at this one. He's doing yoga in front of the Lift Bridge at sunset."

Vivian snatches the phone, her eyes widening as she takes it in. "Dang, he looks bendy."

I lean over to look and can't help but quip, "Oh, I can personally attest to the bendiness. We did partner yoga on Tuesday night."

The room falls silent, every pair of eyes suddenly fixed on me again. Why can't I just keep my mouth shut?

"I mean, it was unexpected, but ..." I backpedal.

"Partner yoga?" Anna's eyes nearly bulge out of their sockets. "As in, *let's balance our bodies in an intimately close proximity way* yoga?"

Tasia sets her glass down with a clink. "Well, that certainly adds a new layer to *personal training*."

Vivian's eyes glitter with unspoken questions, her earlier teasing taking on new meaning. "So, about appreciating his form ...?"

I let out a nervous chuckle, trying to find a way to reel things in. "Okay, let's not get carried away. It was just a regular session, you know, very ... *professional.*"

Not that my session with the shower afterwards reflected that ...

Lily leans forward, her eyebrows raised. "Carlie, honey, I hate to break it to you, but there's nothing *just regular* about partner yoga with a hot, bendy Instagram star."

I groan, burying my face in my hands. "It wasn't like that. It was all about ... alignment and posture," I mumble, between my palms.

"Seems like your alignment was just fine," Anna says, dryly.

"What does *that* mean?" I ask, dropping my hands.

Anna gives me a sly look and turns her phone back to me. I take it from her, confused.

There, staring back at me, is a picture of the two of

us in a pose that looks more like a game of sexy Twister than professional partner yoga.

I hand Anna's phone back to her as horror and disbelief washes over me.

"Seems like this pic is getting a lot of attention," Anna drawls, apparently flipping through the comments.

"Well, go me. I've managed my viral internet debut," I mutter under my breath, "and not even for a cat video or a steamy book scene. No, I had to go straight to yoga scandal. Just my luck."

"Wait, Adam didn't post that photo," Vivian says, giving the image a thorough once-over from her own phone. "It was posted by a gym-goer. But Adam was tagged in it. Carlie, you're right. It's already going viral."

The laughter and teasing at the table fade into the background as my jaw drops.

Adam had called earlier and even texted a couple of times asking that I call him—which I ignored, thinking he was just following up on my second missed session in a row.

I'd promised him I'd be back today, but when I couldn't even wash my hair without wincing, I figured one more day to let my muscles chill wouldn't hurt.

"I ..." Guilt rolls through me. "Shit, Adam wanted me to get in touch with him today. I thought he was just calling about me skipping our session today. Do you think he was trying to warn me about this?"

Lily's smile goes crooked, and her concern is evident. "Carlie, you should talk to him. Just in case."

Tasia nods in agreement. "Yeah, especially if that

photo was posted without your consent. That's not okay."

I bite my lip, scrolling through my phone to find Adam's missed call and unread messages. There's a text from him, sent just an hour ago.

> Carlie, we need to talk. It's about our session. Call me.

My heart pounds in my chest. The playful atmosphere of the book club now feels a world away. "Yeah, I think you're right. I need to sort this out. I had no idea this photo was taken, let alone shared through the interwebs."

Tasia reaches over, giving my hand a reassuring squeeze. "We're here for you, Carlie. If you need anything, just say the word."

Standing up, I nod, grateful for their support. However, the image from Anna's phone haunts me as I gather my things to leave. The once carefree evening has turned into a storm of anxiety and uncertainty.

We never even got to talk about dirty books.

Everyone says their goodbyes as I leave the group and head home earlier than anticipated.

As I step out into the cool night air, my mind is a whirlwind of thoughts. The picture, the exposure, the implications—it's all too much.

I need to talk to Adam and find out how this happened. Glancing at my watch, I realize it's too late to reach out now. I'll have to talk to him before my session. It'll give me some time to think of the right words to say.

I take a deep breath, steadying myself. This wasn't just a simple case of a leaked gym photo. It was about privacy, trust, and if I'm honest, the unexpected direction my relationship with Adam was taking.

What if something like this could get him fired?

We weren't even doing anything wrong, but it suddenly feels like it. The photo, taken out of context, could easily be misconstrued.

"Great, from zero to scandalous in one yoga pose," I grumble, my knack for landing in awkward situations reaching new heights.

I start walking home, each step heavy with apprehension and the knowledge that the conversation with Adam will be inevitable—and crucial.

The last thing I wanted was to create drama at the gym, and yet here I am, potentially stirring up a storm totally unintentionally.

CHAPTER 11

Adam

The morning air is crisp, almost biting—having dropped back into the forties last night, despite it being June.

Stupid bipolar Minnesota weather.

I pace back and forth in front of St. Mary's Hospital. I couldn't even bring myself to wait in the gym where the temps are climate-controlled. I need to be the first thing Carlie sees when she gets here.

It's barely dawn, the sky finally exploding into a sea of colors, but sleep is the last thing on my mind. My phone is burning a hole in my pocket—the screen lighting up with notifications I'm too anxious to read.

I thought the first tagged image was bad. There have been more cropping up now, like we were stalked by the goddamn Paparazzi. And one in particular has hit its mark.

It's clear in the image I have a thing for Carlie—it's practically written across my face in flashing neon lights.

The whole thing is a nightmare.

Now, there are comments accusing me of abusing my position, of being an 'eligible bachelor' who takes advantage of his clients.

What really twists the knife is the way people are talking about Carlie—judging her, making assumptions about her. *About us.*

So much of it is vile.

If I knew who snapped the pictures and posted them the way they did ...

Anger courses through me as I clench my fists at my sides.

To add insult to injury, Carlie is ghosting me.

I don't know if that means she's seen the post or if she's pissed.

I've tried calling and texting her, but she hasn't responded since the last one saying 'she'll be here today *for sure.'*

If she's seen the posts, I can't blame her for ignoring me. She must be feeling blindsided by all this. And the stupid part is, it's my face, my name tied to everything, even though I had nothing to do with it.

It's like watching a car crash in slow motion, and there's not a damn thing I can do to stop it.

I glance at my watch.

Carlie's session is in thirty minutes. I need to talk to her before she walks into a gym buzzing with rumors and stares. Hell, I need to apologize, explain—*do something. Anything.*

As I turn to head back inside, a flicker of movement

—a flash of red hair—catches my eye. My heart seizes as Carlie approaches me, her pace hesitant.

"Carlie," I call out, my voice steadier than I feel.

She looks up, almost as if she's trying extra hard not to trip over her feet. Surprise is etched on her face and I can almost see the walls going up—the defenses she's putting in place.

Shit. She knows.

"Adam," she practically whispers, her voice low as she walks up to me.

I swallow hard, wishing like hell I didn't have to have this discussion. But I hear myself say, "Carlie, we need to talk."

She nods, as if expecting my opening sentence. "I saw the posts."

I exhale, feeling the weight of her gaze as my shoulder sag. "I'm so sorry, Carlie. I had no idea someone was taking photos, let alone posting them."

"It's getting a lot of attention." She wraps her arms around herself, looking smaller, more vulnerable. In the movement, I realize she's not in her workout gear. She ends with, "Not the good kind."

"I'm sorry," I say, fighting the urge to reach out and touch her.

She gives me a small, wry smile, her humor peeking through despite the gravity of the situation. "I always thought if I went viral, it'd be for something cool, like rescuing kittens or accidentally starting a flash mob. Not ... *this.*"

I can't help but crack a small smile at her attempt to

lighten the mood, even though my heart is heavy with guilt. "I know, and it's all my fault. I should have been more aware. I wasn't even thinking about—" I run a hand through my hair, my frustration getting the better of me.

Carlie shakes her head and bites her lip. "It's not your fault, Adam. But ... I don't want to be the reason your career suffers. Or your celebrity status, it seems." A flicker of a smile graces her lips before dying out.

"That's not going to happen," I say quickly—too quickly maybe. "I'm not going to let some idiot with a phone dictate who I train or the methods I use. I could tell yoga was going to help—or at least, I thought it would. You're here to train and I'm going to help you hit your goals. That's what matters."

"But the things they're saying about me ..." her voice wavers and it hits me straight in the center of my chest.

I didn't realize just how self-conscious she is but it's right there—in the tears brimming in her eyes.

"They're just words, Carlie. Hurtful, yes, but they don't define you. And they certainly aren't how I see you," I say, hoping to convey the sincerity I feel.

Her lips twitch again into that small, uncertain smile. "Thank you, Adam. That means a lot."

I'm about to say more when my phone rings. I glance at the screen—it's James, my manager. My stomach knots.

"I have to take this. Wait here for me?"

Carlie nods.

As I'm about to step away to answer the call, Carlie,

with a slight twinkle in her eye despite the situation, quips, "Hey, if they're calling to offer you a movie deal for this dramatic saga, remember, I get to play myself. No one else can capture my unique blend of awkwardness and accidental scandal."

"I'll make sure to put in a good word for you," I reply with a wink. Then, I move a few steps away, pressing the phone to my ear. "Hello?"

"Hey, Adam. Glad I caught you before your first client," James's voice comes through, heavy with concern. "Look, we need to have a discussion. Now, if possible. How soon can you meet me in my office?"

I glance back at Carlie, who's watching me with an expression caught between concern and her recent attempt at humor.

"Sure. Yeah, I'll be there in a few minutes," I respond, my voice steady despite the turmoil inside. "I'm just outside."

"Great. See you then," James says before ending the call.

I return to Carlie, trying hard not to read into whatever that was. "I have to go in. But we're not done here, okay? We'll figure this out. Together."

Carlie gives a small, brave nod. "Sure."

"Good." I jab an index finger toward her outfit. "Now, go get changed. You can't workout in that."

She shakes her head. "Actually, I wasn't planning on—"

I look at her through lowered eyebrows. "We're not going to let some assholes dictate things. Right?"

Her eyes widen and she tips her head slightly. "Right."

I smile, the tension easing slightly as I let slip, "That's my girl."

Her mouth drops open slightly.

"I mean..." I backpedal, my forehead creasing and heart galloping away. "Uh, you know what I mean."

That slip of the tongue felt a bit too personal, but there's no way to take it back now.

Carlie gives a small laugh, her eyes lighting up for a moment. "Got it, boss. I'll change." She hesitates for a second, then adds, "Thanks, Adam. For not giving up on me over all of this."

I nod, feeling a tightness in my chest.

"Always," I say, more to myself than to her.

We walk into the hospital together, the conversation and drama still lingering between us. Watching her turn to head towards the locker room, I'm struck by her resilience, and her ability to find humor in the midst of this kind of shit storm. I've been in the social media spotlight for years and I don't think I'd be able to.

Hell, who am I kidding? I *haven't* been able to.

I shake my head, then make my way to James's office, my mind tumbling through so many thoughts. The situation with the viral post, my growing concern for Carlie, and now, this unexpected meeting.

I don't want to admit it, but having a conversation this early doesn't bode well.

I knock on James's office door, bracing for the worst.

"Come in," he calls.

Entering the office, I find James with the kind of grim expression that says to close the door. So, I do.

The usual pleasantries are absent as he gets straight to the point. "Adam, we've got a serious problem."

I nod, steeling myself. "I know about the posts. I've been trying to—"

"Look, we knew your growing status on social media might become a problem, but you've always been so good at keeping things professional," James counters. "It's not just the posts. It's the backlash, the comments about you and your new client. The newspaper has already called for a statement and …" he pauses, pinching the bridge of his nose. "It's blowing up, and not in a way that paints our program and what we do here in a good light."

My heart sinks. "I didn't do anything wrong, James. Neither did Carlie. It was strictly professional, despite how it looks."

He sighs, leaning back in his chair. "I believe you, Adam. But it's not about what I think. It's about public perception. And right now, the perception is damaging. For us, you, and her."

I clench my fists, feeling a sense of injustice. "So, what happens now?"

James looks at me, his eyes filled with regret. "The board had an emergency meeting this morning and—"

My jaw drops open and I gawk at him.

He sighs heavily, like it pains him to say whatever comes next. "Look, they can't ignore this kind of negative attention, so they've made a decision. I'm sorry, Adam, but we have to let you go."

The words hit me like a physical blow.

Fired.

Over a misunderstanding—a twisted narrative that couldn't be further from the truth. "This is unfair, James. You know that. When Jillian—"

He nods, his expression somber. "I know. But what she did never impacted the integrity of our gym. The only ones who witnessed it were the ones paying attention. My hands are tied here, Adam. The board's decision is final."

I exhale, anger and disbelief coursing through me. "Fine. I'll clear out my stuff."

James's voice is soft as I leave. "I'm sorry, Adam. For what it's worth, you're a great trainer. You'll end up on your feet. I'm sure another company will snap you up."

I huff a laugh.

Fuck that.

I'm done.

I don't even respond, I just shake my head and walk out.

When I hit the hallway, I feel the weight of his words settling on my shoulders. Each step through the gym echoes with a finality I can't shake off.

I glance around at the familiar equipment, the trainers and clients, all oblivious to the storm raging in my life.

I need to find Carlie so I can fill her in on what's happened and tell her none of this is her fault.

My gut churns at the thought of how this news might impact her.

I spot her exiting the locker room, now dressed in her workout gear, and a determined look on her face. The sight of her like that, ready to face the world head-on despite everything, strengthens my resolve and breaks my heart all at the same time.

"Carlie," I call out, my voice betraying a hint of the turmoil inside.

She turns, her expression shifting from determination to concern when she sees my face. "What's wrong? Did something happen with your manager?"

I take a deep breath, steeling myself for what I need to say. "Yeah, something happened. I ..." I blow out a slow breath. "I was just fired."

Her eyes widen in shock. "Shit. No—"

"Board decision," I say, feeling a bitter edge creep into my voice. "It's about the gym's image—about public perception. They can't have one of their trainers embroiled in a scandal, even if it's baseless."

Carlie's face falls, her eyes brimming with guilt. "Adam, this is all my fault. If I hadn't—"

"What are you talking about? No," I cut her off firmly, taking a step closer. "Don't you dare blame yourself. This is on me. I'm the one who brought you to yoga. I could have had us leave when we found out it was a class for partners. I should've been more careful—more aware of how things might look from the outside."

Yet, a part of me really wanted that extra time with her.

She looks up at me, her expression tumbling through sadness and resolve. "So, what now? What will you do?"

I shrug, a humorless laugh escaping my lips. "I don't know. Maybe it's time for a change. My brother and best friend have been on me to start my own gym. Maybe this is a sign."

"But ..." Carlie starts, then hesitates, biting her lip.

"But nothing changes for *you*." I give her a small smile. "You're going to keep training, and keep moving forward. The desk will find you a new trainer and if that doesn't work out, I'll help you find another way."

She nods, her eyes glistening. "Thank you, Adam. For everything."

As we stand there, a silence settles between us, heavy with unspoken words and shared regrets. The gym buzzes around us, unaware of the small, personal drama unfolding in its midst.

Then, my phone vibrates with a message, breaking the moment. I glance at the screen, and my heart sinks further. It's a text from the gym's HR department, asking me to turn in my badge and clear out my locker.

I look back at Carlie. "I have to go take care of this. But we'll talk soon, okay? I promise."

"Okay." She nods, a brave front masking her turmoil.

As I turn to leave, the reality of the situation hits me like a wave.

I'm not just leaving a job—I'm stepping away from a chapter of my life that helped me get to where I am now. Instagram would never have been a thing had St. Mary's not hired me and let me do my thing.

Yet, despite all of that, the hardest part is walking away from someone who has unexpectedly become important to me after just a couple of visits.

How did she manage that?

My steps are heavy as I head to the locker room, each one echoing with the finality of an era ending. I'm not just clearing out a locker—I'm saying goodbye to a part of myself.

As the locker door shuts with a definitive clang, the sound seems to linger in the empty space.

In the reverberating silence that follows, a deeper worry gnaws at me.

What's going to happen to Carlie?

Our paths had just begun to intertwine, and now, with this abrupt exit, I'm haunted by the possibility that I might never see her again.

CHAPTER 12

Carlie

I'm standing outside the gym, decked out in what I optimistically call my 'beast mode' attire.

Honestly, though, it's more like *'slightly disgruntled house cat mode,'* but who's checking?

It's not my favorite workout outfit, but it's the backup in case I ever raced out of the house like my hair was on fire and forgot where I was going. It seemed likely earlier in the week.

The door seems heavier now as I push it open.

Had I known things were about to go monumentally sideways, I would have made more of an effort to make it to my workout sessions with Adam the past two days.

The surprise of him getting fired over me—*over those stupid posts*—it isn't sitting well.

As I enter the space, I half expect to see him with his trademark grin (no seriously, there are posts online about it) and a dumbbell in hand, waiting for me.

Which is stupid, because I just saw him leave the building with a box in his arms.

Instead, it's just the regular gym buzz—treadmills humming, weights clanking, and no Adam in sight.

I head to the main desk, nearly tripping along the way.

"Hey, um, weird question, but I need to find out who my trainer is today? I was working with Adam, but I just heard ..." I let my voice drift off, trying to sound casual but probably failing spectacularly.

They must all know at this point that I'm the problem child.

The receptionist, a girl with a ponytail so tight it could double as a facelift, gives me a once-over.

"Just a sec," she says, tapping away at her computer like it owes her money.

I stand there, shifting weight from one foot to the other, mentally preparing myself for a workout session with some newbie who will want to break me because they have something to prove.

"And you are ...?" Ponytail asks, squinting at the screen.

"Carlie. Carlie with a 'C' and an 'ie.' Not a 'y.' It's a whole thing," I ramble, immediately regretting it.

"Right, Carlie with a 'C'. Your trainer today will be Jillian."

"Jillian?" The name seems familiar, but my scrambled brain can't figure out why.

I try to hide my disappointment.

It's so weird to think back to the beginning of the

week—*the week!*—when I sincerely hoped my trainer would be a woman.

I was pleasantly surprised to find out that Adam was pretty awesome. He could handle my clumsiness like a pro and even enjoyed some flirty banter.

However, no Adam means no more banter and no more pretending that I know what I'm doing with those scary-looking machines.

"Yep, Jillian's great. You'll like her," Ponytail assures me, but she might as well be telling me I'll enjoy a water-boarding session.

"Great, looking forward to it," I lie, plastering on my best fake smile.

I turn away from the desk, bracing myself for an hour of awkward introductions and overly enthusiastic *'You can do it.'*

As I wait, I can't help but feel like I'm on the edge of a cliff, about to dive into the unknown. I shake my head, trying to clear it.

Come on, Carlie, it's just a workout, not a space mission or brain surgery.

But as I spot a figure approaching me, clipboard in hand and a professional smile on her face, I can't shake the feeling that my world's about to get a whole lot more complicated.

Jillian is the super-fit woman I originally pegged as Ada.

Great.

Jillian extends a hand, her grip firmer than I expected.

"Carlie, right? I'm Jillian. Looks like I'll be taking

over your training sessions." Her voice is crisp, but there's a frigid edge to it that I can't quite place.

"Nice to meet you," I reply, trying to match her professionalism. But inside, my stomach is doing some serious butterfly flutters—and not in the way Adam invoked in me, either. This is more the 'escape and flee' kind.

Jillian's eyes are sharp, like she's sizing me up for a boxing match rather than a training session.

"So, it looks like you haven't really done much." She looks over the clipboard in her hand, then directs me into the gym.

We head over to an open mat section, and Jillian starts outlining the day's workout. From the little glimpses I catch, it's more intense than anything Adam had me do so far.

"We're stepping up your routine," she announces. "Time to see what you're really made of. We'll start with a comprehensive fitness test."

I nod, though I'm fairly sure my *'slightly disgruntled house cat'* mode attire is ready for whatever fresh hell she has planned.

"You know, most clients find they get better results when they stick to a regular schedule. Consistency really is key," she says, a pointed look in her eyes as she points to the mat. "Even if your muscles are sore."

I feel a flush creeping up my neck.

Is she referring to the workouts I missed with Adam?

I bite back a retort, and instead, drop to the mat and wait for her instruction.

"Okay, let's start with two minutes of sit-ups. Let's see how many you can do," she says, pulling out her phone and bringing up a timer app.

"Uh, okay." I nod, trying to remember the form Adam showed me because I'm getting the distinct impression nothing short of perfect will do for this woman.

Jillian taps her phone, and the timer starts.

"Go," she says, her tone clinical.

I do as she proclaims, acutely aware of the fact that I have way more padding in my midsection than she has on her entire body. Without Adam's encouraging presence, each sit-up feels twice as hard.

I can tell I'm crunching more than sitting up, and it's not up to Jillian's standards by the way she tsks under her breath.

"That's not a sit-up, Carlie. Adam should have taught you better. You need to sit all the way up, and your lower back should be lifting off the ground," Jillian says, her words sharp like darts. I can feel her eyes on me, cold and evaluating. "Come on, push through it. You can do better than that."

I push harder, trying to ignore the burn in my abs and the growing embarrassment.

"I'm ... *trying*," I gasp out between attempts, but it sounds weak even to my own ears.

If sit-ups are this hard, I'm convinced they're a form of medieval torture.

"No, you're still not lifting your back off the ground. Go slower if you need to, but make the full sit-up," she says, continuing to flit her gaze from me to the phone.

Swallowing hard, I make another attempt, but only make it halfway before my abs give out.

Jillian checks her phone.

"Time," she announces, and I collapse back onto the mat, panting. "Well, that was ... a start."

There's no mistaking the disappointment in her voice.

I use my arms to sit up, feeling a mixture of frustration and defeat.

"I know I'm not exactly a fitness model," I say, trying to inject a bit of my usual humor into the situation, but it falls flat.

Jillian just raises an eyebrow. "This isn't about being a model. It's about effort, Carlie. I need to see you're committed." Her tone is firm, and I can't help but feel like I've just been scolded by a schoolteacher.

Jillian glances at her clipboard and then back at me.

"Next up, two minutes of push-ups. Let's see your form," she says, a challenging note in her voice.

With a sigh that's half resignation, half theatrics, I move into position.

My hands are planted firmly on the mat, and I can't help but think to myself how my relationship with gravity has always been a bit like a bad romance—intense and slightly unbalanced.

And now, here I am, about to prove it with push-ups.

Just as I'm about to drop to my knees, Jillian stops me.

"No, on your feet. Real push-ups," she instructs, her tone leaving no room for argument.

I hesitate for a moment, then awkwardly shift to support myself on my toes. I have no clue when the last time was I attempted a full push-up, but I can already feel every muscle in my body protesting.

"Begin," Jillian commands, starting the timer.

I lower myself down, my arms shaking like I'm in an earthquake. I barely make it halfway before I have to push back up, and even that feels like lifting a mountain.

"Your form needs work, but at least you're trying," she comments, her voice dripping with what feels like reluctant approval.

I manage a few more shaky push-ups, each one harder than the last. My arms are screaming, my breath is ragged, and I can feel sweat trickling down my back.

Jillian's voice cuts through my concentration. "Remember, this is about pushing your limits. You're stronger than you think," she says, but it sounds more like a challenge than encouragement.

When the timer finally beeps, signaling the end of the eternity that was two minutes, I collapse onto the mat, chest heaving.

I've never been so grateful to hear a beep in my life.

Jillian makes a note on her clipboard, her lips pursed.

"We have a lot of work to do," she says, her tone business-like. "But you've got potential. We just need to tap into it."

I nod, too exhausted to speak. As I lie there, trying to catch my breath, I can't help but wonder what I've gotten myself into. This new training regimen with Jillian is going to be nothing like my sessions with Adam.

It's going to be tougher, more demanding, and, I suspect, a lot more impersonal.

Exhausted from the push-ups, I try to get up too quickly and end up tangling my feet in my own shoelaces. Stumbling forward, I catch myself on the mat with the grace of a hippo ballerina.

Smooth move, Carlie. If there were an Olympic event for clumsiness, I'd be a gold medalist.

Jillian raises an eyebrow but doesn't comment. I quickly untangle my feet, pretending my face isn't burning.

Note to self: *add 'learning to walk' to the workout routine.*

Regaining my composure, I stand up, ready for whatever fresh torture Jillian has planned next. She looks over at the pull-up bar, and then back at me with a skeptical expression.

"We'll skip pull-ups for today. I doubt you'd manage even one," she says, her words blunt and unapologetic. "Instead, we're finishing with a three-mile run. Or walk, if that's more your speed."

Her tone is dismissive, but I can't deny the relief washing over me.

No humiliating pull-ups?

Fine by me.

"Okay, three miles. Got it," I say, following after her.

Every muscle in my body is screaming already, but

I'm determined not to show any more weakness in front of Jillian.

Granted, I might need an ice bath and a vat of vodka after this.

We head over to the treadmills, and Jillian sets one up for me.

"I want you to alternate between running and walking. I have it set to start with a brisk walk, then jog. Try to maintain a steady pace," she instructs.

She puts a heart-rate monitor on my arm without a word. Probably so she can make sure my heart doesn't give out in the middle of the run.

I nod, stepping onto the treadmill with less enthusiasm than a kid on their way to the dentist.

I start with a walk as Jillian promised, the pace brisk but manageable. After a minute, the machine increases the speed to a jog. It's been a while since I've run, and my lungs start to burn almost immediately.

Jillian stands nearby, her arms crossed, watching me with those discerning eyes of hers.

"Keep your back straight, and don't slouch. Good posture is key," she calls out.

I straighten up, focusing on my breathing and trying to find a rhythm. The treadmill hums beneath my feet, and I fall into a pattern of walking and jogging. It's tough, but not impossible.

I can do this, I tell myself.

As long as I don't trip…

The thought alone is enough to unleash a torrent of fear in me as I think back to my first session with Adam.

Please, please don't be a klutz. Please please please.

As the miles tick by, I start to find my stride. My breathing evens out, and the initial burn in my legs fades to a dull ache.

I'm not breaking any records, but I'm doing it.

I'm *actually* doing it.

When the treadmill finally beeps to signal the end of the three miles, I'm sweating and out of breath, but there's a sense of accomplishment that wasn't there before. I've pushed through, and I've survived.

Jillian makes another note on her clipboard.

"Not bad, Carlie. Not *great*, but better than I expected," she says, her tone slightly less frosty than before.

I step off the treadmill, trying to catch my breath and focusing on not falling over.

"Thanks, I guess," I reply, unsure whether to be insulted or encouraged.

Jillian's final words are brisk, "I expect you to be here at our designated time on Monday. No excuses. Be here on time."

Then, she's off, leaving me there to gather my things.

I drag myself out of the gym, feeling both physically and emotionally drained.

The session was all business, no banter, and a whole lot of thinly veiled criticism.

I can't shake the feeling that Jillian's attitude is about more than just my fitness level. There's something personal in her jabs, something that goes beyond a trainer-client relationship.

And I'm almost scared to find out what it is.

Adam

The air inside *Jaded Brews* is thick with the aroma of hops and barley, a familiar comfort that does little to ease the turmoil churning in my gut.

I'm slumped at the bar, a half-empty pint of the brewery's signature ale in front of me, and I'm totally lost in thought.

The past week has been a whirlwind.

One week ago, I'd been a bundle of nerves, getting ready to go to an event that would totally rock my world. I just didn't know it yet.

One week ago, I'd forgotten about the shitstorm my life had become, thanks to Jillian and her infidelity.

One week ago, I'd had the most mind-blowing sex of my life—all with a mysterious woman I know I'll never have the opportunity to see again, thanks to Club Nocté's rules.

Then ... *in walked Carlie.*

All thoughts about the woman from Nocté left my

brain and instead, had me focusing on her. I can't help but think about how differently things could have turned out if only …

My thoughts are abruptly interrupted as Dylan slides onto the stool beside me, his arrival marked by a cheeky grin.

"Adam, my man, staring into your beer won't give you answers. Tried it last week. All I got was a headache and a weird conversation with a barstool," he teases, tipping his chin in hello to my brother.

"That barstool probably made more sense than you on most days." Brian, ever the keen observer and part-time philosopher behind the bar, fires back.

I manage a half-smile, still lost in my own world. "You guys wouldn't understand."

"Man, try me. I can't go through another Friday night with Mr. McMopey," Dylan comments, signaling Brian for a drink. "You look like someone ran over your dog"

"More like someone ran over his pride," Brian mutters, eyeing me with a combination of concern and amusement. *Fucking siblings.*

I shoot them both a glare and place my palm over the center of my chest. "Thanks for the support, guys. Really, *truly* touching."

Dylan leans in, his eyes glinting with curiosity. "So, what's got you all twisted up? Daydreaming again about the mystery woman from last weekend?"

I turn to him, incredulous. "What? No, you asshole. I got fired."

He winces and part of me can't help but feel smug about it. "Oh, shit. Sorry, man. I figured this was woman trouble again. What happened?"

"PR nightmare," I offer, returning my gaze to the bottom of my beer.

"The IG situation didn't hit right with the hospital?" Dylan guesses.

I shake my head.

"Shit, now I wish you were daydreaming about last weekend," he mumbles into his beer.

Brian pauses in the middle of pouring a beer and looks up sharply. "Are we talking about the one-night stand Adam won't talk about?"

Apparently, his interest is piqued, because he forgets about the drink he's pouring, causing it to overflow. He shuts it down quickly, cursing under his breath.

"I'm not gonna discuss this," I mutter, trying to wave off the subject. The last thing I want is for my brother to dive into my love life—or lack thereof on top of all the other shit.

Dylan, however, isn't one to let things go. "Come on, man. Maybe you should find her again. Have another wild night to get your mojo back. Nothing shakes off some bad luck like a good shag."

I shake my head, taking a sip of my beer. "It's not that simple. I can't see her again."

"Why not? Did she turn into a pumpkin at midnight?" Brian jokes, still wiping away the overflowing beer.

I roll my eyes. "Funny, Brian. No, it's just ... *not gonna happen*. I can't really explain why."

"Well, what about that new client you seem to have the hots for—what did you say her name was? Carmen?" Brian interjects, throwing his wet dishrag under the bar and grabbing a fresh one.

"Carlie," I respond before I can think better of it. I wince, bracing for it.

Dylan turns to face me, his left eyebrow arched high. "Wait, wait, wait ... *Carlie*—as in the infamous woman from said IG scandal? You have *the hots* for her?"

I groan.

Brian, however, smirks mischievously. "Adam let slip that Carlie reminds him of his mystery woman."

"Interesting ..." Dylan says, waggling his eyebrows. "Tell us more about this Carlie."

I sigh, taking a sip of my beer. "Carlie's ... *she's* real, you know? There's no pretense with her. It's refreshing —but confusing as hell."

Brian leans back, his expression thoughtful. "Sounds like she's got you all twisted up. What's the plan, then? You gonna pursue her or what?"

I hesitate, the image of Carlie's smile flashing in my mind. "I don't know. After losing my job and dragging her into this mess, I'm not sure she'd appreciate that."

Dylan claps me on the shoulder. "First step, stop moping. Second, maybe your brother is right for once. You've already done the damage. Maybe you should see if she'd be willing to give the rumor mill something real to gossip about."

Brian chuckles, shaking his head. "That's Dylan's solution to everything—face it head-on with a dash of reckless optimism."

Dylan grins unapologetically, the lenses of his glasses refracting the lights behind the bar. "Hey, it's worked more often than not."

I rub the back of my neck, feeling the weight of their words. "It's not just about what I want anymore. This whole situation with the gym, Jillian ... it's messed up. And Carlie, she's caught in the middle of it. She's just trying to get her confidence back up. I can't fuck all that up."

"That's the thing about being in the middle, though," Brian comments, leaning on the bar. "Sometimes you get a clearer view of both sides. Maybe she sees something in this mess worth exploring."

Dylan snickers and a shitty grin replaces his features as he giggles darkly. "In the middle. Now there's a picture."

I roll my eyes, though the thought of being in the middle of two redheads could certainly be worse ...

"Get your minds out of the gutter," Brian dictates, lowering his eyebrows as he stares Dylan down.

Yet, it's pretty damn clear we're all thinking it, now.

Dylan clears his throat and itches the side of his head. "Anyway ... speaking of messes, guess who strutted into the coffee shop today, complaining about having to pick up extra work?"

My interest is piqued despite myself and I hate it. "Shit, let me guess ... Jillian. What did she say?"

Dylan takes a sip of his beer, watching me carefully. "She was ranting about having to cover for someone who got fired. Little did I know that was you. Thanks, by the way. Ever heard of sending a text, man?"

"Sorry," I mumble, rubbing my temple with my middle finger.

He harrumphs, but continues, "She was irritated because she had to pick up the slack and train *'some floozie.'* Piecing it all together, that's gotta be this Carlie, I'd wager."

My heart sinks at his words. "Yeah, I'm sure that's her. Dammit."

The thought of Jillian, with her manipulative ways, training Carlie makes my skin crawl. It was different when Carlie was just a new client with no association.

But now... Fuck, Jillian will put the screws on Carlie and probably injure her in the process—all because she's a vindictive bitch.

Dylan downs his beer and extends the glass to Brian for a refill. "She seemed pretty ticked off about it. Made it sound like she was doing the world a gigantic ass favor by taking over the extra clients."

My fist clenches around my beer. "Fuck, I never wanted Carlie to have to deal with Jillian's ... *Jillian-ness.* Especially not after everything else. I should have tried to convince James to have Marc take her on when I was leaving."

"Too late now," Brian mutters.

Dylan leans forward, his expression serious. "Man, you can't let Jillian or this situation dictate your next move. If you like this Carlie, you should ask her out. You've always been the guy who makes his own path. See where it leads. If nothing else, you could help her find a different trainer."

I sigh, the truth in his words resonating within me. "I know, I know. I just … I don't want to make things worse for her."

"Sometimes, the risk of making things worse is worth the chance of making them right," Brian says as he shakes a cocktail mixer—the clanging of ice temporarily drawing my attention.

Dylan clinks his glass against mine pulling my focus back to him. "You've got an opportunity here, Adam. Don't waste it living in regret and what-ifs."

Brian, who passes the cocktail to a woman at the other end of the bar, gives me a sly look. When he returns, he says, "You know, Adam, for a guy who's usually so sure of himself with women, you're awfully hesitant about this Carlie chick. What's the deal?"

I shake my head, trying to mask my frustration with a half-hearted chuckle. "It's just … *complicated*, you know? With the job situation and now this IG bullshit. Seriously. Why won't you guys drop this?"

Dylan, now with a freshly refilled beer, leans in. "Complicated, huh? Is that what they call it these days? I recall a time when *'complicated'* was Adam-speak for *'I'm attracted but too stubborn to admit it.'*"

I can't help but smile, despite the turmoil inside. "All right, maybe there's some truth to that. But it's not just about being intrigued or stubborn. There's a lot at stake here."

Brian nods, adding, "Yeah, like your reputation and your heart, for starters."

Dylan snorts into his glass. "His heart? Since when did we start talking about that mushy stuff at Jaded Brews? Aren't we supposed to be stone-cold *heartbreakers?*"

I roll my eyes, but there's a lightness in my chest that wasn't there before. "Since my life turned into a daytime soap opera, apparently."

Thankfully, the conversation shifts as Dylan and Brian start to reminisce about past escapades and misadventures, each story more exaggerated than the last.

They poke fun at my previous romantic endeavors, bringing up hilariously failed dates and my inability to write even the simplest of social posts without at least one misspelled word.

I find myself laughing, the sound is genuine and freeing after one of the crappiest days I've had in a long time. It's moments like these, with my brother and best friend, that remind me life isn't all doom and gloom.

Even when it feels like everything is falling apart.

Brian, joining in the laughter, suddenly turns to me with a mischievous glint in his eye. "Hey, Adam, remember that time you tried to impress that jujitsu instructor with your MMA expertise when you were nineteen?"

Dylan howls with laughter, nearly spilling his beer.

"Oh man, I'd forgotten about that! She handed him his ass in the first three minutes of sparring with him."

"Yeah, yeah, laugh it up. Let's not forget Dylan's karaoke disaster on his birthday last year," I say, jabbing a finger in his direction.

Dylan holds up his hands in mock surrender. "Okay, okay, we've all had our moments."

"Some more than most," I say, shooting him a pointed look.

He only nods in agreement. "Speaking of moments ... Seriously, Adam, back to Carlie. What's your game plan?"

I take a deep breath, feeling a sense of clarity. "You know what? I'm going to talk to her. I just don't know how to make it right with her. You know?"

Dylan snickers, then takes a quick swig of his beer. "You're kidding, right? You're Adam Fuckin' Foxx, for crying out loud. Do you own your platform or what? Make a statement on your account. Go big or go home."

I blink, surprised. "What?"

"Make it right, you big baby," he says so flippantly, that I doubt he realizes what kind of gift he just handed me.

I look up, their words stirring something within me. A flicker of determination starts to replace the helplessness I've been wallowing in.

Holy shit. *He's right.*

I can't just sit here brooding. I need to take control of the situation, for my sake and for Carlie's.

The laughter and reminiscing fade into a comfortable

silence, and I find myself staring into the depths of my beer, my mind racing with how I'll do it.

"What's the plan, Adam?" Dylan's voice cuts through my thoughts, bringing me back to the present. "I can see the wheels turning in that head of yours."

I look up, feeling the weight of my decision. It's not just about making a move—it's about making the *right* move.

"I don't know, man," I admit. "I mean, what would I even say? '*Hey, sorry I got fired and dragged you into a gym scandal. Want to grab coffee?*'" I huff a dry laugh.

Brian chuckles, but his eyes are understanding. "It doesn't have to be perfect, Adam. Just honest."

Dylan nods in agreement. "Yeah, and who knows? Maybe she's waiting for you to make the first move. Girls love that sorta shit. You won't know until you try. She followed you into partner yoga, after all."

Their words resonate with me, and a plan starts to form in my mind.

I could call her, but that might be too forward given the circumstances.

A message, perhaps?

Casual, but direct. Something that shows I care without overwhelming her.

Besides, I told her I'd be in touch.

I take a deep breath, a sense of purpose slowly replacing the uncertainty. "You're right. I need to do this. I'll send her a message. Keep it simple—see if she's open to talking."

Brian slaps me on the back, a broad smile on his face. "There you go. That's the Adam we know."

Dylan raises his glass in a toast. "To Adam, stepping out of his comfort zone and with a little luck, into the bed of another redhead."

I roll my eyes, snickering softly.

When I leave the bar I'm a bundle of nerves and anticipation.

The message to Carlie is already forming in my head.

It's a risk, but Dylan and Brian are right.

It's time to stop living in the shadow of what-ifs and take a chance on something real. I mean, it can't get much worse, right?

The cool night air hits me as I step outside, and I pull out my phone.

This is it.

The first step towards hopefully mending things with Carlie, and maybe, just maybe, towards something more.

CHAPTER 14

Carlie

Every muscle in my body screams in protest as I try to find a comfortable position at my desk. Yesterday's fitness test with Jillian has left me feeling like I've been hit by a truck.

A very big, *very mean* truck.

And here I thought I was sore on Wednesday, silly, *silly* woman.

I glance at the calendar on my wall—thank goodness it's Saturday.

No gym, no Jillian, no ... *Adam.*

I wince, not just from the pain but from the thought of him. I still can't believe how horribly wrong things went over something so innocent.

It's not like he was the guy from Club Nocté and we were photographed in one of our *many* sexy entanglements.

God, if word somehow got out that I went there the

Friday before—now *that* would have been something for the hospital board to freak out over.

News Flash Duluth Citizens! Super hot fitness trainer caught with hussy, who was last seen at a mysterious sex club in Superior.

I shudder at the thought.

At least that's one secret I'll take to my grave.

I open my laptop, staring at the blinking cursor on the blank page. My book deadline is looming over me like a dark cloud, but ever since the fiasco with Michael, the words have been a slog.

It's been three months and still, writing is just ... *meh*.

I've had a few hits of inspiration, but for the most part, writing has lost some of its luster.

A part of me no longer believes that love and sex go hand in hand. And while the night at Nocté certainly helped me gain some perspective on mind-blowing sex, it's done nothing to truly mend my heart.

I can't even see the man again.

"You've let yourself go. I mean, look at you. I just can't be with someone who doesn't at least make an effort."

Michael's words still haunt me. And to think he had the gall to come back here, thinking we could try again.

What a home-invading asshole.

I hadn't realized how much the stress I've been under impacted my weight until that moment.

Instead, I was just focused on building my author career and getting my books out there. I thought he was on board. That he had my back.

I kept thinking that if I could just prove I was worthy

by earning big, then it meant I was worthy of other things, too.

That went well.

I may have gotten the notoriety and money to prove I can write a dirty book, but my relationship with the man I thought I'd marry dissolved.

Definitely for the better, now that I look back. But it doesn't mean his words don't sting.

I rub my temples, trying to focus on the outline and the scene I'm supposed to write next. However, with every minuscule movement, my mind snaps back to my aching body. Then to Adam's last training session and how different his session was from Jillian's.

Where Adam was encouraging, Jillian was ... well, *demonic* comes to mind.

And then, of course, my traitorous brain decides to remember just how handsome he is. Those gray eyes, that cocky smile.

I shake my head.

Focus.

But it's no use. The muscles in my neck scream from the movement and even blinking feels like work.

I wonder what Adam's doing now?

After the Instagram blow out, after getting fired. Is he okay? What's he planning to do next?

I don't know why it matters or why I'm so curious, but I am. Hopefully, he lands on his feet. I mean, how could he not with that IG following?

My phone rings, snapping me out of my reverie. For the briefest of moments, I actually think that maybe it's Adam. He said he wanted to talk later, right?

It's not.

It's Grandma, also known as my landlord and the no-nonsense matriarch who lives on the first floor of the old Victorian duplex we share.

I know better than to ignore her call. She'll keep trying until I pick up because she's a persistent pain in my ass.

Sighing to myself, I brace for the call and answer. "Hi, Grandma. What's up?"

"Carlie, darling, come downstairs for a chat," she demands, not waiting for a response before hanging up.

I groan, not just at the prospect of navigating the stairs right now but also at whatever Grandma has in store for me.

Her *'chats'* are never just chats.

They usually involve stories of when she was younger and progressively get more uncomfortable as she describes her escapades with Grandpa when he was alive.

I stare at my computer and make a face.

A break from this writer's block might be what I need, though.

I brace myself and slowly stand up. My arms nearly give out and my abs scream bloody murder when I manage to get upright.

But all of that is a walk in the park compared to my legs.

You'd think three minutes on a treadmill wouldn't be a big deal.

However, you'd be wrong.

There are muscles in my legs and ass I didn't even know I had. And every single one of them is singing a chorus of *'What were you thinking?'*

With a deep breath, I inch my way to the door, each stutter step is an exercise in pain management.

This old house, with all its charm and character, suddenly feels like my worst enemy. I curse under my breath for choosing the second floor when I moved in.

Sure, Grandma making it up and down these stairs seemed unreasonable at the time, and the view of the garden is lovely, but right now, I'd trade it for a ground-floor studio in a heartbeat.

I reach the top of the steep staircase and peer down. It looms before me like a mountain.

"Who needs a gym when you have Victorian architecture?" I mutter sarcastically to myself. I'm only half-kidding.

Taking the first step feels like a leap of faith. I clutch the railing, my knuckles white, as I gingerly make my way down, gasping the entire time.

Halfway through, I have to pause. Each step sends jolts of pain through my sore muscles, reminding me of every sit-up, or crunch, I guess. Every relentless minute on the treadmill under Jillian's unforgiving gaze.

"This better be worth it," I grumble. "One word about Grandpa's penis size ..."

Finally, I reach the bottom, breathing heavily, feeling like I've just completed a marathon. I straighten up, trying to compose myself before facing Grandma.

I can't show just how sore I really am—not with her. She's the kind of woman who survived wars, outlived a husband, and still does her own gardening at the age of eighty-two.

I knock softly on her door, bracing for her usual brand of 'tough love' mixed with inappropriate comments.

The door swings open, and there she is, Grandma Elsie, in all her glory. Her white hair is pulled back in a tight bun, her dark blue eyes sharp as ever.

"Took you long enough," she huffs with a mock frown, but her eyes are twinkling.

"I had to battle a dragon on the stairs," I reply, stepping inside.

"Hmmm," she mutters, eyeing me suspiciously, like she knows the truth.

Her living room is a cozy time capsule, filled with antique furniture, countless photos of family, and trinkets from her travels.

She ushers me to sit, then perches herself on her favorite armchair, eyeing me with a mix of concern and curiosity. "You look like you've been through a war, child."

I collapse onto her plush sofa, groaning. "I'm okay, Grandma. Yesterday was a tough workout."

She tuts, leaning over to hand me a cup of her trademark strong, black coffee.

"Exercise is supposed to invigorate, not incapacitate. But let's talk about something more interesting. How's that handsome trainer of yours? Have any more *bendy* sessions with him? Adam, was it?" Her grin turns feline as she takes a sip from her own cup.

I nearly spit out my coffee. "It wasn't … I mean, he's just my trainer. Or *was*. He got fired yesterday."

My eyes slam shut.

Please don't ask why.

Her eyebrows shoot up. "Fired? That's a shame. From what you've told me, he seems like a good egg."

I blush, trying to steer the conversation away from dangerous waters. "Yeah, he's nice. But, Grandma, I've been struggling with my book. I can't seem to …"

However, Grandma cuts me off, "Speaking of nice and struggling, when's the last time you had a good roll in the hay? A young woman like you needs to …"

"Grandma—" I choke out, my face now matching the crimson shade of her curtains. "We've talked about this. Can we please not talk about my sex life?"

"It's not like I can hear a thing, you know." She winks at me and then waves her hand dismissively when she takes in my expression. "Fine, fine. But mark my words, a good romp does wonders for creativity, too. Ask me how I know." Her eyes sparkle, daring me to ask.

"No," I mutter, shuddering internally.

She shrugs. "Suit yourself. Now, what's this about your book?"

I take a deep breath, grateful for the change in topic. "It's just … I'm stuck. I can't seem to find the right words, and the deadline is creeping up on me."

Grandma Elsie nods sagely, her gaze softening. "Writer's block, eh? Happens to the best of us. When I used to write letters to your grandpa during the war, sometimes it was hard to find the words."

I blink, surprised. "You wrote Grandpa letters?"

"Oh yes, love letters, mostly. Some were quite steamy, if I do say so myself. The original sexting, you know." She winks again, and I can't help but giggle despite my embarrassment. "Probably where you got your writing chops."

She's not wrong. Goodness knows I didn't get it from Mom.

However, I find myself saying, "Grandma, I'm not sure steamy love letters are what my publisher is looking for."

"You'd be surprised," she says with a chuckle. "But seriously, darling, sometimes you just need to step away from it all. Clear your head. You're too cooped up in this house all the time. I worry about you."

"I know, but with the gym and everything ..." My voice trails off as I think about Adam again, and I feel a pang in my chest.

Grandma leans forward, placing a hand over mine. "Listen to me, Carlie. Life is too short to be spent in regret. If this Adam fellow has caught your fancy, maybe you should explore that feeling. Who knows, it might just unlock that creativity of yours. Do you have his number?"

I sigh, considering her words. "Yeah, I mean, he's texted me a couple of times."

"Oooh, see. That's something," she says, wiggling her eyebrows as she takes another sip of coffee.

"I don't know that he sees me that way, though," I admit, feeling the warmth flood to my cheeks.

Grandma shrugs. "Only one way to find out."

At that moment, my phone buzzes. I glance at it, and my heart full-on skips a beat.

It's a message from Adam.

> I know things have been complicated,
> but I'd really like to see you, Carlie.
> Are you free for coffee later?

I feel a flutter in my stomach. "Um, Grandma, Adam just texted. He wants to meet for coffee."

Her eyes light up. "Well, there you have it. Destiny has stepped in, girly. You should definitely go. And who knows, maybe you'll come back with more than just coffee."

"Grandma—" I exclaim, half-scandalized and half-amused.

She laughs heartily. "I'm just teasing you, dear. But seriously, go. Have fun. Life is too short to hesitate. Trust me on that."

I smile, feeling a sense of lightness for the first time since I found out about the Instagram fiasco. "Okay. I'll go."

She nods approvingly. "Good girl. Now, off you go. And remember, don't take life too seriously. No one gets out alive anyway."

I roll my eyes at the serious level of corniness.

Coffee with Adam.

Maybe this is exactly what I need.

As I slowly make my way back upstairs, I can't help but feel hopeful. That maybe something good can come out of all of this.

This coffee with him isn't just a casual meet-up—instead, it feels like a *crossroads.*

Or a chance to confront the what-ifs that have been haunting me.

Reaching my apartment, I sink back into my chair, the aches in my body a stark contrast to the flurry of butterflies in my stomach. I stare at the message on my phone—Adam's words causing a mixture of excitement and uncertainty.

My fingers hover over the keypad, the usual witty retort replaced by a flutter of something deeper—more earnest.

I type out a reply, my fingers hesitating over each letter.

Confirming our coffee date feels like stepping into uncharted territory, filled with possibilities and risks. My heart races as I hit send.

The moment lingers, suspended in time.

Maybe this is the beginning of a new chapter, one where I'm not just a character in someone else's story, but the author of my own.

As I sit there, lost in my thoughts, my phone buzzes again.

It's Adam, confirming the time and place and I'm thrilled to see his suggestion happens to be my favorite coffee shop.

A small smile forms on my lips. This coffee date, this

simple act of meeting up, suddenly feels like a pivotal moment in my life.

With a deep breath, I stand up, a sense of determination washing over me despite the shooting agony in my muscles.

Maybe, just maybe, this is where my story really begins.

CHAPTER 15

Adam

I can feel myself bouncing in my seat.

Even though the air in *Bean There, Done That* is infused with the rich aroma of freshly ground coffee, all I can smell is my own anxiety. I'm sitting across from Dylan, trying to steady my jittery hands by wrapping them around a steaming cup of black coffee.

I don't think the caffeine is helping one bit.

If anything, it's making things worse.

"Dude, *relax*. It's just coffee, not a marriage proposal," Dylan says, but his casual tone does nothing to calm my nerves. "Now, if you were meeting up for drinks at *Jaded Brews*, that woulda sent a different kind of message ..."

My fingers instinctively rake through my hair, tangling in the locks as I second-guess each thought racing through my mind. The gesture, almost a nervous tic at this point, does little to ease the knot in my stomach.

"What was I thinking, Dylan? Inviting Carlie out like this after everything …"

Dylan leans back, studying me. "You're overthinking it, man. It's just two people having a conversation, getting to know each other outside the gym. That's normal, bro. It's how relationships are supposed to start. Or at least, so I've heard."

"Yeah, I suppose. It's just—"

Before I can get the rest of the sentence out, the bell over the shop's entrance jingles, and in walks Carlie. She enters with a careful grace, her movements slightly measured, and each step seems a tad deliberate.

The casual elegance of her frilly shirt and ripped up jeans contrasts with the tentative way she tucks a loose wave of red hair behind her ear. A fleeting moment of hesitation flashes in her eyes before she offers one of her pretty smiles that makes her dimples shine.

I rise to my feet, a genuine smile forming effortlessly as I'm struck by her natural, unassuming beauty.

Dylan's gaze shifts to Carlie, and I notice a flicker of recognition in his eyes. He grins broadly. "Well, look who's here."

My stomach tightens. "You know her?"

God, please tell me they didn't date.

He waves off my concern and rush-whispers. "Relax, it's not what you think. She's a regular here—always typing away on her laptop. An author or something. I'll explain later."

Carlie approaches our table, her smile widening. "Hey, Adam. Dylan."

Dylan stands up, giving Carlie a friendly nod. "I'll leave you two to it. Adam, chill out, will ya?" He pats my shoulder before sauntering off to the counter.

I lean over, pulling out a chair for her. "Hi, Carlie. It's good to see you."

She grins, a rosy pink gracing her cheeks. "It's only been a day, Adam." She eases into the chair with a barely noticeable wince, but I catch it. Her muscles are sore but she's trying not to show it.

I rub at the back of my neck. "I know ... It's just, uh—"

An awkward silence envelops us as I drop into my seat, and tap my middle finger on the table beside my coffee.

Carlie's gaze flickers around the cozy interior of the coffee shop.

"This place has the best coffee. I'm here a lot," she admits, trying to ease into the conversation. "I was excited when you mentioned meeting up here."

"Oh, shit—did you want something? I can order—" I begin, flagging Dylan to come back. What an idiot. It should have been the first thing I did.

She shakes her head. "You don't have to do that."

"I asked you here. It's my treat," I say, motioning to Dylan that he should focus on Carlie. "Can you get Carlie whatever she wants? Put it on my tab."

Dylan's lopsided grin emerges, probably at my usage of the phrase 'put it on my tab.' Especially since there is no such thing here.

"Sure, the usual, Carlie?" he offers, with the tilt of his chin.

She beams. "That would be great. Thanks."

Dylan flicks his eyebrows at me and disappears to make her drink.

I lean forward conspiratorially. "So, what *is* the usual?"

I have to admit, the fact that Dylan knows what that is and I don't rubs me wrong.

"Caramel macchiato with two shots of espresso and almond milk," she says, her green eyes sparkling. However, they dim just as quickly. "I mean, I probably shouldn't knowing the calories and sugar content. But you know ..."

My eyebrows pinch in tight and I reach out, placing a hand over hers. "Hey, don't do that. That mind-fuckery won't do you any good."

Her eyes meet mine and she inhales a quick breath. Something zaps between us—like a kind of acknowledgment or appreciation.

"Here you go, Carlie. Make sure my man here takes some deep breaths, would you?" Dylan says, setting her drink in front of her.

The spell between us is broken and Carlie pulls her hand from mine, blinking hard. "You uh—you two are friends?"

"BFFs for life," Dylan assures her, patting me on the shoulder again before heading back.

I chuckle, trying to play it cool. "Yeah, Dylan and I go way back. He's the younger brother I never had."

Carlie nods, a smile playing on her lips. "That's nice. It's good to have friends like that." She takes a sip of her drink, her eyes closing briefly in appreciation.

I watch her, admiring the way her face lights up with such a simple pleasure.

"Carlie," I start, my voice a bit more serious now. "About the whole Instagram thing … I just want to say I'm really sorry for how it all went down. You didn't deserve—"

She looks up, her expression a mix of surprise and something else I can't quite place. "Oh, Adam, it's … it's okay. I mean, it wasn't your fault. It just got blown way out of proportion. Besides, you got the brunt of it, being fired and all."

I shake my head, feeling the weight of the situation. "No, but I feel responsible. That picture, the comments … I hate how it made you a target. They should never have done that. People can just be such assholes."

Her reaction is subtle yet revealing. Her eyes, usually so expressive, widen a fraction, and there's a slight tremble in her lower lip, like the faintest ripple on still water. The whole thing betrays her real feelings on the impact of the incident.

"Yeah, they really can be," she says, her voice coming out in a breathless squeak. She clears her throat and adds, "That's why I've been avoiding Instagram."

I feel a twinge of guilt strike me in the stomach. Based on that comment alone, I can tell she hasn't seen my response post to the trolls.

"I'm sorry, Carlie." It's all I can think to say.

She gives me a small, sad smile. "Thanks, Adam. That means a lot."

"So," I whisper, eager to know more about her and shift the conversation, "I wanna know more about your writing. You've been so vague about it."

She opens her eyes, the spark returning. "You're going to think it's dumb."

My forehead creases. "No, I won't."

She levels me with a stare, then sighs. "All right, but don't say I didn't warn you."

"You can trust me," I press, hoping like hell the sincerity filters into my tone.

Her lips twist to the side for a second, then she says, "I write romance novels. It's a bit cheesy to most people, I know, but I love it. There's something about creating stories where everything works out in the end that makes me really happy."

I can't help but smile back. "Sounds interesting, actually." I lean in, genuinely interested. "And writing romance doesn't sound cheesy. It sounds hopeful. We could all use a bit of that."

"Thanks, Adam." A bloom of soft pink spreads across her cheeks, and she momentarily finds the swirling patterns on the coffee table more interesting—a telltale sign of her modesty in accepting compliments. "It's just ... well, sometimes life isn't like the books, you know?"

I nod, understanding all too well. "Yeah, I get that. Life's thrown me some curveballs, too. *Obviously*."

While I meant it in terms of getting fired—my

thoughts stray back to Jillian's betrayal and the fact that her infidelity led me to Club Nocté.

That certainly was no romance novel. More like a steamy erotic short story.

But it was certainly a curveball, nonetheless.

Carlie's gaze meets mine again, and there's a shared understanding in her eyes. "Life's messy, isn't it? But that's what makes it real, I guess."

"Very true." I chuckle, feeling more at ease. "Speaking of real, you do a lot of your writing here?"

Carlie nods enthusiastically. "Yeah, this place is my second home. Sometimes my Grandma can be a bit much—she's my landlord and ..." She breaks off, dropping her gaze to the table and shaking her head. "A-anyway, it's peaceful here. Perfect for writing. Plus, I love people-watching. It gives me inspiration for characters."

"Characters, huh? Ever base one on a clueless fitness trainer?" I ask with a playful grin.

She laughs, a genuine, heartwarming sound and a part of me feels like it memorizes it. "Not yet, but there's always a first time for everything."

"That there is," I say, my eyebrows flicking upward. "You know, I have a secret love for fantasy novels. Sarah J. Maas is actually one of my favorites," I whisper. "But don't tell Dylan. He'll never let me live it down."

Her entire demeanor shifts at the mention of books. Her eyes, a vivid green, sparkle like emeralds under the coffee shop's warm lighting, and she leans forward, the enthusiasm radiating from her as if it's the most exciting secret she's heard. "No way. I love her books too! A

Court of Thorns and Roses is one of my all-time favorite series. But Crescent City is a close second."

"Mine too," I admit, feeling a connection that goes beyond trainer and client. "Her world-building is incredible."

"So are her sex scenes," she says, then clasps her hand over her mouth.

Her cheeks turn the color of her hair and I have to laugh, even while a certain part of me takes note. There were definitely some strong female sex-positive scenes in those books.

"You like the sex scenes, huh," I tease with more of a shitty grin than I intended. "Noted."

Carlie's blush deepens, but she manages a shy smile. "Well, they are ... creatively inspiring," she says with a playful glint in her eye.

I lean back, chuckling. "I'll have to remember that. Maybe I can learn a thing or two for my own ... *creative endeavors.*"

She runs her lower lip between her teeth, but she doesn't say anything to that. Yet, I can't help but feel the atmosphere between us has definitely shifted a bit.

We talk more about books, diving into more of our favorite genres and authors. I find myself surprised at how much we have in common, and how easily the conversation flows when we leave the Instagram fiasco behind.

"So, Carlie, tell me something about you that most people wouldn't guess at first glance," I ask, curious to know more—dive deeper.

She pauses, pondering the question. "Well, I'm kind of a closeted geek. I love video games and comic books. Not something people expect from a romance author, I guess."

I raise an eyebrow, impressed. "Really? That's pretty cool. I used to be big into gaming myself. Haven't had much time for it lately, though."

"Yeah, it's my way of unwinding after a long day of writing. Sometimes, you just have to shoot some shit," she says, her eyes lighting up. "Do you have a favorite game?"

"Used to be a huge fan of The Witcher series," I admit. "I could get lost in that world for hours. Haven't watched the show, though."

Carlie nods enthusiastically. "The storytelling in that game is phenomenal. I love how immersive it is."

Our conversation drifts to other topics, from our favorite movies to our hobbies. I find myself more and more intrigued by this woman—by the depth of her interests and the warmth of her personality. There's a magnetic quality about her that I could totally get sucked into.

Eventually, the topic circles back to fitness, when I ask her how her latest session went. Carlie's expression turns a bit more somber.

"Jillian's session ... I have to admit, it was really tough. Not just physically, but mentally too. Is she always like that?" She makes a face and I can tell instantly that whatever Jillian did with that fitness test, it was not her normal behavior.

I lean forward, concern flooding in. "I'm sorry to hear that. I wish I could've been there to make it a better experience for you."

She gives a small, appreciative smile. "Your sessions were so different. Encouraging, you know? I wasn't even expecting that when I first walked in."

I nod, feeling a mix of pride and frustration at her comment. "You know, I've been thinking about starting my own fitness business, but turns out I have this non-compete clause."

Since I was let go, I've been doing a lot of contemplation into what comes next. For research, I was looking over my old contract with St. Mary's and I found the non-compete clause. At the time, I didn't have an Instagram following or any intention of creating a gym. So, none of that mattered.

But now ...

Even if I wanted to get Foxx Fitness going, there's a good chance St. Mary's would sue if I don't wait until it expires.

"That's ridiculous. They can fire you and still expect you to stick to a non-compete?" she asks, concern etched in her features.

I shrug. "Looks like. I mean, it runs out in a couple of years, though."

"Well, that's stupid." Her eyes shine with sympathy and support. "Screw them. You should go for it—you know, better to ask forgiveness than permission. You'd be great at running your own place. I'd sign up in a heartbeat."

"You would?" I ask, trying to mask the sudden excitement in my voice.

She nods, her emerald eyes sincere. "Absolutely. Your approach to training is … different. It's more personal, more empowering. You know?"

I sit back, mulling over her words. The idea of her being one of my first clients in a new venture sends an unexpected thrill through me—even if the non-compete clause looms over me like a dark cloud.

I need to find a way around it.

"You're right. I'll figure something out," I say, more to myself than to her. "I can't let a piece of paper stop me from doing what I love. Right?"

"That's the spirit," she says, beaming back at me. "When you do start your own thing, let me know. I'll race right over. Okay, well, maybe not race, because chances are I'll still be in pain from Jillian's workouts, but you know what I mean."

The promise in her words fuels a new determination within me. I need to make this happen, not just for me, but for potential clients like Carlie who want what I have to offer.

The conversation continues, and I find myself not wanting it to end. There's a comfort in her presence, and a sense of ease I haven't felt in a long time. Maybe ever.

However, as our coffee date draws to a close, I take a deep breath, mustering the courage to ask, "Carlie, would you … I mean, can we do this again? Maybe grab dinner next time?"

She smiles, the corners of her eyes crinkling in a way

that tugs at my heart. "I'd like that, Adam. Dinner sounds great."

"How does tomorrow night sound?" I ask, wanting to pin her down before she leaves.

She nods. "Sounds perfect."

As she stands to leave, there's a moment's hesitation —a subtle bracing herself before she moves. Carlie's gait, usually fluid, albeit a bit off-center, carries a hint of carefulness as she takes slow, backward steps toward the door.

Her gaze holds mine, brimming with unspoken words. A tender hope, fragile yet resilient, blossoms in the space between us as she makes her way to the door and waves as she exits.

Dylan comes over, dropping into the seat Carlie just vacated. "So, how'd it go, Casanova?"

I grin, feeling more hopeful than I have in a long time. "Better than I could've imagined. She's amazing, Dylan."

He laughs, shaking his head. "I told you, man. Just two people having coffee."

I stand up, feeling like a weight's been lifted off my shoulders. "Yeah, just two people having coffee."

But I think it might be the start of something more.

CHAPTER 16

Carlie

Every piece of clothing I own is mocking me.

When I agreed to dinner with Adam, I clearly wasn't thinking about the fact that my wardrobe consists mostly of sweatshirts and comfy, stretchy pants.

The life of a writer really doesn't have to consist of much else, let's be honest here.

Sifting through my closet, every movement is a reminder of Jillian's workout from hell and it makes me regret every single attempt at a sit-up. I groan, trying to reach for a dress but ending up clutching my side instead.

God, I hope Adam wasn't able to sense just how bad this is.

"Why does everything hurt?" I groan to myself, grimacing at the colorful array of clothes that seem more like a puzzle than fashion choices at this point.

As I'm about to give up and head for the store, my phone buzzes.

I pick it up from my nightstand.

"Hey, Lily," I answer, trying to disguise my agony.

"Hey, Carlie. I just got your message. What's up?" she asks, her voice so even-keeled compared to my internal anguish. "Everything okay?"

"I'm in a bit of a bind." I let out a chuckle mixed with a sigh. "Adam asked me out for dinner and, well, I'm clueless about what to wear. Also, I'm still aching from the hellacious workout from his replacement," I confess, sinking down slowly onto my bed.

"Adam asked you out? That's fantastic—" Lily exclaims, her excitement crackling through the phone like a burst of sunshine.

"Yeah, it's great but overwhelming," I admit, closing my eyes, the mattress feeling like a cloud compared to my sore body. "I'm just ... lost for what the hell to wear, you know?"

"Don't worry, I'm coming over," Lily says, her voice filled with determination. "I'm no Vivian, but we'll sort this out together."

"Thanks, Lil," I say, a sense of relief washing over me. "Just be prepared, I'm moving like a hundred-year-old tortoise here."

She laughs and we hang up.

In the wake of her call, I lie back on the bed, staring at the ceiling, contemplating the irony of life.

Here I am, a romance writer, yet completely at a loss when it comes to real-life romance.

As it is, my room currently feels like a battleground strewn with rejected outfits, each discarded piece a testament to my growing despair.

Every attempt at getting up sends a sharp reminder of Jillian's torture session. The mere thought of standing up again makes me grimace.

How I'm going to make it through this date without crying in pain is beyond me.

Maybe I should have postponed until next weekend?

"Why did I ever think taking on fitness was a good idea?" I mumble to myself, throwing an arm over my eyes. Then, instantly regret that movement, too.

A few minutes later, Lily arrives, bursting through my door like a fairy godmother. Let's hope she's one well-endowed with a fashion sense. Because I'm clueless.

"Okay, let's see what we have in this disaster zone to work with," she says playfully, surveying the scattered clothes with a critical eye.

I attempt to sit up. "Lily, I think I'm officially broken. If Adam wanted to see the real me, he's in for a treat tonight," I say, half-joking, half-wincing.

She chuckles, her eyes scanning my wardrobe. "The real you is fantastic, Carlie." Lily starts picking up pieces of clothing, holding them up for scrutiny. "So, what's the vibe for this date? Casual chic? Elegant but approachable?"

"I don't even know," I confess, watching her. "I just want to look nice, not like I'm trying too hard, but not like I just rolled out of bed either."

"Adam's seen you in workout attire, right? How bad can it be to find a dress that will knock his socks off?" she teases, dropping the stuff on my bed and instead, turning to the depths of my closet without so much a single wince.

I happen to know for a fact that she's had many *'workout sessions'* with her new boyfriend, London, and she's not even in pain from the strenuous activity.

Oh, to be her.

"It's not just the outfit," I continue, biting my lip and redirecting my brain. "What if he's just feeling sorry for me? You know, after the whole Instagram thing?"

Lily pauses, a pink dress in hand, and gives me a look that's part reality check, part sympathy. "Did he come across like that's what it was?"

I think back to the coffee date. Honestly, it was fun and flirty—and we had way more in common than I expected.

"No, I guess not," I admit, shaking my head.

"That's what I thought." She winks at me, a twinkle of something in her eye that says more than her words.

"But ..."

"Carlie, from what you've told me, Adam's not the pity date kind. He likes you. And he *should*. You're a fine catch," she says, twisting back to the closet. "Now, let's find a dress that screams confidence, not crisis."

I give in, trusting her to find me a magical unicorn outfit from the clothes I've been staring at since yesterday.

She offers a few options, each one not quite the vibe I'm going for.

Finally, Lily holds up an emerald dress I've only worn once. "This one. It's *perfect.*"

"Uh," I hedge, not wanting to explain that the dress in her hands is the one I used to embody Zoey Cummings at the club where her new boyfriend works. "I don't think so."

Lily arches an eyebrow, still holding the dress. "Why not? It's gorgeous, and I bet you look stunning in it."

I shift uncomfortably, memories of that night at Club Nocté flooding back. "Let's just say it's not the first impression I want to make on this date."

She places the dress back with a knowing nod. "Got it. We'll find something else." She rummages through my wardrobe, her enthusiasm undiminished. "How about this one?"

She pulls out a simple, elegant black dress with a flattering, low neckline.

"Shows off the girls quite a bit," I laugh, hoisting my boobs up and letting them drop.

She cackles at that, her eyes sparkling. "Why not give him something to stare at? Isn't that the sentiment Vivian's been trying to drum into you?"

I shake my head at the dress and point back to the closet. "Maybe on date two."

Her eyes twinkle again, but she doesn't press it.

I haven't known Lily long, but the transformation her personality has undergone since I first met her is pretty astounding. I guess divorcing the wrong guy so you can end up with the right one will do that to you.

"So, how are things with you and London?" I ask, extremely curious and only slightly jealous. Their love story is the stuff of one of my dirty books.

"They're good—*really* good actually," Lily responds with a warm smile. "London's just so … understanding, you know? He gets me. He's more than I could have ever dreamed of."

"That's so great to hear," I say, genuinely happy for her. My thoughts drift to Adam, wondering if we could ever have that kind of understanding. "I suppose it doesn't hurt that the sex is mind-blowing, too."

"Carlie," Lily gasps, a grin on full display.

I shrug. "I write erotic stories. A girl can tell."

She laughs again and shakes her head. However, I swear as she turns back to my closet, she whispers, "That definitely doesn't hurt."

Lily holds up a simple yet stylish navy blue dress. "How about this? It's classy, but not over-the-top. It will make your red hair stand out and your eyes pop. Pair it with some cute boots, and you're set."

I eye the dress, a hint of a smile forming. "That could work. As long as I can actually get into it without contorting my body too much."

"I can help you into it, but if you need help getting out of it …" Her grin widens and turns totally mischievous.

"Oh, stop," I say, feeling the heat creep into my cheeks. "It's our first date. I'm not going to jump his bones on the first date."

She shakes her head. "For a romance author, you're pretty cautious. Put on your sexiest lingerie, just in case."

Rather than argue, I do as she says, trying to ignore

the fact that I'm wearing a sexy silver bra and underwear when Lily helps me get the dress on.

As I get ready, we chat about everything and nothing.

It's a welcome distraction from the knots of anxiety in my stomach.

"How do I look?" I ask, running my hands over my thighs and straightening the bottom of my dress.

Lily steps back, her eyes lighting up. "You look beautiful, Carlie. Really. Adam won't know what hit him."

I glance at my reflection, surprised at how the dress seems to transform me. Not quite Zoey-level transformation but certainly better than gym-goer Carlie.

The top is an elegant sleeveless number that rises up across my clavicle. It has a small slit that shows off just enough cleavage and not a single trace of the birthmark that drives me nuts.

Lily was right, it was a good choice. It's comfortable yet chic, striking the perfect balance.

"Thanks, Lily. I ... I feel good in this," I whisper, but butterflies burst in my midsection and I let out a jagged breath.

Lily grins, then ushers me over to the bed. "Okay, distraction time. Tell me more about this session with Jillian. It sounds like she was being a bit of a drill sergeant."

I wince just at the memory. "It was brutal. As someone who's just getting into fitness for the first time, she had me doing things I'm pretty sure were designed for Olympic athletes. And now, I'm paying the price. Every. Single. Muscle. Aches."

"Well, you know, they say the best way to relieve muscle tension is through ... *other* physical activities." Her grin widens suggestively.

I blink at her. "Lily, I already told you, I'm not going to sleep with him on the first date—" My face heats up at the thought. It's not like I haven't slept with someone with far less between us than a first date.

"Who said anything about sleeping?" Lily retorts with a laugh that turns into a soft snort. "I was going to suggest a hot bath, but your mind went straight to the gutter, *Miss Romance Writer.*"

"You *so* were not going to suggest that." I roll my eyes, but can't suppress a giggle. "A hot bath does sound heavenly, though."

Lily nods, her expression turning more serious. "But on a more practical note, have you tried any pain relief gel or something? Might help with the soreness."

"Yeah, I probably should have slathered myself in it before you helped me into this dress," I say, imagining the glamorous picture that paints.

Lily rummages through her purse and pulls out a small tube. "Here, take this. It's a lifesaver. Just don't ... you know, confuse it with your toothpaste. Or use it on any ... sensitive parts, if you know what I mean."

Shuddering slightly at the thought of confusing it for toothpaste or lubrication, I take the tube and read the label.

"Thanks, but I think I'll be okay." I say handing the tube back to her, a sudden thought striking me. "Wait, has London been giving you these muscle soreness survival tips?"

She grins, a blush tinting her cheeks. "Let's just say he's very ... *resourceful.*"

We both burst into laughter, the tension in the room easing. It feels good to laugh, to not take everything so seriously for a moment.

As Lily helps me put everything back into my closet, I can't help but feel grateful for her presence. And for her ability to make me laugh even when I'm a bundle of nerves.

When I walked into the Dirty B's book club a few months ago, I didn't quite know what I'd find.

But I've been pleasantly surprised to find at least one really good friend. Not that the others aren't—but Lily just seems to understand some of my weird quirks.

It's nice to have a friend like her again. Especially after what Sasha did with my stupid ex.

"So, back to the date," Lily says, pulling me from the sudden sour mood that threatens to take me under. "I really think you need some boots paired with this dress. Do you have any?"

I nod, pointing to the back of the closet. "Yeah, I think I have some calf-high ones. Back there."

Lily bends down and fishes them out. "These?" She holds up my brown leather boots that haven't seen the light of day in years.

"That would be them." I nod.

She stands up and hands them over. "They'll look great. Put them on."

I smile, feeling a surge of confidence as I do as she asks, only wincing once. "Thanks, Lily. I don't know what I'd do without you."

She gives my shoulder a gentle squeeze. "What are friends for? Now, remember, just be yourself. Adam's *lucky* to be going out with you."

"Let's hope he thinks so," I whisper.

"I *know* he will," she fires back with a seriousness that says there's no room for argument.

I can't help but admire how the boots really do add a touch of edginess to the outfit. The combination of the navy dress and the boots somehow feels like me, but *more*. Lily's definitely got an eye for this sort of thing.

"Lily, this looks ..." I say, shaking my head in surprise.

"See? You look amazing. Totally date-worthy." Lily steps back, appraising my look with a satisfied nod.

I twirl around slowly, chuckling. "I feel like a new person. Thanks to you."

"Seriously, it was nothing. I'm happy to help," she beams, as her phone buzzes in her purse. She glances at it and smiles. "Sorry, gotta take this. It's London."

As she steps out of the room to answer the call, I take the moment to breathe. In the mirror, I see a reflection of myself looking confident, almost daring.

Not quite my alter-ego daring, but I'll take it.

It's a nice change from the usual gym clothes or my writer's uniform.

The sound of my own phone ringing snaps me out of my reverie. I glance at the caller ID and see it's Grandma.

Picking it up, I brace myself for her usual blend of bluntness and inappropriateness.

"Hey, Grandma, what's up?"

"Carlie, dear, there's a very hunky young man with enormous arms looking lost on our porch. Is he for you?" Grandma's voice is laced with mirth.

I freeze, my heart doing a little skip. "Uhm, might be."

"Hubba hubba. He's easy on the eyes. You want me to keep him entertained until you get down?" Her tone suggests she wouldn't mind one bit.

"Grandma, no. Dear god, *no*. I'll be right down," I say, panic and excitement nearly making me jump out of my skin.

Adam's here.

Already.

I glance at my bedside clock as my heart picks up speed.

He's early.

Rushing to give myself one last look in the mirror, I smooth down my dress and take a deep breath.

This is it.

My first real date in what feels like forever.

I could not have predicted this a week ago.

Lily says her goodbyes to London and hangs up as I make my way to the door. "Lily, I gotta go. He's here—"

Lily claps, her grin dazzling. "Go get him, tiger. I'll lock up and let myself out once you're gone. And remember, *breathe*. Have fun!"

"Breathe, right," I say, trying and failing at doing it.

A flurry of hummingbirds take flight in my stomach but I step out of my room, grab my purse and keys, then make my way down the stairs. Each step is filled with a blend of eagerness and trepidation as my muscles remind me they still haven't forgiven me.

As I reach the door, I pause, taking another stab at a deep breath.

I can do this.

It's just Adam.

The same Adam who's seen me sweat and struggle at the gym. We engaged in partner yoga and went viral on Instagram.

He's also the same Adam who made me laugh over coffee yesterday.

This is just another step.

I open the door, and *there he is.*

His eyes light up when he sees me, and any remaining jitters I have melt away.

"Hi, Adam," I say, my voice steadier than I feel.

"Hey, Carlie. You look ... *wow.* Amazing," he says, his gaze taking me in.

I feel a blush creeping up my cheeks but manage a smile. "Thanks. You look—" My eyes sweep over his form. He's dressed in a pair of faded black denim jeans with a few rips here and there. They're form-fitting enough that I can't wait to see him from behind.

His button-up shirt is a dark purple—or is it blue? Whatever it is, it shimmers slightly in the light. And the way his sleeves are rolled up to his elbows reminds me of all of the sexy heroes I've written about in my books.

swoon

It's then that I realize, I'm practically drooling.

The grin on his face widens and he tilts his head to the side. After a beat, I realize he's waiting for me to finish whatever Godforsaken comment I was in the middle of before …

What was it? What was I saying?

Oh!

"Good. You look really, *really* good," I cough out.

Adam's chuckle is a soft rumble, warm and inviting. He offers his arm, and I take it. As I tentatively place my hand on his bicep, I'm hyper-aware of the muscles beneath his shirt. There's a reassuring strength in his hold, a sense of security that sends a pleasant shiver down my spine.

He leans in, his voice low and teasing. "You know, I think we have an audience."

I turn slightly and sure enough, there's Grandma Elsie, peeking through the curtains with an unmistakable grin on her face. I can't help but laugh.

"Yeah, that's," I sigh, "my grandma."

Adam laughs too, his eyes crinkling in a way that makes my heart flutter. "Well, I guess by the way she's grinning, we have her approval then."

I nod, feeling a rush of excitement. "It would appear so."

We turn to head out, but not before I give Grandma a little wave. She responds with an enthusiastic thumbs-up—her antics bringing another round of laughter bubbling to my lips.

CHAPTER 17

Adam

The road to New Scenic Café is a winding ribbon along the North Shore—with Lake Superior sprawling endlessly to my right. The view is breathtaking, but not nearly as gorgeous as the woman in the seat beside me.

A knot of excitement mixed with nerves twists in my stomach as I sneak glances her way. It's been a while since I've been on a first date, and never with someone like Carlie.

The women I've always gravitated toward have been beautiful, sure. But they often came with a whole lot of maintenance. They were all into fitness or modeling and while that's great, I've definitely had trouble connecting over more than just the physical.

I can't help but wonder if that's where my problems really stem from—choosing women simply because I won't have to explain my eating and workout habits.

In the car, the silence is comfortable, but I feel a

conversation bubbling just beneath the surface. Glancing over at Carlie, I can't help but notice she looks as nervous as I feel.

Time to break some ice.

"So, your grandma seemed pretty … invested in tonight's proceedings," I start, a grin tugging at the corners of my mouth.

Carlie lets out a laugh, nodding. "Oh, you have no idea. She's like the neighborhood watch, but for my love life. She probably called every one of her friends the second we left."

I chuckle, imagining the scene. "She seemed to approve, though. Gave us a thumbs-up and everything."

Carlie rolls her eyes playfully. "Yeah, her approval ratings are notoriously easy to win. Just be hunky and not a serial killer, and you're golden."

"Good to know," I say, feeling a sense of warmth spread through me. "So, does that mean she thinks I tick both of those boxes?"

She huffs a laugh. "Oh, yeah."

"Really?" I say, sneaking another glance in her direction. "And what about you?"

Carlie's hesitant as she turns to face me. "Well, the jury's still out on the serial killer part." She narrows her gaze and continues, "But as for the hunky … let's just say I wouldn't argue with Grandma's assessment."

I can't help but laugh. "I'll take that as a compliment."

"You should," she says, her eyes meeting mine for a moment before she looks back at the road, a playful smirk on her lips. "But I reserve the right to make my own final judgment."

"Fair enough," I reply, focusing back on the drive. The atmosphere in the car is light and comfortable, somehow the perfect blend between playful teasing and genuine connection.

Hunky.

I can't fight the grin that floats to my face.

I've been told I'm good-looking over the years, but for some reason, hearing it fall from her lips hits me a little different.

"But if you think Grandma was a menace tonight, just wait until she starts asking about our wedding plans and future grandkids when you drop me off," she says, her tone painted with humor.

I let out a surprised laugh, glancing at her. "Is that a common topic of conversation?"

"Only every other day," she replies with mock seriousness. "I think she's got a bet going with her bingo friends about when I'll finally settle down. But don't panic. No need to rush for bingo's sake."

"Rushing for bingo's sake," I muse aloud, chuckling. "Now, there's a new one for the books."

Carlie's smile is radiant, lighting up her whole face. "Just wait, it gets better. She's even got names picked out for the grandkids."

"That's ... pretty forward-thinking of her." I chuckle at the thought.

"Oh, you have no idea," Carlie says, her laughter subsiding into a soft smile.

The conversation turns to other topics, and we share stories about our families, finding common ground in the quirks and endearing traits of our relatives.

It's moments like these, simple and honest, that make me feel like there could be something so much deeper between us.

Before too long, we pull into the parking lot of the New Scenic Café. The quaint, rustic appearance of the place, with its warm lighting spilling out onto the patio, creates a cozy, inviting atmosphere. The ambiance promises an intimate evening, and I can sense Carlie's excitement mixed with a touch of nervous anticipation as I park. Or maybe that's my own.

After I shut off the car, I hurry to open her door, and Carlie greets me with a smile that's both thankful and slightly sheepish.

"Chivalry isn't dead, I see," she quips, her tone light and playful.

"I try my best," I reply, offering her my hand to help her out. She takes it, but not without a small grimace. "You okay?"

"Yeah, just still feeling the aftermath of Jillian's boot camp," she says with a wry grin. "I'm pretty sure she was secretly training me for the Hunger Games."

I chuckle at her remark. So many book references. "Well, I'd say *may the odds be ever in your favor,*' but I'm not sure it will help."

"Don't I know it," Carlie laughs, wrapping her hand around my bicep as we walk toward the restaurant.

I can't help but notice Carlie's slight hobble. It's

endearing in a way, seeing her push through the discomfort.

However, her hand on my bicep sends a warm sensation through me, and I'm acutely aware of her closeness. There's something about her touch, even as light as it is, that sets off a flurry of nerves inside me. I glance at her, and she's looking ahead, seemingly unaware of the effect she has on me.

Kinda glad about that, to be honest.

She catches me looking and rolls her eyes. "Don't mind me, just embracing my new life as forever sore."

I clear my throat, trying to refocus. "Well, hopefully, tonight will be less Hunger Games and more ... tranquil dinner date. I promise, no surprise yoga or dance-offs."

She snickers under her breath, the soft glow of the café lights reflecting in her eyes. "I'm holding you to that."

As we walk inside, the host greets us with a warm smile. "Table for two?"

"Yes, please," I reply with a quick nod.

The inside is bathed in soft lighting, creating an inviting atmosphere. It's perfect for a first date, even if I do say so myself.

We're led to a small, intimate table near a window overlooking the lake. The view is spectacular—the vast expanse of water shimmering against the warmth of the sunset.

Carlie's eyes drift out to the view.

"Wow, this is stunning," she murmurs, her attention momentarily captivated by the scenery.

"I thought you might like it," I say, pulling out her chair for her. "I've heard great things about their menu, too."

"Thank you," she says, as I help her sit.

Despite her earlier jokes about her soreness, I can tell she's genuinely struggling a bit. I make a mental note to keep things slow and easy for her tonight. If we were past the first date, I'd even offer to run her a hot bath and give her a massage.

The thought has me sitting down quickly, as I shake the image away.

Once we're seated, a server approaches and hands us menus.

"Can I start you off with something to drink?" he asks.

Carlie orders a glass of white wine, and I go for a craft beer from Jaded Brews. Gotta admit, I'm happy for my brother. It's good to see his stuff in other restaurants in the area.

After the waiter leaves, I should be looking over the menu, but instead, I find myself looking at her, still somewhat in awe of how effortlessly gorgeous she is.

Her red hair is like liquid fire as it cascades over her shoulders. The dim light of the restaurant complements her features, casting soft shadows that add an air of mystique.

She catches me looking at her and tucks a strand of hair behind her ear with a curious expression. "What?"

I shake my head. "Nothing. I was just—"

"Here we are. Are you two ready to order?" the server interrupts, setting our drinks down in front of us.

We both blink hard, breaking our gaze from each other to face the server.

"I'd love to try the smoked pork shank, please," Carlie says, handing the menu to him, and then turning to me.

I glance down at the menu in my hand. "I, uh—"

"I'm sorry, Adam. I should have waited," Carlie mutters, shaking her head. "I thought you were ready."

"No, it's cool. I'll have the seared duck," I say, handing him my menu as well.

He tips his head and stalks off, leaving us again in comfortable silence.

Carlie takes a tentative sip of her wine and I reach for my beer.

"I'm so curious. What's it like to craft your novels? Seems like it would be hard to keep track of everything," I venture, eager to know more about her.

Carlie's eyes light up, a hint of passion flickering behind them. "It's like being a puppet master, in a way. You get to create these worlds, these characters, and then make them fall in love. It's exhilarating, and frustrating, and utterly rewarding. At least, it is when the words flow easily."

Her words peter out a bit and I take that as a sign her writing hasn't been going so well lately.

Rather than take her down a path that feels like a sore spot, I lean in and say, "Sounds amazing. You must have an incredible imagination."

"I mean, I guess?" she says, then her expression shifts to something more playful. "There's also a fair bit of ... *research.*"

I can't help but raise an eyebrow. "Research? That sounds ... *intriguing*. Do tell."

She laughs, a sound that stirs something deep inside me. "Well, you have to know what you're writing about, right? Experience is the best teacher."

The innuendo isn't lost on me, and I feel a warmth spread straight through my lower half. "I suppose that means your books are ... quite authentic?"

She takes another sip of her wine, her eyes never leaving mine. "Oh, I strive for authenticity. But there's always room to learn more. Wouldn't you agree?"

"Oh, yeah," I say, my voice nearly cracking.

There's something in the way she speaks—like sex and intimacy is more than just an act. It's something to be truly relished in.

To be *experienced.*

The air between us crackles with unspoken tension, and I take a long sip of my beer, trying to cool the sudden heat I'm feeling. This conversation is veering dangerously close to territory that's both exciting and nerve-wracking.

Just then, our meals arrive, and we both turn our attention to the food. Carlie's pork shank looks incredible and my duck is nothing short of heavenly.

She must like it, too, because she moans after a bite. "This is ... so good—in a *'my tastebuds are on a rollercoaster'* kind of way."

"Sounds interesting. Trade you for a bite?" I suggest, offering her a taste of mine.

She agrees, and as we switch plates, our hands briefly touch, sending a spark of electricity between us. For a moment, we lock eyes, and there's a silent acknowledgment of the chemistry we're both feeling.

"So, how did you end up in Duluth?" I ask, wanting to know everything I can about her.

"Well, I grew up in central Minnesota—a small town not really worth mentioning. But after college, I was trying to figure out where I wanted to live and Duluth seemed like a fun place. My mom grew up here and my grandma—yes, the same one—still lived here. So, I figured why not give it a try?" She says, a ghost of a smile flitting to her lips. "Grandma's getting older and needed a renter. I wanted to spend more time with her while I still can. So ..."

"So, you moved upstairs," I finish for her. "That's really awesome of you."

She chews on her bottom lip before taking another bite of her food.

It's obvious she cares a lot for the people around her and based on the way she talks about her books, she desperately wants to find a kind of love and connection others only dream of.

Yet, there's a hint of something—something dark that sometimes lingers and I can't help but wonder who hurt her.

One thing's for sure, she's been through a lot, and yet she's still here, still standing strong.

We talk about our favorite places in the city—our shared love of the Lift Bridge. The conversation flows effortlessly, and I find myself losing track of time.

It's as if the world outside this little café has ceased to exist, and it's just Carlie and me, sharing a piece of our lives with each other as we share a meal.

I don't want the night to end. I want to keep talking to her—keep learning about her. Keep sharing more of myself.

As we finish our meal, Carlie looks out the window thoughtfully. The sun has set long ago and a bright crescent moon shines over the lake.

"You know, I always thought romance was something you only read about in books. But tonight feels like I'm living in one of my own stories," she whispers. "Does that sound dorky?"

"I'm glad to be part of your story," I say sincerely, reaching out to place my hand over hers.

She glances down at where our hands meet and a grin floats to her features. "Me too."

"Would you like to go for a walk?" I ask as the server clears our plates. "The lake looks beautiful this time of night."

Carlie's eyes light up at the suggestion, but then she hesitates. "I'd love to, but fair warning, I might wobble more than walk."

I smile, reaching out to take her hand. "I've got you. We'll go slow. Let's go make some memories."

She grins. "Okay."

We walk toward the shore, the rhythmic sound of the waves providing a serene soundtrack. Carlie's hand in mine feels just right, and as we walk, she leans into me slightly. Her warmth is a welcome presence.

"Adam," she starts, her voice tinged with humor. "If I accidentally pull you into the lake, just remember, it was nice knowing you."

I laugh, squeezing her hand gently. "I'll take my chances."

Under the starlit sky, with the gentle waves as our witness, I feel a connection with Carlie that goes beyond anything I've experienced before. It's not just about attraction—it's more than that.

A bond forming.

As we approach the water's edge, the moonlight dances across the waves, casting a magical glow over our surroundings. I find a spot on the shore, a flat rock that serves as a perfect seat, and help Carlie sit down beside me.

Resting there, with the sound of the waves gently lapping at the shore, Carlie turns to me, her eyes sparkling in the moonlight.

"You know, I didn't expect tonight to be like this. I mean, I didn't really know what to expect," she sighs. "It's ... nice."

"Nice?" I echo, playfully feigning disappointment.

She nudges me with her shoulder, a smile tugging at her lips. "Okay, more than nice. It's been wonderful."

I chuckle, locking my gaze with hers.

The proximity between us narrows as we both lean in, drawn together by an invisible force. Her breath mingles with mine, and the world seems to hold its breath. Just as our lips are about to meet, a fleeting memory flashes in my mind—the sensation of a similar, electrifying moment.

But it's Carlie's reaction that pulls me back to reality. She pauses, her eyes widening slightly as she inhales sharply. There's a flicker of something that crosses her face but it's gone before I can pinpoint what it means.

"You okay?" I ask, pulling back just a bit.

She nods, but her voice betrays a hint of uncertainty. "Yeah, just ... never mind. It's nothing."

I study her for a moment, wondering what's going through her mind. There's a sense of familiarity, a connection that seems to reach beyond just this evening. But before I can ponder it further, Carlie leans in, closing the distance between us.

Our lips meet in a tender, hesitant kiss. It's a gentle exploration—a promise of something more—as her tongue softly caresses my bottom lip.

My heart is ready to drum itself right out of my chest as I raise my right hand to the side of her face and I edge in closer.

There's something about her kiss ...

"Oh, wow," she breathes out, pulling back just a fraction, her eyes wide and shimmering in the moonlight. There's something in her eyes—a question, maybe—but she quickly masks it with a shaky smile.

I study her for a moment. "Carlie? Are you sure you're okay?"

She nods quickly—a bit too quickly. "Yeah, everything's fine. Just ... the moon is really bright tonight, isn't it?"

Her attempt to deflect is clear, and I decide not to press her, sensing she needs a moment.

"Definitely," I agree, following her gaze to the moonlit lake.

The air between us has shifted, charged with an unspoken understanding that something significant just happened—but I have no idea what it was.

CHAPTER 18

Carlie

Lying in bed, I stare at the ceiling—the darkness of the room doing nothing to soothe the whirlwind of thoughts spinning through my mind. The faint moonlight seeping through the curtains casts ghostly shadows, mirroring the turmoil inside me.

I basically got zero sleep and it's all because I can't shake off the feeling from last night's date with Adam—the haunting sense of familiarity that's now clinging to me like a second skin.

He *smelled* like the guy from Nocté, or at least so similar that it leaves enough room for doubt to creep in, making me question my own senses.

And that kiss ...

It sent the same electrifying thrill through me, a sensation I thought was unique to that mysterious encounter.

Before our lips touched, there was an inhalation from Adam—like he was bracing himself for the inevitable. It was a small, yet significant detail. One that jolted a memory so vivid, *so potent,* it left me reeling.

I mean, when I first met him the comparison was there. But I thought it was because the memory of that night was so fresh.

Every man I met was suspect.

But now...

I roll onto my side, hugging the pillow tighter.

The idea that Adam might *really* be the guy from Nocté feels both exhilarating and terrifying.

I wasn't the same person that night.

I mean, physically, I was. But mentally ...

Zoey was my ride-or-die and if he is the guy from Nocté, I think dying might be my only option.

I'm not that woman.

But he could certainly be the man.

How is it even possible?

The coincidences stack up, building a case my writer's brain can't ignore.

Lying there in the early morning shadows, my thoughts are chasing their tails.

Adam.

That kiss.

The tantalizing possibility that he's Mr. Nocté—it's like a plot twist in one of my novels, except I can't peek at the last page to see how it ends.

I'm wide awake, despite my best efforts to trick my brain into slumber.

With a groan, I roll out of bed, feeling every bit the

protagonist in a romcom who's accidentally switched lives with a circus clown.

"Let's hope Jillian's bootcamp today is more forgiving than my overactive imagination," I mutter, pulling on my workout clothes.

Of course, in my sleep-deprived state, I manage to put my sports bra on inside out and backward.

"Fantastic start, Carlie. Super job," I mutter under my breath.

After a quick change and a glance in the mirror that confirms I'm at least presentable, I decide to grab coffee at *'Bean There, Done That.'*

I need caffeine if I'm going to face Jillian's torture—*er, training*—session.

Plus, it's on the way to the gym. Win-win.

❧

As I enter the coffee shop, Dylan, Adam's apparent best friend and the world's most infuriatingly smug barista, greets me with a grin that's too cheeky for this hour.

"Morning, Carlie. I'm assuming the usual?" he asks, setting to work as if the half-awake look on my face already told him *yes*.

"Hey, Dylan. Make it strong enough to resurrect the dead, please," I say, attempting a smile but probably looking more like I smelled something foul.

His grin widens, and I can't help but wonder if he's thinking about Adam and me.

Does he know anything? Did Adam talk to him

about our date and the way it ended? Do guys discuss that sort of thing? Or is that reserved only for hookups?

My face heats.

Oh, god. If he's the guy from Nocté, would he have told Dylan about that night?

Is this all a part of the cosmic joke the universe is playing on me?

As Dylan hands me the coffee with a casual flick of his wrist, his expression is playfully sardonic. "Strong enough to wake the dead. Keep it up, and we might start calling you the local necromancer."

I grin back at him. "Thanks, Dylan. If it works on me this morning, you can call me anything you want."

I turn to leave, only to collide with another patron in my haste. The lid pops off my coffee cup, and hot liquid cascades down my front.

"Ouch! Hot, hot, hot!" I dance back, dropping the cup as I fan my now coffee-stained shirt.

Dylan rushes over, napkins in hand. "Whoa, are you okay?"

"Just peachy," I grumble, dabbing at the boiling hot liquid and tugging my shirt away from my body. "And they say writers lead boring lives."

He chuckles, his eyes sparkling with amusement. "You sure you don't want to switch to iced coffee?"

I shoot him a look that's half annoyance, half amusement. "Hilarious, Dylan. I'll remember this the next time you want book recommendations."

On the upside, at least my mortifying mess didn't expand to the brick wall of a guy I ran into. Instead, he just steps around me and my disaster, and walks up to the counter.

"Don't worry, sir, it's not you, it's me," I mutter under my breath. It really doesn't matter if he hears me or not. "I'm just a walking calamity."

I help Dylan clean up the mess on the floor while the other barista helps the guy oblivious to my plight. When every trace of coffee is erased, Dylan heads back to the machines and makes me another drink.

With a little luck, I'll be able to actually swallow down some of that resurrection potion this time.

Rushing back home, I'm a chaotic whirlwind. The idea of being late for Jillian's session, especially after my coffee debacle, sets my nerves on edge. I take quick sips of the scalding coffee, wincing as it burns my tongue.

"Great, now I'll be tasting everything with a side of charred tastebuds," I mutter, fumbling with my keys.

Once inside, I hustle to my room, peeling off the coffee-stained shirt with a grimace.

"You had one job, shirt. One job—" I toss my shirt into the hamper, hoping it doesn't hold a grudge. Grabbing a fresh workout outfit, I hop around trying to get the old one off as quickly as possible, nearly face-planting in the process.

"Balance, Carlie, it's not just for flamingos," I scold myself, finally getting the new shirt over my head.

I gulp down more of the coffee, feeling it jolt my system like a live wire.

Caffeine goodness ... *yes,* I need that more than life itself right now.

"Who needs a functioning tongue anyway?" I muse out loud.

But then last night's kiss flashes into my mind.

Okay, yes, a tongue is useful ...

I shudder the thought away, tossing on a pair of leggings and nearly tripping again.

"At this rate, I'm going to need a helmet just to make it through the day," I mutter.

With one last glance in the mirror—a quick assessment that I'm not inside out or back to front—I make a dash for the door.

The coffee cup is now half empty, or half full if I'm being optimistic. I take a big gulp, trying to channel its caffeinated power—willing it to bring me to life.

Necromancer, indeed.

As I lock the door and hurry down the stairs, I can't help but think, *Jillian is either going to be impressed by my commitment or convinced I'm a lost cause.*

Finally ready (again), I make my way to the gym, my mind still a whirl of questions and coffee stains.

If this is how my day is starting, I shudder to think what Jillian's workout has in store for me. At least I can't accidentally spill a treadmill.

Take a spill and have my face sanded off, though? *Sure.*

I groan at the thought. Knowing my clumsy capabilities, that's a total possibility.

After a quick walk, St. Mary's looms ahead—a place where I'll either find my focus or provide entertainment with my newfound *uber*-clumsiness.

I take a deep breath, bracing myself for the former and secretly praying it's not the latter.

Jillian, of course, is already in full drill sergeant mode when I arrive. Her piercing gaze zeroes in on me the moment I step through the door.

"You're late, Carlie," she chides, though I'm perfectly on time.

By two minutes.

Hallelujah.

"Sorry, Jillian. Traffic," I lie, not wanting to admit the way my morning has technically gone.

She doesn't look like she buys it but simply nods, directing me to warm up. I start with stretches, but my movements are jerky and uncoordinated.

I can literally *feel* Jillian's eyes on me, scrutinizing every awkward movement.

"Focus, Carlie. This isn't a dance recital," she barks, and I can't help but wish it was. At least then my two left feet might have a fighting chance.

As we move on to more rigorous exercises, it's painfully obvious my mind is elsewhere, replaying last night's kiss, the lingering scent of Adam, and all the questions in between.

It doesn't help that every time I glance at Jillian, I half expect her to morph into a demonic trainer from one of my more vivid nightmares. She'd fit the part perfectly.

"Carlie, for heaven's sake, lift your knees higher," Jillian's voice cuts through my daydreams.

I try to comply, but my coordination is off. My foot catches the edge of the mat, and I stumble, barely catching myself before my face splatters onto the gym floor.

I can't even bring myself to care.

I just lay there, like hugging the mat is my number one priority.

"Seriously?" Jillian exclaims, her tone mixed with frustration and disbelief. "What is with you today? You're not even trying."

Slowly—so slowly, I push myself up, feeling a flush of embarrassment heat my cheeks.

"I *am* trying," I protest, but even to my own ears, it sounds weak.

Jillian shakes her head, her hands on her hips. "This is a gym, not a playground. If you can't take this seriously, you shouldn't be here."

I bite my lip, trying to focus, but it's like my body has forgotten how to function properly. Well, *properly* might be a stretch for me, come to think of it.

With a huff (from both of us), we move on to weights, and that's when disaster really strikes. My grip slips and the weights clatter to the floor with a resounding thud that echoes through the gym.

Everyone's attention snaps in our direction and Jillian's patience snaps like a rubber band.

"That's it! You're a hazard to yourself and others. Get out—" Her index finger points in the direction of my walk of shame.

Her words sting, but part of me feels relieved to have an escape route. I gather my things, my hands shaking slightly.

As I walk out, I hear Jillian muttering something about "hopeless cases."

And "can't believe he'd be seen with *that*."

I can only assume she means Adam and the whole Instagram thing. Unless rumor has already reached the gym that we went on a date last night. Wouldn't be surprised, actually.

Outside, I lean against the wall, taking deep breaths.

"Great job, Carlie. Really nailing the whole fitness thing," I mumble to myself.

The thought of going back home and working out there, where the only judgment comes from my grandma, suddenly seems very appealing.

As I walk home, my mind is hijacked by the blur of embarrassing and frustrating memories at the gym. Jillian's words echo in my head, but there's a small, defiant part of me that whispers, "I'll show her."

Maybe I'm not cut out for gym life, but that doesn't mean I can't find my own way to stay fit.

By the time I reach my apartment, I've made a decision.

I'm going to cancel my training sessions and start working out at home.

It might not be as fancy, but at least I'll be in my

element. And who knows, maybe I'll actually enjoy it more without the fear of public humiliation.

As I step inside my apartment, the quietness envelops me like a comforting blanket. Dropping my gym bag by the door, I let out a long, tired sigh.

My reflection in the hallway mirror catches my eye. Hair disheveled, outfit sweaty—I'm a hot mess in the most literal sense.

Kicking off my shoes, I shuffle towards the kitchen, the desire for fresh coffee and the promise of solitude pushing me forward.

After brewing a fresh pot, I fill my mug with coffee, the steam rising in lazy swirls. Taking a cautious sip, I wince as it scalds my still-fuzzy tongue.

"Perfect," I mutter, setting the cup down. I lean against the counter, closing my eyes for a moment trying to center myself.

From my pocket, my cell phone buzzes, jolting me from my thoughts.

It's a text from Adam.

My heart leaps, then sinks.

What if he heard about the gym fiasco? What if Jillian's comments were about us and he knows?

I hesitate, then open the message.

> Morning, Carlie. I had fun last night. Hope you're having a better day than me. Spilled my protein shake all over my shirt. Guess you're not the only one with a talent for chaos. 😅

I can't help but laugh. The tension eases from my shoulders.

He's just as human, just as prone to mishaps as I am. It's strangely comforting.

And maybe ...

Just maybe—he was up last night thinking about me, too.

Quickly typing a reply, I tease him about joining the 'clumsy club.'

I don't fill him in on today's fiasco, hoping that's something he never has to learn about.

His response is immediate and light-hearted.

We banter back and forth, and for a brief moment, I forget about Jillian, about the gym, about the doubts plaguing me.

Setting my phone aside, I glance around my apartment. It's small, cozy, a reflection of my life—a little chaotic, a lot colorful.

I make my way to the living room, pulling out my yoga mat. Maybe it's time to take my fitness into my own hands. Since I never got the chance to cool down at the gym, I'll start by stretching.

As I reach for my toes, feeling the tension leave my body, I can't help but think about Adam and our partner yoga session.

The mystery of Mr. Nocté still hangs over us, but right now, it doesn't matter.

I'm Carlie, a writer, a hopeful romantic, and a survivor of the most disastrous gym session in history.

I'm also ready to embrace whatever comes next.

With a renewed sense of purpose, I finish my routine.

There's a story waiting to be written, a life waiting to be lived. I grab my laptop, open a new document, and start typing. The words flow a little easier today, mirroring my newfound resolve.

No matter what the future holds, I'm ready for it. With or without Adam, with or without the gym, I'm just getting started.

Bring it on, universe.

I'm ready.

CHAPTER 19

Adam

I'm lounging on my couch, phone in hand, trying to think of something witty to text Carlie.

For some reason, she pulls that side out of me. The side that wants to prove I'm more than just a muscle head who cares more about my protein intake than intelligence.

I want to see her again, *soon*.

Settling for simplicity over wit, I type out:

> Hey Carlie, want to catch up Friday night? Dinner and maybe something fun afterward?

I hit send before I can second-guess myself.

Let the waiting game begin.

I'm not usually this antsy about a date, but with her, everything feels different, more ... *something*. I can't put my finger on it.

To distract myself, I decide to grab a coffee from

'Bean There, Done That.' Dylan always has a way of putting things into perspective.

I pull on a light hoodie and grab my keys, deciding a drive might help clear my head.

As I get into my car, my thoughts drift to the severance package I received from St. Mary's. It's a decent amount—enough to keep me afloat while I figure out my next move.

But right now, my career isn't what's occupying my thoughts—it's Carlie.

Our date went well—*really well,* actually. But there was something in her demeanor after our kiss.

She was slightly off, almost cryptic about what she was thinking. It's like there's a puzzle piece I'm missing, and it's driving me nuts not knowing what it is.

Pulling into the small coffee shop parking lot, I shake off the thoughts.

I need to focus on the here and now—and right now, that's grabbing a coffee and shooting the breeze with Dylan.

Stepping inside, I'm greeted by the familiar, comforting scent of freshly brewed coffee. Dylan's behind the counter, his usual confident self, but today there's an extra spring in his step.

"Hey, Adam. I wasn't expecting you today," he greets with a wide grin. "Your usual?"

"Yeah, thanks," I reply, leaning against the counter. "You look like you're in a good mood. What's up?"

Dylan chuckles, his eyes gleaming as he sets to work. "You might say I'm feeling hopeful. Met this woman yesterday. Blond, total knockout. Wrote my number on her cup. Classic, right?"

I laugh. "That's one way to do it. She called you yet?"

"Not yet," he says, shrugging nonchalantly, but I can tell he's excited about the prospect. "Fingers crossed for this weekend."

"You'll have to keep me posted," I say, smiling.

As he hands me my coffee, Dylan's expression turns curious. "So, speaking of weekend dates ... How'd it go with Carlie on Sunday?"

I pause, my thoughts snagging again on that kiss.

"It went great," I say, keeping it vague. I'm not one to kiss and tell, even with Dylan.

"Come on, man, give me something more than that," Dylan protests, but he's smiling. "If blondie doesn't call, I gotta live vicariously through someone.

"Well, it's not gonna be me, Dylan. That's all you're getting," I reply, shooting him a lopsided grin.

He rolls his eyes but thankfully, lets it go. He knows me well enough by now to know that some things never change. This being one of them.

Then, his expression shifts, becoming more serious. "Actually, speaking of Carlie, Jillian was in here earlier. Why I let that woman come in, is a mystery, come to think of it." His expression turns quizzical, like he's trying to parse out his own logic.

It would be laughable if my protective instincts weren't immediately on edge.

"Focus, Dyl. What did Jillian say about Carlie?" I ask, snapping my fingers in front of his face.

He shakes his head and refocuses on me. "Oh, right. She was talking to some guy—I'm guessing from St. Mary's. I've never seen him before."

I roll my hand, urging him to get on with it.

He narrows his gaze and flattens his expression, but thankfully, continues, "I was gonna text you about it. I just got swamped with the morning rush."

"Dylan," I groan.

"Yeesh, panties in a bunch, I see," he snorts over his own wit and continues, "She said something about how the *'woman Adam got fired over'* couldn't even last a week at the gym before quitting. Seriously, how that woman doesn't realize I can overhear her in this tiny coffee shop is beyond me. Not much in the brains department, that one."

My grip on the coffee cup he hands me tightens. "She was talking about Carlie?"

"I'm assuming. Unless you got fired because of some other girl," Dylan says, raising an eyebrow in mock exasperation. "Jillian's got a mean streak a mile wide."

I frown, thinking things through. If it's true, and Carlie quit her sessions, something's not right.

"Adam, you still with me?" Dylan's voice pulls me back from my thoughts.

"Yeah, just thinking," I say, rubbing the back of my neck, my gaze drifting off.

The conversation I had with her last week about wanting to open my own gym floats to mind. Her immediate response was light but sincere—she said that if I ever opened my own gym, she'd be my first client.

As sweet as that was, I still hadn't given it a whole helluva lot of credence.

But now … it ignites something in me, a spark of possibility that hasn't been there before. Even for as much of the not-so-subtle nudging Brian and Dylan have offered, pointing me in this exact same direction.

I don't have a gym—at least not one like St. Mary's.

But I have my home, equipped enough for personal training.

It's not the sprawling fitness center I've imagined, but it could be a start.

Could I really train Carlie at my place?

Would she even be comfortable with that?

I find myself weighing the pros and cons, trying to gauge how she might react.

Especially knowing how things went down with Jillian—and our developing relationship.

Maybe she wouldn't even want my help anymore.

However, the idea of training her, helping her on her fitness journey in a way that's supportive and positive *feels right.*

It's personal, yes, but it's also a chance to prove to myself that I can do this—that I can be more than just another employee at a gym.

"Dylan, maybe it's time to bring Foxx Fitness to the world," I start, turning back to face him. "I think I might have my first client. At least, I hope so."

Dylan's eyebrows shoot up as surprise and excitement light up his face. "You're serious? Man, that's great! Who's the client? Wait, don't tell me …"

His grin widens.

I nod, feeling a rush of adrenaline at the prospect. "Yeah, Carlie. But it'll have to be at my place for now. Just gotta run it by her."

"Your place, huh?" Dylan leans in with a conspiratorial gleam in his eyes. "That's one way to get personal training on a whole new level."

I chuckle, shaking my head. "Not like that, Dylan. I want to help her. She deserves better than Jillian. Who knows what kind of bullshit she pulled to get Carlie to quit."

"Right?" Dylan agrees, his expression turning serious for a moment. "You know, Brian's gonna flip when he hears about this."

"Yeah, well, let's not get ahead of ourselves. Don't clue him in just yet," I warn, giving him the stink eye because I know Dylan's propensity for running his mouth off. "I've still got to ask Carlie if she's even up for it."

"You got this, man," Dylan says, giving me an encouraging pat on the shoulder. "And hey, if you need any help setting up or anything, you know where to find me."

I nod, appreciative of his offer. "Thanks, Dylan. I might take you up on that. But for now, I think I have what I need."

"Good, because I had no idea how I'd help," Dylan chuckles, wiping down the counter.

"You know, I'm gonna head over to Carlie's," I say, a sense of purpose in my voice as I take a big swig from my coffee cup. "Talk to her about this personal training idea and make sure she's okay."

Dylan's eyebrows lift in surprise, then he chuckles. "Right now? Man, you're not wasting any time."

I nod. "Yeah, I want to catch her before she gets wrapped up in her day or finds another gym to go to. And I need to do this face-to-face."

"Bold move," Dylan approves, grinning. "She's a lucky girl, having someone so *dedicated looking out for her.*" He flutters his eyelashes and clasps his hands under his chin like he's a heartsick lovebird.

I can't help but shake my head and smile back. "Thanks, Dylan. Wish me luck."

"Always, man. Go get 'er," he replies, giving me a supportive nod.

I push off from the counter, feeling more determined with each step. "Catch you later, Dylan. And thanks for the coffee."

"No problem, Adam. Let me know how it goes—" Dylan calls after me as I head for the door.

"Will do," I respond back as I swing the door open.

Stepping outside, I take a deep breath of the fresh morning air.

This is going to work.

The drive over to Carlie's apartment isn't long, but it gives me enough time to organize my thoughts and mentally prepare for the conversation ahead.

As I navigate through the streets, my mind whirls with possibilities and plans.

This isn't just about offering Carlie personal training.

It's a chance to start something new—deepen the connection between us ...

And maybe, in the process, lay the foundation for my dreams.

Turning onto her street, my grip on the steering wheel tightens. There's an excitement bubbling inside me, mixed with a not-so-subtle hint of nervousness.

Will Carlie see this proposition as too forward—too presumptuous? Or will she understand the genuine intention behind it?

Parking the car, I take a moment to collect my thoughts. Sneaking a glance at my phone, I notice Carlie texted me back.

Of course, I'd love to see you Friday.

A smile inches across my face and lightens the pressure on my chest. No matter what happens, or what she says about the training—we still have this.

I head towards Carlie's house, rehearsing in my mind the words I want to say. When I reach the deck, I walk to her door and press the doorbell before I lose my nerve.

I'm so focused on my thoughts that I almost miss the sound of another door opening.

I turn to find Carlie's grandmother, her eyes sharp and assessing as she looks me over. "Well, well, if it isn't the famous Adam," she says, her voice tinged with humor.

I offer a polite smile, slightly taken aback by her directness.

"Hi, you must be Carlie's grandma. It's nice to meet you," I say, holding out my hand.

She eyes it, then swipes my hand back. "Around here, we hug."

Before I know what's happening, the tiny woman wraps her arms around me and squeezes tight.

"My, you're a solid one, aren't you?" She says, practically giving me a pat down.

I chuckle, opting not to step into that one. "I'm here to see Carlie. Is she around?"

As she steps back, she crosses her arms, giving me an assessing look. "She's upstairs. But before you go up to see her, I have a few questions for you, young man."

I nod, understanding the protective nature of her interrogation. "Of course. What do you want to know?"

"What are your intentions with my granddaughter? And what exactly are you doing here so early?" she asks, narrowing her gaze and raising her chin.

"I, uh—" I hedge. I don't mind telling her any of it—it's just I want Carlie to find out from me what my idea is.

Truthfully, it's kinda sweet she cares so much.

"'Uh' is not an explanation, Adam. Cat got your tongue?" she fires back, her focus never straying from my face.

Just as I'm about to explain the idea of offering personal training to Carlie at my place—because let's face it, that look her grandma is giving me means business—I hear footsteps descending the stairs.

Carlie appears in her doorway, looking relaxed and

comfortable in a rumpled t-shirt and sweatpants. It's a stark contrast to some of the other outfits I've seen, and it adds a new level of interest to her.

I read her shirt, which says, "Piss me off and I'll kill you ... *in my books.*"

Despite myself, I have to chuckle.

"Adam, what are you doing here?" Carlie asks, her eyes lighting up with surprise.

I turn to her, feeling her grandmother's scrutinizing gaze on me. "I wanted to check in on you and see how you're doing. And I have something to propose to you."

"Grandma, you can go," Carlie says, looking past me with a pointed look.

Carlie's grandmother narrows her gaze on me, then raises two fingers to her eyes and flicks them in my direction.

Carlie lets out an exasperated sigh.

Her grandma grins broadly at Carlie, then excuses herself, leaving us to talk.

Carlie rolls her eyes, then steps closer, a curious expression now on her face. "What's this about a proposal?"

Taking a deep breath, I begin, "I was thinking ..."

Her green eyes lock with mine and for a brief moment, I almost get lost in them. She raises her eyebrows expectantly.

"Sorry," I say, shaking my head to clear it. "I was thinking about the conversation we had last week about you being my first client if I opened a gym. Now, hear me out—"

Her eyes widen. "You're doing it? You're opening your own gym?"

"Yes, I mean—sorta. Right now, I'd have to train you at my place. But it's a start. Dylan told me you might have quit your sessions and I thought—" I exhale another breath. "I thought maybe Jillian pushed you over the edge. She can be a great trainer, but sometimes, she can also be brutal. You deserve better."

Carlie watches me intently and after a moment, she smiles, a look of relief and excitement crossing her features. "I think this is a fantastic idea, Adam. You're right, I couldn't stomach any more sessions with Jillian. Not after—" She pauses, her eyes finding mine. "I'd love to be your first client."

The tension I hadn't realized I was holding onto melts away. "Great! We'll start fresh next Monday. How does that sound? It'll give you some time to rest up and I'll get everything organized on my end."

Her smile widens, and she nods in agreement. "Sounds like a plan. A fresh start."

"A fresh start," I agree with a nod.

As we finalize the details and I head out, I can't help but feel a sense of accomplishment and anticipation.

Monday won't just be a new beginning for my career —it's a new beginning for my life. And Carlie seems to be an integral part of it.

But first … I have a date to plan.

CHAPTER 20

Carlie

Four days have slipped by since the night at New Scenic Café.

It's hard to believe, but then I think back to the absolute clusterfuck that was Monday with Jillian and I remember, yes, it's been one hell of a week so far.

On the upside, each day has been filled with a whirlwind of texts from Adam. His messages have been so playful and encouraging and it keeps reminding me of how much has changed between us.

The thought sends a flutter through my stomach.

Our conversations are easy, filled with laughter and teasing, and a smidge of innuendo. But there's an undercurrent of something deeper, something that's been steadily growing since Sunday.

It's exciting and terrifying all at the same time, especially when I think about the personal training sessions he proposed.

Starting Monday, I'll be stepping into a new kind of

routine with him—one that's both about fitness and something more personal.

And then there's tomorrow …

We have another official date—this time at Hanabi for sushi.

The thought sends another flutter through my stomach, but it's mixed with a growing unease that I haven't been able to fully shake off.

That moment at the end of our kiss continues to haunt my mind. It was the stirring of a realization I can't quite seem to wrap my head around.

His scent, up close and personal, reminded me so much of the sexy, mysterious man from Nocté.

It was a powerful, potent thing that made my heart race and my nether regions heat up in unexpected ways.

And then there was that quick inhalation—it was so subtle, but it was identical to the way the other man reacted before our first kiss.

I'm used to my overactive imagination. Usually, I know when to dismiss it.

But no matter what I do, I can't shake the thought away.

Could Adam be the same guy from Club Nocté?

It seems ludicrous, yet it clings to me, refusing to be dismissed.

My writer's brain is screaming *'alert, alert!'* and it's very rarely wrong. At least—where books are concerned.

But this is no book.

It's *real life.*

As I walk the street, my mind continues to twist through scenarios.

If he was at that event at Nocté, then that would mean he was cheated on, too.

That's how their rules work.

It's a painful thought, and part of me aches for him, *for both of us.* If it's even true.

But it's a wild tangent, isn't it?

The odds are—well, let's just say I should play the lottery before something like this could be real.

Shaking my head, I try to stuff all of the questions aside.

Tonight is about escaping into the world of books at the Dirty B's book club. Hanging out with those crazy ladies is quickly becoming my safe haven. It's a place where romance isn't just a possibility—it's a certainty, neatly contained within the pages of our latest read.

When I'm finally standing in front of Dirty Books, I take a deep breath, ready to dive into discussions about fictional love stories—and forget my tangled thoughts for a beat. It's easier to think about someone else's heartache and happiness.

As I walk in, the familiar scent of books and the laughter of my fellow book lovers greet me.

"Carlie? Is that you?" Tasia calls out from the book nook.

I step up onto my tiptoes, trying to get a view of them. But the shelves are too high.

"Yep," I call out.

"Can you lock the door?" she fires back.

I nod, more to myself, since she can't see me. "Sure thing."

Locking the door behind me, I attempt a smooth turn only to fumble with the book in my hand. It clatters to the floor with an echoing thud that seems to announce my arrival more effectively than any words could.

I don't know why I'm still surprised.

Bending down to retrieve it, I mutter under my breath, "Smooth move, Carlie. First rule of the book club —don't break the book."

Straightening up, I can't help but let out a small chuckle, hoping no one noticed my little mishap, but in the back of my mind, I know everyone heard. How could they not?

As I walk through the rest of the store and step into the cozy warmth of the book nook, I tuck the rebellious book under my arm, reminding myself that the night is about relaxation and camaraderie—not about how gracefully I can walk.

The lively chatter and the comfortable clutter of books and cushions immediately set me at ease. It also helps that there's wine being poured.

Oh yes, come to momma.

Per usual, Tasia and Vivian are sitting in two of the three cushy wingback chairs, while Lily and Anna are nestled on the loveseat, deep in conversation.

Lily, with her ever-present sense of calm, is flipping through the pages of her book, while Anna's face is buried in her phone, her brows knit in concentration.

As I approach, Anna glances up. "Hey, Carlie," she

greets casually. Then, her demeanor shifts as she sets her phone in her lap and turns to Lily with her jaw clenched. "Joel *fucking* Price is playing at Nocté next month? Did you know about this?"

Lily looks over at her, a flicker of interest crossing her face before she shrugs nonchalantly.

But I caught that look.

She definitely knew.

"Um, who's that?" Vivian asks, her gossip radar clearly on high alert.

Anna takes a deep breath through her nose and from here, it looks like she's fighting hard not to roll her eyes. "Only the most obnoxious musician on the planet."

"Joel Price? I think his music is pretty good," Tasia admits, her focus narrowing in on Anna.

I take my seat quietly observing and accepting the glass of wine Tasia offers.

"Thanks," I whisper to her with a grin.

Anna picks up her phone, shaking her head in disgust. "He's so ... *irritating.*"

"Isn't he from Duluth?" Tasia asks, taking a sip of her wine.

Anna practically snorts. "Yeah. That matters why?"

Vivian leans in, her head tilting slightly. "Dish, Chang. What's got your panties in such a twist about this guy? He an ex or something?" she asks, her eyes sparkling as she starts tapping her knees with her fingertips.

"Anna has exes?" Tasia quips, a knowing glint sparking in her gaze.

Anna's eyes narrow and she practically spits venom. "Fuck no. I wouldn't touch that man with a barge pole."

"That's not what it sounds like," Vivian counters with a smug grin.

Anna's intense reaction has piqued everyone's interest, but she waves off the inquiries with a dismissive gesture. "Let's just say I've had enough of his type. All show and no substance." She huffs a heavy sigh, then turns her attention back to her phone. "Anyway, we're not here to talk about my personal grudges. I was just curious if *Lily* was aware."

"I'll ask London about it," Lily offers with a shrug, but her gaze flits to mine for a moment and this time, I'm sure of the look I receive. There's a hint of something hidden in their depths and she thinks I know something.

Do I know something?

"Cool." Anna offers a curt nod. Under her breath, she mutters, "Then I'll know whether or not I need to plan a trip to Fiji that weekend."

We all shoot her a confused glance, but Tasia claps her hands together. "Alright, ladies, let's get down to business. Tonight's discussion is about *'Whispers of Desire'* by Isabella Hartley. Everyone finished?"

Vivian, always the first to dive into book discussions if she can steer it toward the steamy sex, leans forward, her eyes alight. "I loved it. The chemistry between the main characters was off-the-charts hot. And that scene in the rain? Whew! Who wouldn't love that?"

I chuckle, sipping my wine. "It was pretty steamy. Hartley really knows how to write sexual tension."

Lily nods in agreement, her expression thoughtful. "It's not just the physical stuff she nails, though. The emotional depth she brings to her characters ... It's *compelling.*"

Tasia nods, her fingers tracing the book's cover. "I appreciated the subplot with the heroine's career. It wasn't just a love story—it was about her journey, too."

Anna, now more relaxed, chimes in. "True. And the way Hartley portrayed Brock's vulnerability? *That* was refreshing. Not all ambition and no heart—or *brains*," she adds with a huff.

"Like a guy with heart, huh?" Vivian teases, then hides her grin behind a sip of wine.

Anna shoots Vivian a glare, but there's a hint of amusement in her eyes. "Yeah, well, who doesn't appreciate a little depth in their characters, right?"

"Depth, huh?" Vivian continues, wiggling her eyebrows suggestively.

Anna shakes her head and continues to scroll through her phone.

The discussion meanders through various aspects of *'Whispers of Desire,'* from character development to plot twists. I find myself joining in, laughing, and sharing opinions, yet part of me is still preoccupied with thoughts of Adam.

Midway through the conversation, Lily, with her innate ability to observe and reflect, subtly shifts the topic.

"Sometimes, we see what we want to see in people," she says thoughtfully, her eyes meeting mine for a moment. "We paint them in the colors of our past experiences—for better or worse."

Her words resonate with me, echoing my own conflicted feelings. It's as if she's peering right into my soul, seeing the turmoil I've been wrestling with.

Tasia nods, leaning back in her chair. "True. We can get so caught up in our own narratives that we forget to see the person right in front of us. Daniel would say I've been known to do that."

Lily chimes in, her voice gentle. "It's a delicate balance, isn't it? Trusting your instincts while giving someone new a fair chance. How are things with Daniel, by the way?"

Tasia offers a small one-sided shrug. "The same."

Lily's expression turns thoughtful and it's clear there's more understanding between the two of them than what the rest of us are privy to.

"Is Daniel your boyfriend?" I ask, since this is the first time his name's been brought up.

Tasia practically snorts into her wine. "No, not for a long time."

"Daniel's Tasia's husband," Lily offers with a smile.

"Oh," I say, nodding in understanding.

Though, why it's taken me four months of meeting weekly to come to that understanding, makes me think things are not going stellar in their relationship.

Anna, now looking up from her phone, adds, "Relationships are complicated. Sometimes what you think you know about someone—*or how you feel*—it changes over time."

Vivian nods, her voice more of a whisper than I've ever heard from her. "And sometimes, you realize that the person you thought you knew never really existed. They were just a figment of your imagination."

Anna drops her phone looking impressed, though she doesn't say so.

The conversation becomes a blend of personal experiences and philosophical musings. Tasia talks about the evolution of her relationship with Daniel, how they've grown and changed together, and the challenges they've faced.

She loves him, that much is evident. Yet somehow, she still feels like the relationship is missing something, but she can't figure out what.

"It's about growing together, but also allowing each other to grow individually," Tasia says softly. "It's not always easy, but I think in the end, it's worth it. At least, I think."

"With Seth, for a long time, I lost myself trying to be what I thought he wanted. I guess he was doing the same for me, come to think of it. With London, it's different. I can be myself, weird and quirky even, and that's made all the difference," Lily says with a love-struck sigh.

Something stirs in my chest and I realize I'm so happy for Lily. Getting to where she is with London took a big leap of faith.

"I've learned the hard way that trust is a fragile fucking thing. It takes a lot to rebuild once it's broken," Anna offers, her lips pressing tightly.

Vivian nods. "Trust is like a mirror. Once it's shattered, you can try to piece it back together, but the cracks will always show."

Again, Anna glances at Vivian like she's grown a second head.

I can attest to her words, though. Especially when I think back to my relationship with Michael. Those cracks never faded away. They grew bigger and bigger until they practically consumed my soul.

As the discussion winds down, I find myself reflecting on my situation with Adam.

The insights from these women, each with their own unique experiences, help me see things from a different perspective. It's not just about my fears or insecurities—it's about giving Adam, and myself, a chance to discover what could be.

Even if he's the guy from Nocté?

That thought strikes me and a jolt of panic courses through my veins.

The man from Nocté met a completely different woman that night.

I'm nothing like Zoey …

And I'd hate for Adam to be that man, only to discover—I'm *not* that woman.

CHAPTER 21

Adam

The cool evening air brushes against my skin as we step out of Hanabi. The buzz of our laughter mingles with the sounds of the bustling city, making my heart beat faster.

I glance at Carlie, her face is illuminated by the soft glow of the setting sun.

She's radiant.

Her eyes sparkle with a joy that echoes in my chest.

"So, did the sushi live up to your expectations?" I ask, hoping to keep the light, easy vibe we've had since I picked her up.

Carlie's smile widens. "Absolutely. That was some of the best sushi I've ever had. Thank you for introducing me to that restaurant."

Her gratitude is sincere and unguarded, and it deepens the warmth I've been feeling all evening.

"I'm glad you enjoyed it," I say, taking her hand in mine, despite the flip it causes in my stomach. "Now, for the next part of our evening, as corny as it might sound, I thought I'd show you where our training sessions will be held on Monday. If you're up to it, that is." I try to sound casual, but the truth is, I'm eager to see her reaction to the surprise I've set up back at my place.

She looks at me, narrowing her gaze, as a mixture of curiosity and excitement lights in her eyes. "Um, sure. That sounds great."

I beam back. "Great. I was hoping you'd say yes."

Her gaze drops as her smile widens.

I wish I could tell what she was thinking—but hopefully whatever it is, she won't realize what I'm really up to.

The drive to my house is a blur of anticipation, despite how short it is.

Every now and then, I steal glances at Carlie, her presence filling the car with a comforting yet exhilarating energy. It's hard to believe how quickly things have progressed between us, but I can't even bother to question it because it all feels so right.

I've never felt this way about anyone—and truth be told, it's as unnerving as it is awesome.

Pulling into my driveway, I park the car and turn to her. "So, this is it. Your new gym."

Carlie looks around, her eyes taking in the quaint charm of my house.

It's a classic Craftsman bungalow, typical of Duluth's older neighborhoods, with its low-pitched roof, wide eaves, and exposed wooden structural elements. The exterior, thankfully, is a harmonious blend of natural stone and warm, earthy tones, exuding a cozy, inviting vibe.

At least to me.

Of course, there's the small front porch, adorned with a couple of rustic chairs that completes the scene. I don't know how many nights I've sat out there with Dylan or Brian, drinking beers and talking shit into the wee hours of the morning.

"This is where the magic happens, huh?" she teases, her tone light.

"You could say that." I chuckle, feeling a flicker of nerves. "Let me show you."

"Okay," she says softly.

I get out, making my way to her door so I can get it for her—it's as much a show that I'm a gentleman as it is a precaution. However, Carlie's been the epitome of balance tonight, which has been interesting.

We walk up to the front door, and I can't help but feel a sense of pride showing her this part of my life. I hope she likes what's inside and doesn't think I'm pushing for anything.

I mean, don't get me wrong, if things were to develop, I wouldn't *say no.*

It's just—*no expectations.*

I just want her to feel special.

My key clicks into place and I swing the door open and I lead her inside.

"Welcome to my humble abode." I grin, stepping aside to let her in as I flick on the light in the entryway.

She takes a tentative step past me and I stuff back the

flutter of nerves happening in my midsection. In just a few more steps, she'll see that my living room—which I've transformed into a romantic oasis, awaits her.

Soft instrumental music plays in the background and dim lights cast a warm glow in the room. Everything provides a simple intimacy, which feels like a stark contrast to the usual straightforwardness of my decor.

I had to make a trip to Pier One to get a few plush cushions and pillows to accent my pretty boring couch, but they were the right choice when I hear her audible gasp.

Carlie's eyes widen as she takes in the scene. "Adam, this is … *beautiful*."

Her reaction eases my nerves, and I find myself smiling as I reach for the lighter and make quick work lighting the candles around the room. "I'm glad you like it. I thought we could relax here for a bit before I show you the training area. In fact, we don't really need to check it out at all, if you don't feel like it. I really just needed an excuse to bring you here."

She chuckles, her gaze lingering on the candles before meeting mine. "I love it. This is so … *thoughtful*. Thank you, Adam. And to think I was just expecting fluorescent lights and the smell of gym socks."

I grin at her and take her hand. "Well, then my plan worked perfectly. Lull you with my allure of smelly socks and wow you with candles and fuzzy pillows instead."

She smirks at me and nudges me with her shoulder.

We settle onto the couch, the plush pillows bringing us closer together than a typical sitting arrangement. I notice how her body language opens up, a relaxed posture that invites conversation. And truthfully, I'm here for it.

Hell, I want to know *all about her.*

"So, how has writing been going this week?" I start, leaning back and watching her with genuine interest. "All good?"

Carlie shifts slightly, her eyes meeting mine with an honesty that's both endearing and a little intriguing.

"Actually, it's been a bit slow," she admits, a small laugh escaping her lips. "I've been … well, a bit distracted, I suppose you could say."

"Distracted, huh?" I echo, a playful note in my voice. I can't help but feel a little thrill at the thought that I might be the cause of her distraction.

"Yeah," she says, her gaze flickering down to where our hands are nearly touching on the couch. "Thoughts of a certain someone have been occupying more than a bit of my mind as of late."

"Plotting Jillian's demise, huh?" I tease.

Again, she laughs and it makes my heart soar. I swear, that sound is swiftly becoming my absolute favorite.

Her eyebrows rise and she shakes her head. "I haven't given that demon a second thought, to be honest. Not since … *you.*"

I can't help the grin that spreads across my face. "Well, I hope I'm not causing *too much* trouble in that creative mind of yours."

Carlie's smile widens. "Let's just say you're inspiring a whole new level of creativity."

I raise an eyebrow and reach out, bridging the gap and taking her hand in mine. The warmth of it spreads to whole new areas of my body. "Oh really? Do tell."

Carlie's laughter fills the room, easing the tension that's been building between us.

"Well, I might just have to keep some of those details to myself," she teases, giving my hand a gentle squeeze. "But let's just say that my latest book might have a certain … *intensity* to it."

"I'll take that as a compliment," I reply, intrigued. I let my thumb brush softly against the back of her hand, a small gesture that draws us even closer. "So, about writing *those* scenes … is it difficult? Do you … um, pull from personal experience?"

Carlie raises an eyebrow, a playful challenge glinting in her eyes. "It's a mix, really. Writing sex scenes can be challenging. You have to balance the physical with the emotional to make it feel real. And as for personal experiences …" she trails off, biting gently at her bottom lip.

I lean in, captivated. "Yes?"

She laughs, the sound light and musical. "Let's just say a writer's imagination is a powerful tool. But sure, experiences, fantasies, a bit of creative license—it all goes into the mix."

My body reacts to her words, and I'm suddenly one hundred percent sure I need to find her books. I shift slightly, trying to ease the pressure building up behind my zipper.

"Sounds like an interesting process." I can't help but chuckle.

"It is," she confirms. "And it's about more than just the act. It's about the connection between the characters, their emotions—their specific vulnerabilities. That's what makes a scene come alive."

I nod, understanding dawning. "That makes sense. It's not just about the physical act, but about the intimacy—the closeness."

"Exactly," she agrees, her gaze meeting mine. "It's about creating something that resonates with the readers—something that feels authentic and true."

Forget readers, her words resonate with me, and I find myself thinking about the connection we're building.

"That's really insightful. It sounds like you put a lot of yourself into your work," I offer, continuing to caress the back of her hand with my thumb.

Carlie smiles, a softness touching the edges of her lips. "I guess you could say that. Each book is a little piece of me."

Curiosity nudges at me, and I decide to venture a little deeper. "So, I've been wondering ... Are your books under your own name? Or do you have a pen name? I'd love to read some of your work."

There's a moment's hesitation, and I can almost see the wheels turning in her head.

"I'm not sure if I'm ready to share that just yet," she says with a playful yet cautious smile. "It's kind of like baring a part of my soul, you know?"

I nod, understanding her need for privacy. "I get it. No pressure. Whenever you're ready—*if ever.*"

Carlie's appreciation for my understanding is evident in her eyes, a warmth there that wasn't present before. "Thanks, Adam. That means a lot." She leans back, her gaze thoughtful. "So, tell me about this idea of opening your own gym. Where did that come from?"

I lean back, feeling the comfort of the couch as I gather my thoughts. "Well, it's always been a dream of mine. But lately, Dylan and my brother have been really pushing me to make it a reality."

"Sounds like they really believe in you," she observes.

I nod. "They do. They've seen me in the gym, working with clients, and they think I have what it takes to run my own place. They both run their own businesses, so I guess it's also kind of innate in their thinking."

"What's your vision for it?" Carlie asks, reaching out and tracing her fingertips over my knee. The contact makes me shudder in all the right ways.

"Well, I want it to be more than just a gym. I want to create a place where people feel empowered—not just physically but mentally, too. I want to build a community where everyone supports each other and it's not just a room full of equipment and guys grunting. You know?"

"That sounds amazing, Adam," Carlie says, her eyes gleaming with enthusiasm. "A gym that focuses on overall well-being. I love that."

I smile, encouraged by her response. "Yeah, I want it to be a better experience for people. Somewhere they can come to improve themselves in a supportive environment. We need fewer Jillians in the world."

"You're not wrong there." Carlie snickers under her breath and nods. Then, she lifts her eyes to mine and I swear they somehow darken to the point where they're giant emerald orbs. "With your passion and dedication, I have no doubt you'll make it happen."

Her words touch something deep within me, and I find myself leaning closer. "Thanks, Carlie. That means a lot—especially coming from you."

Our eyes lock, and there's a moment where everything else fades away.

It's just her and me ... in this *bubble.*

Slowly, almost hesitantly, I lean in closer, closing the distance between us. Carlie's breath hitches slightly, her eyes fluttering closed as our lips meet in a tender, tentative kiss.

The world slows down to this one point of contact.

The kiss is gentle, and exploratory, as our lips move in a delicate dance. There's no rush, no urgency—just a sweet exploration. I savor the softness of her lips, the subtle hint of citrus, and the warmth that spreads through my chest and the rest of my body.

Her hands tug at my hair, doing things to my pulse and the blood flow that rushes southbound.

As we pull away, our eyes meet again, and a silent understanding passes between us. We're both breathing a little heavier, the air tinged with unspoken possibilities.

"I've been wanting to do that for a while now," I

admit softly, my thumb gently brushing against her cheek.

Since the last kiss, actually.

Carlie smiles, a beautiful, genuine smile that lights up her entire face. "I'm glad you did."

The moment feels perfect, but I don't want to push things too far, too fast.

"I ... I should probably show you the workout space," I say, clearing my throat. "I did promise you a tour."

She nods, a playful glint in her eyes, like she knows exactly why I'm redirecting us. "Lead the way."

I stand up, offering her my hand to help her up.

As we walk towards the converted garage, I can't help but be both excited and content. This evening has turned into something far more special than I could have imagined.

My workout space is simple but well-equipped—a testament to my commitment to fitness and personal training, I suppose. I watch Carlie as she looks around, her eyes taking in the weights, the mats, and the small space I've set aside for personal training sessions.

"It's perfect, Adam," she says, turning to face me. "It's got everything I'd need, that's for sure. I can't wait to start training with you again."

Her enthusiasm is infectious, and I find myself grinning from ear to ear. "I'm looking forward to it too. It's going to be great, Carlie. I promise, nothing like whatever Jillian put you through."

As we head back to the living room, I feel a deep sense of anticipation for what's to come—both for our training sessions and for whatever might develop between us.

In the quiet comfort of my living room, with the soft glow of the candles casting a romantic ambiance around us, I find myself stealing glances at Carlie. She's glancing around the room, a contented smile on her face, and I can't help but wonder what she's thinking.

"Everything okay?" she asks, noticing my pensive look.

"Yeah, more than okay," I reply, my voice carrying a sincerity that I don't often reveal. I take a deep breath, deciding to open up a bit more. "I've been thinking ... about us. This evening has been incredible, and I guess I'm just ... I'm really looking forward to seeing where this goes."

Carlie's expression softens, and she moves a little closer—her hand finding mine. "Me too, Adam. There's something special here, isn't there?"

I nod, feeling a rush of emotion. "Yeah, there is. I've never felt this way so quickly about anyone. It's kind of scary, but in a good way."

"I know what you mean," she whispers, holding my gaze with the kind of intensity that could bind planets together.

The honesty of the moment hangs between us, a tangible connection that seems to draw us closer. It's a feeling that's hard to describe—a mix of excitement, hope, and a bit of fear, but above all, a deep sense of connection.

After Jillian's betrayal, I honestly never thought I'd feel like this again.

We sit there for a moment, just looking at each other, letting the weight of our words settle in. I realize then that what I'm feeling isn't just a fleeting attraction. It's something deeper, something that has the potential to grow into more than I'd ever imagined.

Maybe I sensed it before I really had the conscious realization, come to think of it.

I know one thing for sure—I'm totally ready to see where things lead with Carlie.

CHAPTER 22

Carlie

The sky is a bright blue without a single cloud as I pull up to Adam's house—or should I say my new gym?

I'm trying to maintain my excited optimism, but the nervous flutter in my stomach is a stark contrast to the steady rhythm of the upbeat music blaring from my car's speakers.

Taylor Swift's "The Man" can only hype me up so far, turns out.

We've reached our first official training session at his place, and I'm not really sure how I feel.

I mean, it's not like exercise has been a BFF up to this point.

Stepping out of the car, I take a deep breath, trying to quell the butterflies. But it's no use. They keep multiplying.

Adam's already at the door, waving me in with a

warm smile that does something to my heart. He's dressed in his own workout gear this morning—a tight-fitting white tank top and gym shorts.

From here, he's absolutely drool-worthy.

"Morning, Carlie. Ready to get started?" he asks when I get close enough, his voice laced with a playful edge that somehow manages to ease my nerves a bit. I don't know how he does it.

"As ready as I'll ever be," I reply, hoping my attempt at confidence is more convincing than I feel. I should have played "*The Man*" one more time.

Inside, the now familiar scent of his home—a mix of citrus and something uniquely Adam—fills my senses. He leads me past his living room, which no longer has all of the pillows or candles laid about. As I walk past, I can't help but smile at the memory of date number two.

He has such a sweet, romantic side that I can't help but swoon over.

"Do you need water? Coffee before we get started?" he asks over his shoulder.

I shake my head. "No, I'm good. Drank a whole carafe of coffee before I got here. If anything, I'll need the directions to the bathroom soon." I slap a hand over my mouth, mortified I let that one slip out.

He just huffs a sexy laugh and points down the hall. "Well, it's right there when you need it."

I nod like an idiot and follow him to the workout area. He's converted what looks like an old garage into a workout space most people would dream of. It's neat and well-organized, much like Adam himself.

"Okay, may as well stick to what we know, right? Let's start with some basic stretches to get you limbered up," he instructs, taking on his professional tone. It instantly reminds me of that first day at St. Mary's.

God, it feels so long ago.

I nod, trying once again to mirror his movements as he demonstrates but feeling more like a clumsy imitation of a graceful swan—if the swan had two left feet and zero flexibility.

"I'm not exactly the poster child for agility," I joke, wobbling slightly as I reach for my toes.

Adam chuckles, stepping closer to assist. "Don't worry, you're doing great. Flexibility comes with practice. And to be honest, your hamstrings are more limber than mine."

His hands are warm as they guide me gently. I'm suddenly acutely conscious of every point of contact— hell, every breath.

Who knew working out when you're ridiculously attracted to your workout partner is a challenge in itself?

Adam's reassurance is like a balm to my jittery nerves, but it doesn't quite stop the heat from flooding my cheeks.

"Thanks," I mutter softly, trying to focus on the stretch rather than the way his fingers are sending jolts of energy straight to my lady bits.

"We'll start with a total body workout today," Adam explains as we move to the next stretch. "Nothing too intense, just some light movements to get you acclimated.

Plus, this way it should help you with soreness tomorrow."

"Good." I nod, following his lead as we go through a series of lunges and squats.

Each movement is accompanied by Adam's gentle guidance, his voice calm and encouraging. It's a stark contrast to the militaristic drill sergeant—aka Jillian.

Adam's approach is patient, almost ... *intimate.*

I can't tell if it's because it's us—and we're in his house. Or if this is the way he's always been with me. My head's a whirlwind of citrus and sweat and it's messing with all operational systems of thought, if I'm honest.

As we move into more complex exercises, I find myself alternating between trying to impress him and trying not to fall flat on my face. Neither is going as I'd hoped.

"I didn't realize I signed up to be on stage for a comedy show," I quip, nearly losing my balance during some forward lunges.

"You're doing better than you think," Adam assures me, his hand at my back steadying me. "Remember our first session at the gym? You've come a long way."

His words bring a genuine smile to my face, and for a moment, I feel a sense of pride. Me, Carlie the Clutz, actually making progress. Who knew?

We move into a series of squats, and I'm half expecting my knees to give out, but surprisingly, they hold up.

"Hey, look at me, not collapsing into a heap. That's progress, right?" I say, trying to keep the mood light.

Adam laughs, his eyes sparkling with amusement. "Definitely progress. You might be a natural at this one."

I roll my eyes playfully. "Let's not get ahead of ourselves."

My stupid brain goes back to what Vivian said about him getting turned on by squats and I can't help but sneak glances at Adam to see if he's watching.

Of course, he is.

But I'm too afraid to sneak glances elsewhere.

Next, Adam introduces me to some dumbbell exercises.

"We'll keep the weights light. It's all about form and control today. We can increase the weight later," he instructs, demonstrating a bicep curl and pointing out the correct form.

I mimic his movements, feeling slightly less awkward with each rep. The dumbbells are light, but I start to feel the burn, a sign that my muscles are actually doing something.

"I feel powerful. Like I could take on the world ... or at least a small cat," I mutter through my reps.

Adam chuckles, his gray eyes sparkling with encouragement. "You're doing great. Feeling powerful is exactly what we're aiming for. That small cat doesn't stand a chance."

I can't help the way my lips twitch and a full smile spreads across them.

When we wrap up the weights portion, Adam announces, "Let's finish with some light cardio to boost your heart rate. Then we can cool down."

"Okay," I say, suggesting he show the way.

He leads me through a series of exercises that feel more like a dance than a workout—step touches, light jogging in place, and even some playful jumping jacks.

I can't help but laugh as I try to keep up, feeling like a flailing octopus.

Adam laughs along with me, his eyes crinkling at the corners. "See? Working out can be fun."

I'm panting slightly, but there's a smile on my face. "I never thought I'd hear myself say this, but I'm actually enjoying this."

He grins, looking satisfied. "That's the goal. Tomorrow we'll focus on upper body, but for today, you did great."

"Thanks." I beam.

"Let's wind down with some more stretching to keep those muscles from tightening up. Then, we'll be done for today," he says, pointing to the mat where we started.

"Oh, okay." I nod, surprised and a little sad that the session is over so quickly. Then I glance at the clock and realize it's nearly been an hour and a half.

Well, bowl me over.

We go through a new series of stretches, and I find myself increasingly aware of how close we are. It's like the partner yoga in a lot of ways.

However, the way Adam looks at me, it makes me feel seen—in a way that's both exhilarating and a little terrifying. There's an easy back-and-forth between us, peppered with laughter and occasional physical contact that sends tingles up my spine.

With each touch, whether it's a gentle correction or a supportive pat, the air between us seems to crackle with electricity.

"I didn't think I'd ever say this, but I had a lot of fun working out today," I say, panting slightly but grinning.

He smiles back, his eyes softening. "I'm glad to hear that. You did amazing. I'm really proud of you."

If a heart could expand to twice its size, I swear, mine just did.

There's a moment where we just stand there, looking at each other, the air thick with unspoken words.

Finally, Adam breaks the silence. "So, what's next for you today?"

I sigh, thinking of the mountain of writing I have to tackle. "Shower, then barricade myself in my writing cave. Deadlines wait for no one, unfortunately. I guess that's why they're called *dead*lines."

Adam's eyes hold a hint of mischief. "You're welcome to use my shower if you like. I promise I won't peek ... *much*."

I feel a flush rise to my cheeks, but a laugh bursts from me. "That is one tempting offer, but I think I better pass. I need all my willpower for writing, not fending off charming men."

He raises his hands in mock surrender. "Can't blame a guy for trying. But if you change your mind ..."

An involuntary shudder rolls through me and I could *so* visualize that scene.

Hot and sweaty woman who's falling for her sexy,

muscular trainer takes a shower at his place ... only to have wild and crazy sex against the shower door.

I step closer, rising to my tiptoes, so I can plant a quick kiss on his lips before I can enact the scene. "Thanks for everything, Adam. *Really.*"

His expression softens, and he runs his knuckles softly across my cheek. "Anytime, Carlie. It was my pleasure."

With a deep sigh, I gather my things. Part of me really wants to take him up on that offer, but I'm almost afraid to confirm—or hell, even find out he's *not* the man from Nocté.

In some weird way, both bring me anxiety.

"Same time tomorrow?" I ask, turning back to him.

"Absolutely," he confirms, his eyes lingering on me a moment longer than necessary. "I'll be looking forward to it."

Inhaling some confidence from his glance, I make my way back to his front door. Adam follows a step behind and I can feel his presence radiate off of him like a soothing, delectable blanket that wants to embrace you.

When I get to the front door, I turn around and quickly step up to kiss him. Before either of us can get too invested, I step away and open the door. My lips curve into a smile I hope says, 'mysterious woman on the run' and not 'woman scared shitless of her past.'

He stands in the doorway, watching me with his own lopsided smile—hair mussed up and lit by the sunlight.

As I walk to my car, the cool air does little to soothe the warmth spreading through me. My mind is a whirlpool of thoughts, each one about Adam and the undeniable connection building between us.

It's no longer just about the training sessions—that went out the window the second we partnered for yoga, I think.

No, there's something deeper forming between us ... something I can't quite put my finger on, but it's there, palpable and thrilling.

I just need to get my head sorted around this Nocté thing.

As I slide into the driver's seat, I let out a long breath, trying to calm my racing heart. Slowly, I turn on my vehicle and back out of his driveway.

He's still standing at the door, watching me leave, and for a moment, our eyes lock. Even from this distance, I feel the intensity of his gaze, a silent promise of something yet to come.

I wave and as I drive away, a part of me longs to turn back, to run into his arms and explore this budding relationship without fear or hesitation. But the other part—the one that's been hurt and cautious, holds me back.

The road ahead is unclear, but one thing is for certain —Adam is no longer just my trainer. He's become a vital part of my world, and I'm both exhilarated and terrified by the depth of my feelings for him.

I turn up the volume on the radio, letting Taylor Swift's "The Man" fill the car once more, but this time, it's not about hyping myself up. It's about drowning out the questions, the doubts, and the fears.

As I head home, a single thought echoes in my mind: *What if Adam is the man from Nocté?*

The possibility sends a shiver down my spine. The truth, whatever it may be, is out there, and I'm not sure I'm ready to face it.

But ready or not, the truth has a way of revealing itself, and I can't help but wonder—when it does, will it bring us closer together or tear us apart?

CHAPTER 23

Adam

As I roll up the last yoga mat, I can't help but think how quickly this week has flown by.

Each training session with Carlie has been a mixture of hard work and unexpected fun. She has a way of bringing this unique spark of humor to everything she does.

I love it.

I glance over at her as she wipes the sweat from her brow with a satisfied smile, and I feel a twinge of pride.

She's kicked some major ass this week. Even when she didn't think she could go any longer—or move her muscles—she made it happen.

She's a badass.

"You know," I start, as she reaches for her water bottle, "the more you work out, even when you're sore, the faster that soreness will start to fade."

She takes a long sip, then looks at me, a playful challenge in her eyes. "Is that your professional trainer's wisdom or just an attempt to make me feel better about my aching muscles?"

I laugh, remembering my own early days at the gym. "A bit of both, actually. When I first started, I had no idea. I just thought pain was part of the deal. But really, it's about getting your muscles used to the movement."

Her laughter joins mine, and there's an ease between us that feels like it's been there forever.

We start to share a few more stories, and I find myself opening up about one of my early gym experiences.

"So, there I was," I begin, a grin tugging at my lips, "thinking I could handle more weight than I actually could. Young and dumb, I guess. It was my first week in the gym, and I wanted to impress, you know?"

Carlie nods, her green eyes twinkling with anticipation.

"I loaded up the barbell for a bench press. Felt pretty confident—maybe *too* confident. I lift it off, and it's going ... okay. Then, on the third rep, my arms just gave out. The bar came crashing down."

She covers her mouth with her hand, trying not to laugh. "Oh no, did you get hurt?"

I shake my head, laughing along with her. "Nah, the safety bars caught it. But the noise it made ... it was like a gunshot. Everyone turned to look. I was lying there, pinned under the weight, my face fifty shades of red."

Her laughter fills the room, making my heart stutter. God, I love that sound.

"I bet you never made that mistake again," she says between giggles.

"Never," I affirm with a smile. "Learned my lesson about overestimating my abilities pretty quickly."

She leans against the wall, still chuckling. "Well, it's nice to know even pros like you have their moments."

"That we definitely do." I nod, admiring the way her grin lights up the whole damn room.

It's these little connections—these tiny moments really—that make my feelings for Carlie grow stronger by the day.

As our laughter starts to fade, the sound of footsteps stomping through my house catches my attention. There's only one person those loud feet could belong to.

I turn just in time to see my brother Brian striding in, his usual confident swagger on display. He's in his casual work attire, which still looks sharper than most, if I'm honest.

"Hey, Adam—" Brian calls out, but his eyes are instantly diverted from me as they land on Carlie. "And you must be Carlie. I've heard a lot about you."

Carlie straightens up, wiping her hands on her yoga pants. "Yeah, that's me. And you're Brian, right? The infamous brother."

He shoots her a befuddled expression.

She merely shrugs and confesses, "You look a lot like Adam. Just older. I made a calculated assumption and secretly hoped I wasn't wrong."

"Ah." Brian chuckles, extending his hand. "Guilty as charged. Good to finally meet you."

They shake hands, and I can't help but wonder what he sees when he looks at Carlie. Brian has always been a great judge of character. I guess it helps a lot when you work at a bar.

"So, what's up, Brian?" I ask, leaning against the wall. "Did you need something?"

He shrugs, a playful glint in his eyes that makes me cringe internally. "Just thought I'd drop by and see how the fitness empire is coming along. Maybe I should be stealing some of your training secrets."

I roll my eyes, but I'm smiling. "You know my training techniques are top secret. But for a small fee …"

"Atta boy." Brian laughs me off with a wink, then turns to Carlie. "I've seen some of Adam's Instagram posts. You're doing awesome. Keep it up."

Carlie beams, clearly pleased. "Thanks, Brian. I'm just happy when I stay vertical. Adam's a good teacher."

Brian nods, then looks at me with a knowing smirk. "You always did have a way of motivating people. Remember that summer when we …"

I cut him off with a quick, "Not now, Brian," shooting him a pointed look. Some stories are better left untold, especially in front of Carlie.

Brian raises his hands in surrender, but he's still grinning. "All right, all right. I'll save the embarrassing childhood stories for another time."

I can feel Carlie's curious gaze on me, but I just shake my head. "Trust me, you don't want to know."

Brian takes a moment to glance around the converted garage, nodding approvingly. "You've done a great job with this place, bro. It's come a long way since the last time I was in here."

"Thanks, man. It's a work in progress, but I'm getting there."

Carlie picks up her water bottle, turning to Brian. "Well, it's nice to finally meet you. Adam talks about you a lot."

Brian's smile widens. "All good things, I hope."

"Mostly," Carlie teases, and I can't help but chuckle.

Brian's expression softens, and he gives Carlie a friendly nod. "Hey, you two should swing by Jaded Brews sometime. I'd love to show you around the brewery."

Carlie's eyes sparkle with interest. "That's your place? The new craft brewery downtown? I've heard great things about it."

"Absolutely," I chime in, feeling genuinely excited about the idea. "That sounds like a great plan. What do you say, Carlie? Wanna check out the brewery later?"

She nods enthusiastically. "I'd love that. Maybe after our zoo adventure this afternoon?"

Brian grins, clearly pleased. "Perfect. Let me know when you're coming, and I'll make sure to give you the VIP treatment."

"Thanks, Brian," I say as he makes his way to leave. "We'll definitely take you up on that. See ya this evening."

He throws up a hand and walks out. "Have fun."

As Brian exits, I turn back to Carlie. "So, about the zoo this afternoon ..."

Her face lights up. "I'm really excited to show it to you. The Duluth Zoo is one of my favorite places. I adore animals—and it's the safest way for me to love them without having to ensure they stay alive. Which, as it turns out, I'm not great at." She frowns slightly, and I know there must be another story hidden in there.

The idea of spending more time with her, especially in a place that means something to her, fills me with a warm anticipation. "I'm looking forward to it. But first, you mentioned needing a shower. Do you want to just take one here? I know I teased last time about not—"

"Yeah, that would be great, actually," she says with a smile that makes my heart skip a beat.

"All right, let me get you some towels. You can use the shower upstairs," I offer, trying to keep my voice steady.

As we head back into my house, there's a new level of intimacy in the air, subtle but undeniable. I show her to the bathroom, handing her one of my extra towels. "Feel free to use whatever you need."

She accepts the towel, her gaze holding mine for a moment, filled with an unspoken understanding. "Thanks, Adam."

I can tell there's more she wants to say, as she opens and closes her mouth. However, she never speaks the words that seem to be ready to fall from her lips.

Instead, she reaches over and brushes her hand across my jaw. Then, she steps into the bathroom.

There's a zing of electricity that passes through me— like there's a hint of an invitation in her touch.

After Carlie closes the bathroom door, I find myself standing alone in the hallway, caught in a tangle of thoughts. There's this tension in the air—a sense of something unspoken between us. I can still feel the warmth of her smile, the hint of invitation in her eyes.

Should I ...?

No, Adam, don't be that guy, I scold myself.

Full consent only—that's my rule.

And she didn't speak her consent.

But the thought lingers, tantalizing and bold.

The idea of just casually knocking on the door and asking if she needs any company is tempting—really *fucking* tempting. A part of me wants to throw caution to the wind and see if that spark I feel is as strong as it seems.

I run a hand through my hair, wrestling with the urge. It would be so easy to give in, to let this growing connection between us take its natural course. But another part of me hesitates, wary of crossing a line that could complicate things if Carlie's not there yet.

Sure, she writes romance for a living—but doesn't that mean she wants to be wooed? *Romanced?*

As I'm lost in this internal debate, the sound of my phone vibrating snaps me back to reality. I pull it out of my pocket, expecting maybe a message from Brian or a notification from Instagram.

It is an Instagram notification—only it's a comment from Jillian.

My heart sinks a little and the moment of possibility with Carlie abruptly fades.

Opening the notification, I'm met with Jillian's familiar tone of sarcasm and insinuation. She's commenting on one of the Instagram posts I made with Carlie this week—basically telling everyone that Carlie's a lost cause and I'm only using her to jump-start my own business.

There's an edge to her words, a subtle jab meant to rile me up and hurt Carlie.

What a bitch.

I let out a frustrated sigh. There are already hundreds of comments under hers agreeing with her.

This is the last thing I need right now. The last thing I want is for Carlie to be dragged into another Instagram drama—this time with Jillian.

It's bad enough that I still haven't told Carlie I dated her.

I lock my phone, tucking it away with a mix of annoyance and concern. I'll have to deal with Jillian later, but right now, my focus needs to be on Carlie and the time we're spending together.

Shaking off the unease, I head downstairs to take my own quick shower as I wait for Carlie. It's a rinse-off, but I turn the water as cold as I can manage and try to force myself to regain some of the lightness I felt just moments ago.

I focus on the excitement of our upcoming trip to the zoo and even the feeling that we might take this relationship to another level soon.

But Jillian's message lingers in the back of my mind, an unwelcome shadow on an otherwise bright day.

By the time I step out of my shower, I'm nowhere

near as present as I'd like to be. I wrap a towel around my waist and trudge into the bedroom to hunt for clothes.

It only takes me a minute to get dressed and I settle on the couch to wait for Carlie.

When she emerges from the shower, looking refreshed and radiant, I stand up and push all thoughts of Jillian aside. This afternoon is about us, and I'm not going to let anything ruin that.

"Ready for the zoo?" I ask, trying to inject as much enthusiasm into my voice as possible.

She hesitates for a brief moment, then nods, her smile infectious. "Absolutely. Can't wait."

We leave the house, stepping into the sunlight and the promise of a new adventure. As we drive, I steal glances at Carlie, her presence a comforting antidote to the chaos of my thoughts.

However, with every glance, part of me wonders: *What would she think if she knew I dated Jillian? That we were nearly engaged? Would she think I hid it from her? Worse yet, would she believe the lies Jillian is beginning to spread?*

I keep these thoughts to myself, not wanting to spoil our day. However, there's this terrible unease that tightens in my gut. It feels like I'm on the edge of something—either a wonderful new chapter with Carlie or an inevitable confrontation that could change everything.

CHAPTER 24

Carlie

W e're strolling through the Duluth Zoo, but I'm on a mission to chip away at the tension I sense in Adam.

He's been off since I kinda sorta tried to hint that he join me in the shower earlier. I admit, it wasn't my smoothest or clearest of invitations. But it was an attempt at washing away the mixture of sexual tension and straight-up tension I've been feeling.

There's something about that man that makes me feel so comfortable—so at peace with myself—that a part of me doesn't even care if we realize we've done this before anymore.

In fact, *not* knowing if Adam is the man from Nocté is starting to eat away at me. When the realization first hit —I didn't want to know.

I didn't want *him* to know, either.

At least, if it were true.

Now, it feels like if I don't know, things will be far, far worse.

I need to mentally prepare for the fallout and there's only one way to do that.

I need to know if he has the tribal tattoo on his lower abdomen.

And the only way to do that is …

Instead of joining me, however, I showered alone and came out to one hell of a Debbie Downer. It was like someone had run over his dog while I was in there and it doesn't seem like he wants to let it go, either. It's made the whole day trip a little awkward.

We walk through the first couple of zoo enclosures in damn near silence and if anyone knows me, they know silence is my enemy.

"Is there something bothering you?" I ask, hoping that it might allow him the opportunity to talk about whatever's bugging him.

He pauses for a moment, turning to face me as if he's contemplating his words. Then, he shakes his head. "No, I'm okay. Just didn't get much sleep last night."

"Oh," I say with a nod. However, his words don't quite land right because he was totally fine during our workout session this morning.

For the next few minutes, we continue walking in silence—both of us lost in thought, it seems. I barely even notice the otter enclosure as we walk on by.

I don't know what happened while I was sudsing it up in his shower earlier, but I'm determined to bring back the easygoing guy I've come to know.

"So, Adam," I begin, mustering up a playful tone as we pass a group of otters tumbling over one another, "ever think about what animal you'd be? I'm guessing something majestic like an eagle or maybe a bear?"

He turns to face me, giving me the ghost of a smile. "A bear, huh? I can see that. Strong, a bit solitary, but protective."

The way he says that last word makes me pause. It's like there's a hidden meaning there, but I'm not sure I'm privy to the extent of it.

So, instead, I nod enthusiastically. "Exactly—and you get to hibernate, which is basically an extended nap. Win-win! Am I right?"

He laughs, deep and throaty, and the sound is music to my ears. "You do have a point there."

"I typically do. Granted, it's often buried in hyperbole ..." I chuckle.

We continue meandering through my favorite parts of the zoo, and I try to keep the conversation light and whimsical, since it seems to help. When we reach the primate exhibit, I strike a pose, imitating a monkey.

"Check out my primate impression. Do you think they'll accept me as one of their own?" I ask, blowing up my cheeks and crossing my eyes. With anyone else, I'd be mortified. But with him—it's like I can be my total goofy self.

Adam chuckles, shaking his head. "I think they might. You've got the playful spirit down for sure."

My cheeks heat and I drop my arms and uncross my eyes. "If my writing career doesn't pan out, I've always got a fallback as a primate impersonator. I'm sure there's a huge demand for that, right?"

His laughter grows more genuine, and I can tell he's starting to relax a bit.

Thank the lords and stars above.

As we continue to wander from exhibit to exhibit, I can't resist sharing a bit more about myself in the hopes of elevating his mood some more. Each stop seems to pull another quirky story from me, and I'm eager to see Adam's reactions.

"So, I have this thing for cheesy horror movies. I think I told you a little before, but they're bordering on an obsession at this point," I confess as we pause in front of the reptile house, watching a snake lazily coil around a branch. "I'm talking the kind where you can almost see the zipper on the monster costume. Seriously, they're so bad, they're *good*."

Adam grins, the corners of his eyes crinkling. "Yeah, I remember you saying something about that. I have to agree, though. There's something charming about those old-school effects. Makes the whole thing more ... human, I guess?"

"Exactly!" I exclaim, happy he understands. "It's like a time capsule of creativity before CGI took over. By the way, I watched Nosferatu, like you suggested. *Hilarious.*" I grin at him. "Granted, I was making up all the dialogue on my own, but I definitely see what you were talking about."

The creases of his eyes crinkle. "Isn't it great? We should watch it together sometime."

"Oh my gosh, that could be dangerous. Sit me down with a bottle of wine and we'll make up the funniest dialogue for the film. I swear, we'll laugh the night away," I chuckle, bumping him with my shoulder.

"That sounds ..." he huffs a laugh, despite himself, "*interesting*. We'll have to make it happen."

I beam back at him. "Good. I look forward to it."

We move to the next exhibit, and I spot a group of colorful parrots. Their vibrant feathers remind me of a faded memory.

"You know, I once tried to learn the guitar. Wanted to be a pop star or something," I chuckle, remembering back to that time.

Adam raises an eyebrow, clearly intrigued. "Really? How did that go?"

I laugh, a bit self-consciously. "Let's just say my musical talents are ... nonexistent. The guitar is now an art piece on my wall. Holds books and a couple of plants. I'll show you the next time you're over."

He laughs, a warm, rich sound. "I'd like that."

I shake my head and take a seat on one of the benches. "On the upside, I know a little bit about it, so it makes writing rockstar romances feel more authentic."

"I bet," he says, sitting down next to me and giving me a sly side-eye. "Like musicians, do you?"

"I mean, they're okay," I say, feigning nonchalance. "But as it turns out, I'm finding I have more of a thing for personal trainers."

Our eyes lock for a moment, and I can see it there, in his eyes—he wants to say something but he's holding it back. So, I take his hand in mine, stand up, and lead us on.

At the penguin exhibit, I lean close to the glass, fascinated. We watch them for the longest time before I finally admit, "Penguins are my spirit animals. They're awkward on land but graceful in water. Kind of like me, except I'm still waiting to find my graceful side."

Adam stands beside me, his arm brushing mine and causing every hair on my body to vibrate at attention. "I think you're selling yourself short, Carlie. You've got plenty of grace, especially when it comes to handling tough situations."

I glance up at him, touched by his words. There's a softness in his eyes that makes my heart skip a few beats.

"What do you mean?" I ask before I can stop myself.

Adam looks down at me, his eyes reflecting a mixture of admiration and sincerity. "I mean, you handle things with humor and resilience. It's ... *impressive*." He pauses, seemingly searching for the right words. "Like how you dealt with the Jillian situation, and even with the training sessions. You don't let things keep you down—even when it's obviously hard. I wish I had more of that, honestly."

His words send a warm rush through me. "Thanks, Adam," I reply, biting the inside of my cheek. "I try to keep things light. No use in drowning in the heavy stuff. You know?"

He nods, his gaze still holding mine. "It's a good approach. Keeps life ... *fun*."

Our conversation is interrupted by the playful antics

of the penguins, and we both laugh as one of them slides belly-first across the ice and then nearly smacks into the glass.

"And we've found the Carlie penguin," I mutter, running a hand over my face.

"They really are something, aren't they?" he remarks, a genuine smile spreading across his face.

"They are," I agree, still watching the penguins. "They make everything seem so simple and joyful."

As we continue our zoo adventure, Adam slowly becomes more relaxed and engaged. His laughter comes more easily, and his smiles are more frequent. It's as if the zoo has worked its magic on him, melting away the tension and worry.

Part of me hopes that it's a little of my own magic that's helped, too.

Eventually, we find ourselves at the zoo's café, taking a break to enjoy the summer weather and rest our feet. We find a table outside, to enjoy the warmth of the sun on our skin. In Minnesota, when you finally have it, you don't take it for granted.

I order a light salad while Adam goes for a tuna sandwich. We chat about everything and nothing—from our favorite foods to our dream vacation spots.

The café bustles around us, but it feels like we're in our little world, enjoying each other's company and the beautiful day. Adam's mood has lifted entirely, and it's like I'm seeing the Adam I first met—easygoing, charming, and full of life.

As we finish our meal, Adam leans back in his chair, looking more relaxed than I've seen him all day.

"You know, I really needed this," he admits, his gaze meeting mine. "Thanks for bringing me here. I can see why you like it so much."

I smile, feeling a sense of accomplishment. "I'm glad you enjoyed it. The zoo has a way of making everything better."

He chuckles, nodding in agreement. "It really does."

We linger at the café for a while longer, soaking up the sun and each other's company.

After a little while, Adam and I decide to continue our day by heading over to Jaded Brews, since his brother would be looking for us.

I have to admit, the transition from the serene setting of the zoo to the lively atmosphere of the brewery feels like stepping into a different world.

Jaded Brews has a rustic charm and the gentle hum of conversations and clinking glasses sets a relaxed yet vibrant mood.

I spot Dylan, Adam's friend, and the familiar face from the coffee shop, already there, sitting at a reserved table in the corner. He waves when he catches my eye.

Stepping up to speak in Adam's ear, I tell him, "I think we're over this way." Then, I lead him through the crowd and over to where Dylan's grinning at us.

"Hey, you guys made it. Brian said you were meant to show up at some point," Dylan says, greeting us with a warm smile as we approach. "He had to step out for a bit, something about needing more ice? Or was it salt? Whatever, he should be back soon."

Adam and I take our seats, thanking Dylan for saving a spot for us.

The place really is cozy, filled with the soft glow of ambient lighting and the rich aroma of hops and malt. I'm not much of a beer drinker, but I could definitely see hanging out here more often. It feels like a place you take your closest friends to just hang out.

"Adam here said you were meant to go to the zoo today. Did you have fun?" Dylan asks, his eyes twinkling with a mix of curiosity and amusement.

Adam chuckles. "Yeah, we did, actually. Carlie here has a way with animals. Turns out, she's quite the penguin whisperer."

I can't help but laugh. "Well, someone had to show Adam the ropes. He's more at home with weights than wildlife, it seems."

Dylan laughs along with us, and the conversation flows easily. We talk about our day, sharing stories and observations from the zoo. Dylan seems genuinely interested, and his easygoing nature makes it feel like we've all been friends for years.

Just as we're deep into discussing our favorite animals, Brian shows up at our table with a wide grin on his face. "I see Dylan was able to get the party started without me. Hope you're talking all good things about my brewery."

"We were just getting to that," I say, smiling at Brian.

"This place is fantastic. You've done an amazing job with it."

Brian beams, pride emanating from his eyes. "Thanks, Carlie. It's been a journey, that's for sure. But definitely worth it looking back. So, what did I miss?"

Dylan jumps in with a toothy grin. "Just some zoo tales and penguin escapades. You know, the usual."

We all share a laugh, and Brian pulls up a chair, joining our little group.

The evening progresses with more shared stories, laughter, and a few rounds of Brian's finest brews. The camaraderie among us is palpable, and I find myself completely at ease, enjoying the company and the lively atmosphere of the brewery.

As the evening wears on, the conversation shifts from casual banter to plans for upcoming events at the brewery, local happenings, and even a bit of good-natured ribbing between the guys. Brian and Dylan take turns teasing Adam about his newfound appreciation for the animal kingdom, while Adam dishes it right back with anecdotes from their past.

In the midst of their teasing, I see an opening for a bit of my own brand of humor.

With lowered eyebrows, I interject, "Yeah, watch out Adam, I'm picking up all sorts of animal-handling tips. Next thing you know, I'll be wrangling personal trainers."

My remark earns a round of surprised laughter, and Adam's look of mock horror only adds to the fun.

The time flies by, and before we know it, the sky outside has darkened, and my stomach rumbles.

Brian stands up, stretching. "Well, folks, I should get back to overseeing things. You're welcome to stay as long as you like. Drinks are on the house."

"As awesome as that is," Dylan begins, also getting up and giving us a friendly nod. "I gotta bolt, too. Great hanging out with you guys. Let's do this again soon, yeah?"

Adam and I thank them, and after saying our good-byes, we decide it's time to head out as well. Stepping outside, the cool night air feels refreshing after the warmth of the brewery.

The streets are quieter now, the hustle of the day giving way to the peaceful calm of the evening.

"So, dinner?" Adam asks, a hopeful note in his voice.

"Definitely," I reply, feeling a pleasant buzz from the beer and the company. "I'm starving."

We walk down the sidewalk, chatting about the evening and where to grab dinner.

The night is still young, and the possibilities seem endless. I can't help but feel a sense of excitement and anticipation for what the rest of the night holds.

CHAPTER 25

Adam

As I stir the sauce, I glance over at Carlie, who's leaning casually against my kitchen counter watching me with such an intensity, it heats every part of me.

Her presence fills the kitchen, making it feel more like a home than it ever has.

I don't know how she does it.

"Need a hand?" she asks, her eyes sparkling with curiosity. "I promise, I'm less clumsy with a knife than my feet."

I chuckle under my breath. "I'm not so sure I believe that."

She gasps in mock horror, pressing her fingertips to her chest. "I'll have you know my Grandma says I'm the best prep cook she's ever worked with."

"Well, if your grandma can vouch for you ..." With a grin on my face, I hand her the cutting board filled with vegetables. "Chop these for me?"

Carlie takes the cutting board with a smile, her movements confident and surprisingly graceful. She starts chopping the vegetables, and I can't help but admire the ease with which she handles the knife. It's a stark contrast to her self-declared clumsiness, for sure.

"So, did your grandma teach you to cook?" I ask, stirring the sauce slowly, as its aroma fills the air.

She nods, her focus still on the vegetables. "Yeah, she's an amazing cook. Taught me everything from spaghetti to soufflés. Cooking was one of our bonding things. Now, she enjoys embarrassing me more than anything else."

I watch her for a moment, struck by the warmth in her voice. There's a depth to Carlie that always catches me off guard, a complexity that draws me in deeper every time we talk.

I add the chopped vegetables to the sauce, blending them in. "Well, I'm impressed. Maybe you can give me a lesson or two someday. As much as I love to cook, you've definitely got the chopping thing down more than I do. It's not my favorite."

Carlie laughs, a sound that's quickly becoming my favorite melody. "Deal. But be warned, I'm a strict teacher. "She narrows her gaze and jabs a finger my way.

I can't help but laugh.

As I continue to stir the sauce, Carlie finishes up the remaining vegetables with a rhythmic precision that's almost mesmerizing. I can't help but throw a playful challenge her way. "You sure that's not too much onion? We don't want to end up in tears here."

She shoots me a sly look, her knife pausing mid-chop. "Are you questioning my expert judgment? I'm appalled, sir."

I laugh, leaning slightly against the counter, closer to her. "I wouldn't dare. I'm just concerned for our well-being. I mean, what if you want to kiss me later?"

"Oh, you think I'll want to kiss you, do you? I think you have that the wrong way around." Carlie resumes her chopping, but there's a mischievous spark in her eyes. "If you can handle our training sessions, I'm sure you can handle a little extra onion."

I can't resist the banter, and as I add her perfectly chopped vegetables into the sauce, I quip, "Well, to be fair, I've got a pretty good view the whole time."

She playfully rolls her eyes, and there's a comfortable silence as we focus on our tasks. But the air between us feels charged, an electric current that's both thrilling and a little daunting—no hint of the vibe from earlier in the day and I intend on keeping it that way.

After a moment, I decide to step up the playful atmosphere. I sneak a piece of bell pepper and toss it gently towards her. It lands with a soft plop on the counter next to her.

Carlie looks up, feigning shock. "Did you just start a food fight in your own kitchen?"

I hold up my hands. "I wouldn't dare. Just testing your reflexes." Of course, I let my smirk slip through.

In response, she picks up the pepper and pretends to consider throwing it back at me. But instead, she pops it into her mouth with a grin. "Can't waste good food."

The playful ease of our interaction feels natural, and I find myself savoring every moment. It's not just the act of cooking together, but the shared smiles, the light touches as we pass each other, and the unspoken anticipation of what the evening might bring.

As we cook, the kitchen fills with the rich aromas of our meal, and I'm acutely aware of Carlie's presence next to me—her laughter, her casual grace, and the warmth that seems to radiate from her.

This is more than just dinner—it's a dance, a silent conversation, and a building of something that feels like it could be profound by the end of the night.

Once dinner is ready, I plate our meals and set the table. The room is bathed in the soft glow of the candles I lit, turning our casual dinner into something that feels intimate and special.

Carlie takes a seat, her eyes lighting up at the sight of the meal. "This looks amazing, Adam."

I pour us each a glass of wine, the rich red liquid reflecting the candlelight. "You're welcome. Thanks for helping."

"Of course." She grins back at me, reaching for her glass and taking a sip. "You know, they say food can be a sensual experience. This is definitely proving that point."

I pause, feeling a sudden jolt of memory. That phrase echoes in my mind, transporting me back to Nocté, to a night of masked mystery and intense connections. Food was certainly a sensual experience then, too. But I shake off the feeling, focusing on the present.

"Absolutely. There's something about creating a

meal, the flavors, the aromas ... it's all part of the experience."

Her gaze meets mine, and there's a hint of something more in her eyes, a depth that hints at something I can't quite read.

I'm about to ask her what she's thinking when she leans forward with a mischievous grin and whispers, "Let's play a game. Truth for a truth. Are you game?"

Again, the memory of Nocté flares to life at the edges of my consciousness. I suck in a quick breath, watching her for the briefest of moments. But the only thing I see reflecting back from her is curiosity.

"All right." I nod, clearing my throat, and deciding to steer clear of the same truths I gave that night. "I, uh used to be terrified of dogs as a kid. Took me years to get over that fear."

Carlie leans back, pressing the palm of her hand over her heart. "Really? I would've never guessed."

"It's not the highlight of my childhood, that's for sure," I chuckle, taking a bite of my pasta. "Your turn."

She taps her chin for a moment, making a show of searching hard for whatever truth she plans on sharing. Finally, she offers, "I once sang karaoke in a panda costume. It was a hit at the party, but I've never been able to live it down. Grandma's bingo ladies still try to get me to wear it every Halloween."

I laugh, trying hard not to choke on my spaghetti. "Now, this costume sounds like something I need to see."

She shakes her head, scooping up a bite for herself. "Not a chance."

We continue back and forth, sharing truths that range from silly to personal. With each exchange, the air between us becomes charged with an unspoken understanding, a connection that's growing deeper by the moment.

As dinner progresses, our conversation flows effortlessly. It's like I've known her my whole life. Not just a few weeks.

When we've finished eating, we naturally gravitate towards the living room, leaving our plates abandoned on the table. The couch welcomes us with its comfortable embrace, and we sink into it side by side. The dim lighting from the candles left in the kitchen casts a soft glow, adding to the warmth of the moment as I light a couple more around us.

I toss a cushion onto her lap playfully. "For extra comfort," I say with a wink.

She catches it with a laugh. "Thanks, I'm all about the comfort."

We start talking about random things—favorite movies, embarrassing childhood memories, the worst dates we've ever been on. Carlie's stories are peppered with her signature wit, making me laugh more than I have in a long time.

"Okay, your turn. Worst date?" I prompt, leaning in with genuine curiosity.

She groans, rolling her eyes. "Oh, where do I start? There was this one time I went out with a guy who talked about his ex the entire dinner. Like, I knew more about her by the end of the night than I knew about *him*."

I burst out laughing, the sound echoing in the room. "That's brutal. Did you ever see him again?"

"Not a chance," she says, shaking her head. "I noped out of there so fast. There's only so much bandwidth for dating drama and I reserve that for my books."

Her words jolt me a bit, making my insides constrict as I think back to Jillian and her comments on Instagram. But I shake it off, refusing to allow that woman to ruin the wonderful night that's spread out before us.

The conversation continues to flow effortlessly, each story and confession drawing us closer, both physically and emotionally. I find myself sharing things with Carlie that I haven't told anyone. Her presence makes it feel safe to open up.

As we talk, our bodies inch closer, the space between us diminishing until her legs rest over mine and our hands are intertwined. The physical contact sends a torrent of sparks through me, signaling a connection that's deepening with every word we share.

At some point, Carlie leans her head against my shoulder, and I instinctively wrap my arm around her. She fits perfectly against me, as if she's meant to be there.

I'm about to launch into another story when Carlie shifts, her gaze lifting to meet mine. Her eyes hold a mixture of warmth and something more—an unspoken invitation. Her hand gently brushes against my cheek, sending shivers up and down my spine.

I turn my head slightly, our faces inches apart.

There's a hesitation, a moment where everything seems to pause, the air thick with anticipation.

Then, as if drawn by an invisible force, our lips meet in a tentative, exploratory kiss. It's soft at first, a whisper of a touch, but it quickly deepens, fueled by pent-up emotions and an undeniable chemistry between us.

The kiss ignites a fire, and we both yield to it, our movements syncing in a dance as old as time. Carlie's hand finds its way to my hair, tugging gently, eliciting a groan from deep within me. I let my hands roam, exploring the curve of her back, and pulling her closer, so I can deepen the kiss.

We break apart for a moment, gasping for air, our foreheads resting against each other. Our eyes meet, and there's a silent understanding, a shared desire that needs no words.

Carlie's breath hitches slightly as she whispers, "Adam, I want ..."

I nod, my voice a rough whisper, "I know ... Me, too."

We rise from the couch, our hands clasped tightly, as if letting go is not an option.

Every step we take is a silent affirmation of the path we're choosing to walk together—one that means taking things a step further.

As we reach the bedroom door, we pause, our breaths mingling in the charged air between us. There's a magnetic pull—a silent conversation in our shared glances—each one filled with a promise of venturing into uncharted territory.

Carlie's eyes, bright with a mix of desire and something deeper, lock onto mine. She takes a small, almost hesitant step forward, closing the distance between us.

Her voice is barely above a whisper, yet it resonates with a clarity that reaches deep into my core. "Adam, are you sure?"

For a moment, the world around us ceases to exist, and all that matters is the choice that lies ahead of us.

I look into her eyes, seeing the reflection of my own emotions mirrored back at me and without a doubt I know this is the right move.

With a nod, I answer, not just with words but with the conviction in my gaze. "If you're ready—if you want me as much as I want you—then there's nowhere else I'd rather be."

A slow, beautiful smile graces her lips and she pulls me into the bedroom.

CHAPTER 26

Carlie

The moment the bedroom door clicks shut, any worries and concerns from the outside world vanish, leaving only Adam and me in our own secluded universe.

His eyes are so full of emotion and unspoken promises as they lock onto mine, and it sends my heart racing into oblivion. Any thoughts I may have had before this moment flee and all I can think about is how much I want to feel his skin on mine—his mouth on me.

Adam gently cups my face, the tenderness in his touch sending shivers down my spine as the anticipation of this moment takes my breath away. My hands fist the fabric of his shirt and I pull him closer, needing to feel his body against mine.

He obliges, stepping forward until our lips meet in a kiss that's deep and urgent—releasing a torrent of all the feelings we've kept at bay until this moment.

Honestly, his lips are a revelation—each kiss a story

being written in a language only we understand. I'm lost in the sensation, the warmth of his body. But as Adam's hands start to explore, reaching for the hem of my shirt, a flicker of panic sparks in me.

The tattoo.

I need to know if he has the tattoo before I reveal too much of myself.

If he sees my birthmark, there's a good chance he'll be able to connect the dots, too, and I don't know if either one of us is ready for that.

"Adam," I breathe out between kisses, my mind racing. "Let's make this more interesting." I step back, my fingers trailing down his chest, but I hope my voice doesn't betray the chaos of my thoughts. "Keep your eyes closed."

He raises an eyebrow, a curious smile playing on his lips. "Is this a trust exercise? Because you can trust me. I hope you know that."

"Of course," I say, my voice a blend of nerves and mischief. I need to keep him off balance, just for a little longer. "I'm just a little self-conscious."

Not entirely untrue.

He's a freaking god with that body of his and there's definitely a part of me that cringes internally about my own. I swallow down that apprehension, trusting that we wouldn't be here in this moment if any of that mattered to him.

"You don't have anything to be self-conscious about, Carlie. You're gorgeous," he whispers, brushing his knuckles across my cheeks.

My chest heaves with my breaths and desire floods every cell of my being.

"Then, for me?" I ask, biting my lower lip.

His eyes dart to my mouth, following the movement. After a beat, he swallows hard and nods. "Okay."

His eyes close, and his features soften into a blind trust that makes my heart both swell and ache.

I want to be honest with him. Open up to him—

But I'm so scared he won't be able to see past the woman I pretended to be that night.

If, I remind myself, he's the man from the club.

I use the moment to guide his hands to the hem of my shirt, subtly steering them around my back. It's a dance of evasion, each of my movements calculated even though I'm desperate to appear casual.

As his fingers brush against my skin, I can't help but think how ridiculously this mirrors a bad spy movie—dodging laser beams in a high-security vault.

Except here, the treasure is the secret branded into my skin, the very thing that might shatter this fragile, beautiful illusion we've woven.

His hands work their way around my torso as he gently lifts my shirt from my body. The cool air brushes against my skin, but the heat from his touch is all-consuming. Exposed in the soft glow of the moonlight cascading through the window, I feel both vulnerable and empowered.

But if he were to open his eyes ... even for a moment ...

I inhale sharply, torn between wanting more and

fearing the inevitable. My heart is a drumbeat thundering in my chest, loud enough, I'm convinced, for him to hear.

Sneaking another glance in his direction, I smile at his closed eyes and his ghost of a grin. Then, I match his movements, my fingers fumbling with the buttons on his shirt as I revel in the way he feels beneath them.

As I undo the last button, my fingers lightly trace the contours of his well-defined chest, then to the lines of his abs.

Seriously, how many muscles does this man have?

The soft gasp that escapes his lips emboldens me to push the shirt off his shoulders. It falls to the floor, forgotten, as I stand up and brush my lips to his. His tongue sweeps against my lower lip, and a growl rides the simple request.

I open my mouth, allowing his tongue to dominate me, exploring and savoring the kiss.

As his hands pull me closer, mine roam across his chest, down his abs—every touch an exploration, a *discovery.*

The clasp of my bra is suddenly undone and it slides from my body and lands on the floor between us. With each piece of clothing that drops, it feels like we're shedding more than just fabric—we're precariously close to baring our souls.

But my real quest lies hidden, and my hands cleverly work their way to his waistband, feigning a boldness I don't entirely feel.

This is the moment of truth—*literally.*

I'm looking for the tribal tattoo, the silent testament of our shared past.

If we have one—I remind myself again.

As I slide my hands along his waist, I feel his muscles tense under my touch. I glance up at him, his eyes still obediently closed, his expression a mix of anticipation and vulnerability.

For a second, I'm torn—do I really want to know?

Can I handle the truth?

I push the thought aside, steeling myself.

I do. I *need* to know.

Slowly, I start to unbuckle his belt and undo the button on his jeans. My fingers tremble slightly as I work, each motion deliberate yet fraught with nervous energy.

I'm hyper-aware of every breath Adam takes, every slight movement of his body. It's as if my entire world has narrowed down to this single, pivotal moment.

His belt slips free, and the sound of his zipper seems impossibly loud in the quiet room. As I slowly tug the fabric down, my heartbeat pounds in my ears, a frantic rhythm that mirrors my escalating nerves.

There's a tension in the air, thick and palpable, as his jeans hit the floor and he steps out of them.

Adam, perhaps sensing the shift in my demeanor, or maybe holding his own breath in anticipation, remains still.

My gaze flits back to his and his eyes are still closed—his trust in me absolute. It's a trust I'm terrified of breaking, yet I can't turn back now.

I have to know.

In my books, the heroine often faces a moment of truth, usually with better bodies and better lighting. Here I am, living my own cliché, except the plot twist is real, and the stakes are my heart.

Sliding my palm over the top of his briefs, I drag my hand over his length, reveling in the hardness. A low moan escapes his lips and moisture pools between my legs.

God, do I want him.

This man. Not some imaginary figment.

But there's another part of me that's desperate to have him, even if he is the man from Nocté.

Because then ... it's like we're cheating fate.

Or cheating the club.

Ironic, considering how the club works.

I shake my head, forcing all of those thoughts from my mind.

Slowly, I push his briefs down his hips, and as they fall to the floor, my eyes dart to his lower abdomen.

The soft glow of the moonlight spills across his skin, revealing ...

My breath catches and my heart skips a beat.

There it is.

The tribal tattoo is precisely where I remember seeing it that night at Nocté.

A cocktail of shock, realization, and an inexplicable sense of destiny washes over me.

It's him. It's *really* him.

I stand frozen as every emotion under the sun crashes over me.

Part of me wants to laugh at the absurdity of it all—part of me wants to cry.

Another part is grappling with the moral dilemma of not saying something.

Should he know?

But there's no time for any of the questions circling my brain because Adam reaches out undoing my own jeans. They're on the floor as his mouth crashes against mine and I'm swept up again in the moment.

In a desperate bid to regain control of the situation, I gently push Adam back onto the bed, keeping his focus on the movement and away from my own telltale birthmark.

"Keep your eyes closed," I whisper, my voice barely steady. "I want you to focus on how we feel together."

It's the truth, but not the whole truth. I need him to remain oblivious for just a little longer.

Adam complies, a small smile on his face, blissfully unaware of the storm brewing inside me.

I quickly shed the rest of my clothes, careful to keep my back to him as I try to remain upright. The last thing I need is for him to see the birthmark until I know what in the actual fuck I'm going to do—or how I'm going to explain it.

God, how *am* I going to explain everything to him?

Turning around, I slowly climb onto the bed, straddling him between my legs. My heart pounds against my chest and just about everywhere else. Then, I lean down, capturing his lips in a kiss that's fueled by a mixture of passion, desperation, and a newfound urgency.

My hands explore his body, tracing the lines of his tattoo, committing every detail to memory. Then, I wrap my hand around him and squeeze, enjoying the way he groans against my lips.

"It was a stupid college thing," he says breathlessly, breaking our kiss.

"Huh?" I ask, continuing the slow motion, letting his arousal slicken my grip.

He grabs my face, pulling me in for another kiss. There's a smile on his lips when he says, "The tattoo."

Adam's admission about the tattoo, so casually tossed into the thick of our passion, sends my mind reeling.

A stupid college thing.

Little does he know the significance it holds, the secret it unknowingly symbolizes. I force a smile, concealing the tumultuous thoughts racing through my mind.

"The tattoo," I echo, my voice a soft whisper. I continue my movements, but my mind is elsewhere, tangled in a web of emotions and revelations.

He's lost in the moment, his eyes closed, his breaths coming in short, rapid gasps as he explores my body with his hands.

I watch him, this beautiful, unknowing man who's become the center of my world in such a short time. The intensity of my feelings for him, compounded by the truth I now hold, weighs heavily on me.

I lean down, my lips finding his in a fervent kiss, a mix of desire and an attempt to quiet the storm inside me. Our movements become more urgent, a dance of need and longing so powerful I get swept away by it.

The heat between us is undeniable, each touch sending waves of desire coursing through my body.

As our kisses deepen, and his fingers work their magic on my body, I lose myself in the sensations, trying to forget the gnawing guilt and focus on the present. But it's there, lurking in the shadows, the unspoken truth that I've discovered his identity and he's still in the dark.

However, with each caress and stroke of his tongue, a part of me starts to let go.

His bedroom, dimly lit by the moon's soft glow, becomes our world. It's just Adam and me, and the mounting tension that's been building between us from the very beginning.

My worries begin to fade, overshadowed by the raw need pulsing through me.

Adam's hands, strong yet gentle, explore my body with a reverence that makes my skin tingle, and the memories from that night spring to life.

His touch ignites fires in places I didn't even know could burn. I arch into him, craving more of his touch, more of this connection that's growing stronger by the second.

The guilt that's been nagging at me starts to slip away, piece by piece, as his lips find mine again. Our kiss is a silent language that speaks volumes.

The truth about Nocté, about the tattoo, it all fades into the background.

In this moment, nothing else matters but the here and now.

My breath hitches as Adam's hands move with a purpose, his fingers dipping inside me in a way that makes me want so much more.

As we move together, our bodies find a rhythm that's both ancient and new. It's a dance as old as time, yet it feels like we're discovering it for the first time—and in a way, we are.

The world outside, with all its complications and truths, fades into insignificance. All that matters is him—*us*. The beating of our hearts, the warmth of our bodies, and the unspoken promise of something deeper, something *real*.

When he finally slides inside me, it's like the entire universe aligns and fate itself bows to us.

I swear, nothing has ever felt so *good*.

Our movements become more frenzied, more urgent as we move in rhythm to each other. Every touch, every kiss—the intensity of the moment is overwhelming, yet it's exactly where I want to be ...

In the aftermath, as we lay together, our bodies entwined, the reality of what just happened begins to seep back in. The guilt that I'd managed to push aside comes crashing through, stronger and more insistent.

I've given myself to Adam, but I've also kept from him a truth that could change everything.

Would he still want me if he knew?

As he drifts off to sleep, his arm draped protectively over me, the weight of this secret presses heavily on my chest. I watch him in the dim light, his face relaxed in sleep, and my heart aches.

He's the man from Nocté, the one I've dreamt about —*fantasized over.*

And he doesn't know.

He doesn't know that I'm the woman behind the mask. The one who shared that intense, anonymous night with him.

I wait until his breathing evens out, then quietly, I slide out from under his arm, my movements careful not to disturb him. I gather my clothes as I'm wrapped up in a whirlwind of emotions.

I should tell him.

I should wake him up right now and confess *everything.*

But the words stick in my throat, fear and uncertainty holding them back.

Instead, I dress silently, my eyes lingering on his peaceful face one last time.

There's a part of me that wants to stay, to bask in the warmth of what we have. But the larger part, the part gripped by fear and guilt, knows I have to leave. I need to sort this out.

I need to plot the ending ...

With a heavy heart, I slip out of the room, closing the door behind me with the softest click.

As I make my way out of his house to wait for my Uber, the night air feels cooler, *harsher*. I'm leaving behind more than just a man. I'm leaving behind a part of myself, a piece of my heart that I'm not sure I'll ever get back.

The realization hits me like a physical blow, and I pause for a moment, leaning against his front door. Tears prick at the corners of my eyes, but I force them back.

Now's not the time for tears.

Now's the time for decisions—for figuring out what the fuck comes next.

If I were writing this scene, it'd be raining—dramatic, poignant, a metaphor for internal turmoil. But tonight, the sky is clear, leaving me to navigate my own storm.

Stupid, *unreliable* nature.

The road ahead is uncertain, filled with questions and doubts. But one thing is clear—I can't keep running from the truth.

Sooner or later, it'll catch up to me.

And when it does, I'll have to face the consequences of a night that changed everything.

But now the question is ... which one?

CHAPTER 27

Adam

Waking up to an empty bed wasn't what I expected—*especially* after last night.

My body is a confusing combined state of utter satisfaction and bliss—mixed with a worried alertness that wasn't there a minute ago.

The first rays of morning sun filter through the blinds, casting a soft, golden light across my bedroom. But the warmth of the sun does nothing to fill the void left by Carlie's absence.

In fact, she must have left a while ago because her side of the bed has gone cold.

I lie still for a moment, listening for any sign of her in the house as I inhale her scent, lingering in this bed like a ghost.

The stark contrast between the heat of last night and the chill of the morning hits me hard.

I've had one-night stands before. But this—I didn't expect Carlie to be one of them.

I sit up, trying to tamp down my confusion and panic.

Would she really leave without saying goodbye?

Maybe she's in the kitchen? Or the bathroom?

Clutching at straws, I throw back the covers and the cool air of the room wraps around me like a shroud. I ignore it, slipping out of bed and grabbing a shirt from the dresser. As quickly as I can, I pull it over my head, trying to calm the chaos in my mind. But nothing I do helps.

I need to check the house.

Once I tug on my sweats, I pad through every room, just to be sure. My movements are mechanical as I navigate through each silent space, the quiet amplifying my growing sense of unease.

By the time I stop at the kitchen, the realization really sinks in.

But she's not here. There's no note.

No *nothing*.

The house is as empty as the pit in my stomach.

My gaze drifts out to my backyard, now bathed in early morning sunlight

Why would she leave without saying goodbye?

Especially after ...

I run a hand through my hair as the events of last night replay in my mind.

Last night was ...

Fuck, it was *incredible*.

It was more than that. The physical connection was

intense and real—but it was more than sex. I felt it and I sure as hell know she did.

It was there, in her touch and the way she kissed me.

It felt like we crossed a threshold, reaching a level of intimacy that I've only ever come close to once before …

But with that woman, it was all a mirage. An event to take my mind off the fact that I was cheated on and had to deal with that reality every day at work.

And yet, some elements were so similar to that night at the club—the talk of trading truths and the way she wanted me to close my eyes. Being blind left me with the same sensations as having a mask. I had to rely on my other senses and it was hot as hell.

In some ways, it was practically a repeat of that night.

That revelation is strange and sexy, but I shake the thoughts away.

Carlie isn't anything like the woman that night. She's sweet and tentative and clumsy at times.

And yet …

The way she moved on top of me—beneath me. The way she held me and stroked my …

"Fuck," I groan, rubbing my hands over my face.

Why the hell am I comparing Carlie to that woman? Carlie is *real* and tangible.

Not some fantasy of a woman I'll never see again.

But now, the empty house echoes back my confusion.

Why would she leave without a word?

Did I do something wrong? Did she feel pressured?

The intimacy of last night, the vulnerability we

shared—did it mean nothing to her? Or did something scare her away?

In this sudden silence, my mind involuntarily drifts to past relationships.

The relationship with Jillian ended badly—*obviously*. She never thought I had enough ambition and by the end, she used that as her excuse.

Our relationship had been a whirlwind of highs and lows, marked by passionate arguments and equally passionate reconciliations.

But even at our best, it was never like this.

With Jillian, it was a fire that burned too hot, too quickly, leaving only ashes in its wake. There was never emotional depth. Never that connection I've always been seeking, but almost thought was a fantasy.

Carlie, though ... with her, it's *different*.

The connection with her is like a slow-burning flame, warm and inviting. I feel it in the way she looks at me, in the softness of her laugh, the earnest smile lighting in her eyes.

What we have is real in a way that I never experienced with anyone.

Jillian, included. She was more about the image—the *spectacle*.

Walking back to my bedroom, I grab my phone from my nightstand, intending to call Carlie but stop as a flood of notifications catch my eye. My stomach tightens as I open Instagram, only to see my feed blowing up with posts and comments about me and Carlie—*again*.

My heart sinks.

. . .

"Adam Foxx, using a client from his old job to launch his own gym? Sad to see how the mighty have fallen."

"Typical player moves, pretending to care just for the 'gram."

"I'd use the chubby chick, too. Those thighs. Mmmmm."

Each word cuts deeper than the last and I think I'm gonna puke.

They don't know the first thing about what Carlie and I share. They sure as hell don't know anything about *her*. She's funny, and smart, and *fucking gorgeous.*

They've got it all wrong.

Working with her—training her, *dating* her—isn't about publicity or some shallow game.

What I feel for Carlie ... *it's real.*

But then the realization hits me hard—what if Carlie saw these?

Could that be the reason she left?

What if she thinks I'm just using her? *Used* her.

I run a hand through my hair, my frustration mounting. The one time I find someone who ignites something deep inside me, and this social media circus tries to tear it down.

I won't let it happen. *No fucking way.*

I need to set things right.

But how?

I scroll through the comments, each one a mix of speculation and accusation. It's like watching a car crash in slow motion, and I'm the driver, helplessly watching as everything spirals out of control.

There are pictures of us taken out of context. Mashups with my old dating history and the type of women I've been known to date. Stupid theories about how I've been masterminding this for the past few months.

It's all bullshit.

The room feels smaller, the walls closing in as the weight of public opinion bears down on me.

This isn't just idle gossip—it's a targeted attack.

A smear campaign that's not just hurting me, but potentially destroying something that was just beginning with Carlie.

Frustration boils within me—transforming into a potent mix of anger and helplessness. I've been in the public eye long enough to know how damaging these rumors can be, but I never thought they'd seep into something so personal—so *real*.

Fitness was always meant to be fun. To be encouraging and empowering. Not—whatever the hell this is.

Jillian's comment yesterday flashes in my mind, and a bitter taste fills my mouth.

Fucking Jillian.

This has her fingerprints all over it.

I always knew she played dirty, but this ... *this is a new low.*

Dragging Carlie into her petty games, trying to tarnish our relationship with her jealousy and spite. Who the hell does she think she is?

I can't just stand by and let this happen.

No way am I going to let this slide.

I have to fight back, not just for my reputation, but for what I feel for Carlie.

Hell, for Carlie herself.

She needs to know the truth—to see beyond the lies and the rumors.

But how? *How* do I convince her that what we have is real? That it's not just another story for the tabloids?

I hesitate for a moment, my thumb hovering over Carlie's contact on my phone.

No, not yet.

I need advice, a plan. I scroll through my contacts and hit call on the one person who always knows what to do.

"Why in the fuck are you calling me at seven in the morning?" Brian's voice is groggy, betraying the early hour. "Hate to break it to you, but not everyone loves being up at this ungodly hour."

"Brian, man, I need your help," I start, my words rushing out.

I explain everything—Carlie leaving, the Instagram debacle, my suspicion about Jillian's involvement.

"Damn, that's messed up," Brian mutters after a pause. "First things first, bro, you need to put Jillian on notice. You can't let her control the narrative. She's obviously messing with you just because she thinks she can."

"I know, but how?" I ground out, frustration edging my voice.

"Go to St. Mary's. Confront her in person. It's time she knows you're not playing her games anymore. And Adam, if you need me to, I'll go with you. You don't need to face that bitch alone."

His offer is a lifeline in the chaos. "Thanks, man. I'd take you up on that, but I think I need to deal with her on my own. She won't take it seriously otherwise."

"Okay, I get that. Don't wait too long, though. You need to clear this up. I know all too well how bullshit lies can spiral out of control. So, take care of it. Not just for the public, but for Carlie, too," Brian advises. "And about Carlie ... talk to her, bro. Be honest. Tell her everything. She deserves that much."

He's right.

Carlie does deserve the truth.

All of it.

I need to explain the situation and show her that she's more than just a headline to me.

"Thanks, Brian. I'll head over to St. Mary's now. And I'll call Carlie afterward."

"Good luck, Adam. Call me if you need me," he says before hanging up.

Armed with a plan, I feel a surge of determination.

I'm going to put an end to Jillian's antics once and for all. And then, I'll do everything in my power to make things right with Carlie.

Carlie

The moment I step into Lily's living room, my stomach is doing somersaults—and not the good kind. The kind that screams, *"Carlie, you colossal idiot!"*

I'm about two seconds away from a full-blown panic attack, and my brain is stuck on repeat: I used Adam for sex.

I used Adam for sex!

God, that sounds so bad, even in my head.

What is wrong with me?

Lily tilts her head, concern etching her features as she waits for me to explain my reason for barging in so early in the morning.

"Lily, I'm the worst human being on the planet," I blurt out, collapsing onto her sofa like it's my personal fainting couch. I'm half-expecting it to swallow me whole, which, frankly, wouldn't be the worst thing right now.

Lily, ever the calm one, puts down her coffee mug

and sits beside me, her eyebrows knitted in concern. "I'm going to need a little more to go on here. What's happened, Carlie?"

Here goes nothing. *Or everything.*

"I slept with Adam," I blurt out, and it feels like confessing to a crime.

She huffs a laugh and shakes her head. "Was it terrible or something?" Lily leans forward, her eyes sparkling with a mix of amusement and curiosity.

"God no," I say, fanning myself. Definitely *not*. He was hot with a capital H. In a bizarre twist, my brain decides this is a good time to replay every steamy detail of last night, like a highlight reel nobody asked for. "*I'm terrible.*"

"At sex?" Lily counters with a soft laugh.

I level her with a glare. "Look, here's the thing. What I'm about to tell you—*you can't tell anyone.* Not even Tasia or Quinn. Especially not London."

Lily's face shifts from gentle amusement to serious attentiveness, her eyes locking onto mine. She sets her coffee mug down, giving me her full attention.

I itch the side of my eye, trying to find the right words. It shouldn't be so damn hard. I'm an author, for crying out loud.

"I've had sex with him before," I continue, my voice a little more than a whisper, as if saying it louder might make it more real.

Well, there goes my shot at the *'Most Transparent Friend of the Year'* award.

Lily narrows her gaze. "I'm confused."

"That makes two of us," I mutter, trying to steel myself. If I can't even tell one of my closest friends, what chance do I have with Adam?

"Carlie, whatever it is, I won't tell anyone," Lily offers, placing a hand on my knee.

I nod, blowing out a breath. "There was an event …" I chew on my lip, studying Lily's face as if I can somehow telepathically send her the information she needs.

But then, just as I suspected, recognition flickers in her brown eyes. Lily's fingers tap against her chin, a silent signal of her processing the information.

"Oh," is all she says.

It sounds like a full sentence when she says it like that.

I swallow hard. "I think … you planned it, didn't you? At Nocté?"

Lily's face is a study in restraint. She's always been good at hiding what she's thinking, but right now, I wish I could read her mind. "Carlie, I—"

"Because if you did," I press on, not letting her evade the question, "it means you understand how this is a little bit …"

Lily glances toward the hallway, and I remember that London is probably here, somewhere in this house. Her eyes flick back to me, filled with a mix of emotions. "Carlie, I can't talk about …"

Duh, Carlie.

The club has rules for participants. They probably have an NDA or something for the people who work the event.

I could facepalm myself right now.

"I get it," I cut her off, my frustration simmering. "But I'm not asking for club secrets. I'm asking about my life, Lily. My mess of a life that seems to be tangled up in all this."

She takes a deep breath, and I can tell she's choosing her words carefully. "I can't confirm or deny anything about what goes on at Nocté. But Carlie, this is about you and Adam. Whatever happened—*or didn't happen*—at that event, it's your story to write now."

"Oh, it happened. One hundred percent it happened," I mutter, slumping back into the couch.

"How do you know?" Lily asks, her question coming out tentatively.

The memory of his tattoo is etched in my mind—impossible to forget.

"He has this tribal tattoo ..."

"Oh," she breathes out with a nod. Somehow, it's like she understands just how powerful that damn artwork can be.

Come to think of it, London has tattoos.

Focus, Carlie.

I shoot her a pointed stare. "Right?"

"Okay, well ..." She glances over her shoulder again, her gaze flitting to the back porch. When she turns back to me, she leans in close and whispers, "Then you know the rules, right? Is that why you're upset? You want to go back to the club?"

My eyes widen in horror. "No—*no.* I have no intention of trying to hook up with someone else."

Confusion flickers across her face. "Are you worried that Adam wants to—?"

I shake my head, though, if I'm honest, that horrific thought never occurred to me.

Thanks, Lily.

"Then, I don't see the problem. You can just—" she begins.

A strangled breath escapes my lips as I blurt, "*He* doesn't know."

Lily's expression is one of confusion and anticipation as she waits for me to continue my tirade. Before I can continue to pour out my heart, Lily's phone buzzes on the coffee table.

She glances at it, her brow furrowing slightly as she reads the screen. There's a brief flash of something—concern, maybe, or surprise—that crosses her face before she quickly flips her phone over, giving me her undivided attention again.

"It's Anna," she says, meeting my eyes. "She wants to talk about some social media situation, but it can wait." There's a pause, a fleeting hesitation in her voice, suggesting there could be more to it. "Right now, you're what's important. We can check on Anna's news later," Lily adds with a reassuring smile.

Despite her words, my stupid brain flits back to the drama-fest that happened with Adam's Instagram a couple of weeks ago. God, if the internet trolls found out we were actually sleeping together, they'd have a field day.

Speaking of which ...

"Lily, I slept with Adam, knowing who he was—*knowing we'd already—*" I swallowed the confession down like a bad pill as tears threaten to spill over. "I'm going straight to hell."

If there's a handbook on how to mess up potential relationships, I'm pretty sure I'm writing it.

Chapter One: How to Dig Your Own Emotional Grave.

Lily's face softens—something I don't deserve—as a mixture of sympathy and understanding dawns in her eyes. "Carlie," she says gently, "I've been there. Remember everything that happened between me and London?"

I nod, remembering the tangled web of emotions and secrets that had surrounded the beginning of Lily and London's relationship. It was like watching a rom-com but with the added tension of real-life consequences.

"Sometimes," Lily continues, "we find ourselves in these complicated situations because we're afraid. Afraid of the truth, afraid of what might happen if we're honest. But let me tell you something I learned the hard way ... The truth might be scary, but it's also freeing."

I let out a small, humorless laugh. "Freeing, huh? Right now, it feels more like I'm handcuffed to a ticking bomb."

Lily chuckles, but her eyes are serious as she reaches out, giving my hand a reassuring squeeze. "I felt the same with London. But hiding the truth, it's like a slow poison. It eats away at what could be. Opening up, being vulnerable—it's hard, but it's the only way to move forward—to heal. And you're not going to hell. You're *human*." Again with the pointed look. "When I was keeping secrets from London, I thought I was protecting us, but I was just scared. Scared of losing him, scared of facing my past. Scared of moving forward. I have no doubt you're the same. So, maybe you made a mistake, but that doesn't define you. What defines you is what you do next."

"And what should I do?" I ask, feeling the weight of my choices like a heavy cloak around my shoulders.

"Talk to Adam," she advises. "Be honest with him. Tell him about the past, about the event. Explain why you didn't tell him earlier. It won't be easy, but it's necessary if you want to continue to have a relationship with him."

I sigh, knowing she's right. "But what if he hates me for it?"

"Then he's not the right person for you," Lily responds firmly. "But if he cares about you, he'll listen. He'll understand. And who knows, maybe he already knows and has been too scared to tell you, too."

I ponder her words, feeling a sliver of hope amid the chaos of my thoughts. "You think so?"

Lily takes a deep breath, her shoulders rising and falling in the motion. "In my experience, relationships are rarely straightforward. There's always more beneath the surface. The only way to navigate them is through honesty and communication. You're a writer, Carlie. You know people aren't just characters in a story we write.

They have their own stories, their own reasons. You need to talk to Adam. Get his side of the story."

I nod slowly, knowing she's right but hating that it's not easier. Telling Adam the truth, knowing it could hurt him—or hurt our chances at a future—it's terrifying.

"I just ... I don't want to hurt him. Or me. Or us. If there even is an 'us' now," I admit, more to myself than her.

"Then start with honesty," Lily suggests with a shrug. "It's the best foundation you can build on. No matter where the story goes."

I stand up, feeling a little steadier. "Honesty. Right. I can do that." I offer her a small smile. "Thanks, Lily. For what you could say, anyway. I hope I didn't put you in a bad position."

Lily grins at me. "We're good. Thank you for trusting me with this. It means a lot. See? You're already making strides at this whole honest and open thing."

Snickering at her words, I feel a renewed sense of purpose, albeit a shaky one. "Well, I should go. I need to figure out what I'm going to say to him."

She smiles, a knowing glint in her eyes. "Just remember, no matter what happens, you're not alone. We've all been there in one way or another. And we've got your back."

As I leave Lily's house, her words echo in my mind.

Honesty.

Communication.

The truth.

They sound so simple, yet they feel like the hardest

things in the world right now. But I know she's right. It's time to face the music, even if it's a tune I'm terrified to hear.

So here I go, stepping into my own personal opera of awkward. Curtain up on the drama that is my love life.

Encore, anyone?

CHAPTER 29

Adam

I should be back home, naked and in bed with Carlie.

Maybe even going for round two. Or three.

At least, that was the fantasy I had in my mind last night.

Instead, my nerves are frayed and my rage is simmering as I drive to St. Mary's.

Saturday mornings are supposed to be for relaxation —for a brief respite from the week's chaos. But today, I'm anything but calm.

The Instagram fiasco keeps replaying in my head like a bad movie on a loop.

IG has always been my thing. My place where I felt in control of the narrative and helped make a difference in people's lives.

Everyone knows that.

Even exes.

I should've known Jillian was behind the drama lately. It's just her style—subtle enough to deny, but obvious to anyone who really knows her. She must be getting one helluva laugh at our expense.

I pull up on the street outside St. Mary's Hospital. This building, with its state-of-the-art gym, has been a sanctuary for me over the past few years—a place to clear my head and refocus. But today, as I walk through the familiar sliding doors, the hustle of the hospital only adds to the chaos in my head. It feels like just another stop in my quest for answers.

I head directly to the gym, the rhythm of my footsteps matching the rapid beat of my heart. I scan the area, searching for her familiar figure, but Jillian's nowhere to be seen.

Approaching the front desk, I'm greeted by a guy I don't recognize.

He looks up, his expression open and friendly.

"Hey, can I help you with something?" he asks, his eyes briefly scanning me up and down. "Oh, Adam. Hi."

I might not know him, but evidently, he knows me.

"I'm looking for Jillian. Is she here today?" My voice is firmer than I intend, betraying my simmering anger.

He taps a few keys on his computer, his brow furrowing. "Sorry, man, Jillian doesn't work Saturdays. Is there anything else I can help with?"

Not unless he has the power to snap his fingers and erase Jillian from the planet.

I shake my head and pat the counter in frustration. "Nah, thanks, though."

I leave the gym, my frustration and irritation ratcheting up a notch. When I get outside, the morning sun does little to lift the darkness clouding my thoughts.

In my car, I sit motionless, gripping the steering wheel.

Right. *Saturday.* Jillian's sacred day off.

The realization hits me with a mix of irony and anger. If she can stir up trouble from the shadows, then she can certainly face the music—even on her day off.

I start up the car, the engine's hum a backdrop to the turmoil in my mind. As I drive to her house, I can't help but think about how everything has spiraled out of control.

From the moment she cheated on me to right now— Jillian has fucked with me more than I ever thought possible.

She's always craved attention, and playing games has been her forte. But this time, she's crossed a line, and I can't let it slide.

Not when it involves Carlie.

Her house comes into view, and it's a symbol of the life she always wants to portray—perfect, orderly, *unattainable.*

I pull up, my resolve solidifying with every breath. She thinks she can play games with people's lives? It's time she learns that actions have consequences.

I march up to her door, my heart pounding in my chest. This isn't just about setting the record straight. It's about protecting what I've started to build with Carlie— about defending the semblance of peace I've found with her.

I ring the bell, ready for whatever façade Jillian chooses to present because I'm one hundred percent sure she'll pick one.

The door swings open, and there she stands, her expression shifting from surprise to a calculated smile that doesn't quite reach her eyes.

"Adam, what a surprise," she purrs, leaning against the door frame. "What brings you here?"

She doesn't even have the courtesy to look sleepy or disheveled at eight in the morning.

"I need to talk to you. *Now.*" I don't mince words, the urgency is clear in my tone.

"About what?" she feigns ignorance, but her eyes betray her.

"I'm here for the truth, Jillian," I say, my voice steady. "What the fuck do you think you're doing?"

She chuckles—it's an amused, totally obnoxious laugh that makes me want to break things. "You're going to need to be more specific, Adam."

"The Instagram bullshit. The lies about Carlie and me—about Foxx Fitness. I know everything was started by you," I ground out, my fists at my side.

For a moment, her mask falters, revealing the briefest flicker of guilt, but she's quick to regain her composure. "I really don't know what you're talking about. Why would I care about you and Carlie? Or the notion that you'll ever venture out and start your business?"

Her words cut like knives.

She was always so pissed that I didn't start up my

own gym and get out from under St. Mary's. In her words, it's the reason she cheated.

I was going nowhere.

"Don't insult my intelligence," I counter. "It's over, Jillian. Whatever game you're playing, it ends *now*. Stay away from me, and stay away from Carlie."

"Or what?" she fires back, the lines in her jaw hardening. Her challenge hangs in the air between us, her smirk growing as she awaits my response. "Or *what*, Adam? What are you going to do? We both know that taking initiative isn't your thing."

I take a deep breath, steadying my nerves. It's time to play my hand. "Or I'll go to the hospital board with what I know. About your 'extra-curricular activities' with some of the gym clients. It's against the policy, right? Fraternizing with clients in a way that could ... tarnish St. Mary's reputation. It's how I was fired—*thanks to you.*"

It all clicks into place. She's a fucking projector.

Putting all eyes on me to take them off her own indiscretions.

I never said a word about her and that stupid asshole who jumped at her the first chance he got.

But I will. *Oh, I fucking will.*

Jillian's smirk fades, her eyes widening slightly. It's the reaction I was hoping for. "You wouldn't dare," she hisses.

"Oh, I would. And I have enough to back it up," I say, my voice firm. "I've seen the way you operate, Jillian. The flirtations, the private sessions that are a little too close for comfort. It wouldn't be hard for people to believe. Not to mention the clients you push around instead of helping. People like Carlie, for instance ...”

Her façade crumbles, replaced by a look of panic. “You're bluffing.”

I shake my head. “No more games, Jillian. I'm done playing. Leave Carlie and me alone, or I'll make sure the hospital board hears about every inappropriate encounter you've had at the gym.”

She steps back, the doorframe no longer a support but a barrier between us. “You're serious,” she whispers.

“Dead serious. This is your only warning, Jillian. Stay away from us.”

Jillian's façade wavers, but she scrambles to regain her composure, stepping closer with a manipulative glint in her eyes. “Adam, you're upset. I understand. But you need someone who truly gets you. Carlie isn't that person. She's not good enough for you. I mean, look at her.”

“There is nothing wrong with Carlie. And for the record, she's twice the woman you'll ever be—” I spit out through clenched teeth.

She snickers under her breath. “Give me a break. You and I both know you need someone who hasn't let herself go. Someone who has the body you've always seen yourself with.” She runs her hands down the sides of her torso, as if she's actually suggesting *she's* what I need.

I recoil from her advance. “No, Jillian. What I need is for you to stay out of my life.”

Her mask finally slips, revealing the anger beneath. “Fine, Adam. Have it your way,” she spits out, her voice cold. "But don't come running back to me when you realize your mistake."

"You're fucking unbelievable," I mutter.

I don't wait for another word, turning on my heel and walking away. I can feel her gaze burning into my back, but I don't look back.

Not this time.

I walk away from her house, the weight of the confrontation heavy on my shoulders.

In the car, I take a moment to breathe, letting the adrenaline rush subside as I take a deep breath, and try to calm the torrent of anger coursing through me.

From the corner of my eye, I see her front door shut and I slam the butt of my hand against the steering wheel.

"Fuck," I mutter, closing my eyes and taking a few more deep breaths.

I start the car and pull away from the road.

Jillian had always been manipulative, but I never thought she'd stoop this low.

I don't even get it. *Why bother?*

She has her boy toy.

Why fuck with me and Carlie?

As I drive home, I realize this is more than just a fight with an ex—it's a battle to protect the new life I'm trying to build.

A life with Carlie.

When I pull into my driveway, the morning's events are swirling in my mind.

It's a clusterfuck of epic proportions.

I get out, slam my door harder than necessary, then stalk to my front door. However, when I reach it, I notice an envelope tucked under the mat. Picking it up, I recognize the insignia immediately.

Nocté.

A sense of foreboding washes over me as I tear it open.

Inside is a note, its message, succinct and unsettling.

Dear Mr. Foxx,

Thank you for your participation in Nocté's Upper Tier. Your involvement is now concluded and access is revoked.

Into the Night,
Club Nocté

"What the fuck?" I blurt out, my eyes skimming the letter again.

Why would Nocté suddenly cut ties?

And why *now*, of all times?

I mean, it's not like I had any intention of going back —*not after Carlie.* But what the hell?

The letter feels heavy, its words a stark finality to something I hadn't even fully grasped.

Nocté had been an escape—a world away from the

ordinary, and now, just as abruptly as it entered my life, it's exiting.

The timing can't be a coincidence.

That all too familiar frustration bubbles up, hot and unyielding.

Questions race through my mind, each one a dead end. I turn the letter over in my hands, as if the blank backside might hold more answers.

It doesn't.

This is all too closely entwined with everything else —Jillian's machinations, the Instagram chaos, and my deepening connection with Carlie.

Maybe Nocté caught wind of all the bullshit, too, and decided I'm a liability.

Carlie's face flashes into my mind—the way she smiles, the way she looks at me—like I'm someone worth looking at, worth caring about.

The idea that she's being drug into this mess, into the fallout from a part of my life she had nothing to do with, is unbearable.

I take a deep breath, trying to quell the rising panic.

This is a warning—hell, *a sign.*

CHAPTER 30

Carlie

As I head home from Lily's house, I feel like a ship adrift.

My thoughts are churning like stormy seas and all I want is to retreat to my apartment—to be alone with the chaos swirling inside me. But fate, it seems, has other plans, as it tugs at my intuition.

I'm halfway up the stairs to my place when I pause.

The familiar sounds from Grandma's apartment seep through the door—the clink of china, the hum of her old radio.

I know I should just go home and sort through the tangled-up mess in my head, but something pulls me back down the steps and towards her door.

I knock softly, and her voice, warm and inviting, calls out, "Carlie, is that you? Come in, dear."

Grandma's sitting at her kitchen table with a mischievous twinkle in her eye. One that I know all too well.

"Carlie, just the person I wanted to see. I need your help with something."

I can't help but smile despite everything. She always has a way of drawing me in, even when I'm determined to shut the world out.

"What do you need help with?" I ask, walking through her open dining area. When I reach her, I pull my phone from my pocket, set it on the table, and sink into a chair beside her.

Her grin spreads and my insides coil as she replies, "I need enlightenment."

Nothing good can come from that smile.

Why did I think it was a good idea to come here again?

Clearing my throat, I sit up straighter. "Enlightenment on what ... exactly?"

"I noticed you didn't come home last night," she begins, her white eyebrows waggling.

Despite myself, heat rushes to my cheeks and I pat them down, as if somehow, it might keep the blush at bay.

"So, spill it," she continues with a knowing glint lighting up her irises. "Why didn't you come home last night? And don't try to butter me up with some tall tale, young lady. This grandma knows better. I saw the way you've been mooning over that personal trainer of yours. What's his name ... Adam?"

I sigh, sinking back into my chair. Geez, she always had a way of cutting right to the chase. "Yeah, Adam."

My admission hangs in the air, and I brace myself for the inevitable barrage of questions.

Grandma leans in with unbridled curiosity. "So, did Mr. Muscles sweep you off your feet yet? Or should I be sharpening my pitchfork?"

I can't help but chuckle. "No pitchforks needed, Grandma. He's ... he's different."

"Different, eh?" Grandma taps her chin thoughtfully. "That's what they all say, dear. Before you know it, you're knee-deep in gym socks and protein powder."

I roll my eyes, a small smile tugging at my lips. "It's not like that. We just ... *connected*, you know?"

Grandma nods sagely, though there's a knowing glint in her eye. "Oh, I know all about 'connecting.' In my day, we called it—"

"Grandma—" I cut her off, my cheeks flaming again. There's only so much 'enlightenment' I can handle.

She laughs, a hearty, joyful sound that fills the room. "I'm just teasing you, dear. But seriously, is everything okay? You should have that after-sex glow. Instead, you look like—"

Just then, my phone buzzes, derailing our conversation. I glance at the screen—it's a text from Lily.

Carlie, we need to talk ASAP. Call me.

My heart sinks. This can't be good.

I've only been gone fifteen minutes.

"Everything's ... *complicated*," I admit, standing up. "I've got to take this, Grandma. Thanks for the chat."

She reaches out, grabbing hold of my hand and causing me to pull up short. "Carlie, dear, men are like books. Some are open and easy to read, while others have chapters that are more complex and take time to understand. But if he's worth it, you'll find a way to read between the lines."

A smile flickers on my lips and I nod. "That's one way to put it."

But her words resonate with me.

Adam is definitely a book with hidden chapters ... but *so am I.*

Grandma gives me a knowing nod as I step away, phone in hand.

I head upstairs to my apartment and take a seat on my couch while I dial Lily. My stomach twists itself into knots with each ring.

"Hi, Lily, it's Carlie." My voice quivers slightly as she picks up and I have no idea why.

"Carlie, thank God," Lily's voice is tinged with urgency. "Have you seen what's happening on Adam's Instagram?"

My heart skips a beat and my stomach full-on plummets. Instagram hasn't been overly kind to us.

Did someone find out we were both at Nocté?

"No, what's going on?" I breathe, clutching my phone close.

"It's a mess. There are all these rumors swirling around about how he's been using you to kickstart his new fitness biz. Now people are saying that he went to Jillian's place this morning, trying to get back with her, or something. Were they dating?" Lily's words come out in a rush, each one like a blow to my chest. "That's what Anna was trying to text before you left. Had I known …"

I feel a cold chill run down my spine.

No, that can't be true …

"But … he was with me last night." The words are barely a whisper, a plea for this not to be true.

"I know, and that's why I'm worried about you," Lily says softly. "There's something else, Carlie. I wouldn't have believed that he was over there, but I guess Jillian posted a photo of Adam at her door this morning with a really nasty caption."

My fingers tremble as I open Instagram. Part of me is glad that I keep off social media so I can focus on writing —not that it's been going well lately. The other part is kicking myself after the last time.

He's been posting about our workouts and my progress. I should have been following Adam's IG so I can keep tabs on things. If for no other reason than to protect myself from being blindsided like this.

I scroll through Adam's profile. It's a sea of pictures of him, of his new workout routine at home, and images of the logo he's been working on for Foxx Fitness. Then, there are the few Reels and images of our workouts together.

There are comments everywhere claiming he's just using me as a great before and after to launch Foxx Fitness. Some are just fucking rude—saying he's a player —and it's obvious based on his dating history.

I click over to someone else's profile—a conspiracy

post, by the looks of it, but I can't seem to stop myself. It's a collage of his recent dating history. There are fit, muscled women with big boobs and legs for days. They're all blond and perfect and ... *nothing like me.*

I think I'm going to be sick.

"Carlie, are you there?" Lily asks, her voice tentative.

I swallow hard, switching back to Adam's profile. "Yeah, I'm still here."

But my gaze snags on Jillian's comment under a photo of the two of us after a workout.

Way to take one for the team. She's a walking disaster.

It's vindictive—a clear jab meant to hurt.

What the fuck did I ever do to her?

Unless ...

Were they together?

Panic claws at my insides and I tap on her profile.

"Do you need me to come over?" Lily asks, breaking through my inner turmoil.

But I can't take my eyes off of it—her post.

There, in stark clarity, Adam is standing at Jillian's door, the timestamp glaringly clear.

The caption cuts deep:

When your ex shows up unannounced wanting to rekindle

things after slumming it for weeks ... How pathetic. #MovedOn

I stare at the screen, a potent mixture of hurt and confusion swirling inside me.

I mean, I know I hid the truth about our night at Nocté, but ... *this*. This is some next-level shit.

Was everything he said, everything we shared, just a lie?

Do I even know him?

The questions pound in my head like a relentless drumbeat. I thought I knew Adam—thought there was something real between us. But now, all of a sudden, everything I thought about him is up in the air.

The room spins around me. "Lily, I ... I don't understand. Why would he do this?"

"I don't know, Carlie. But maybe there's an explanation. You need to talk to Adam and find out the truth. You know how shit like this can get blown way out of proportion."

I nod, even though she can't see me. "Yeah, I need answers. Thanks, Lily."

We end the call, and I sit there, numb.

The man I thought I was starting to know, *to trust,* is wrapped up in a scandal that paints him in a completely different light. The Adam I thought I knew seems like a mirage, fading away under the harsh light of these revelations.

Doubts cloud my mind, each one a haunting question about who Adam really is.

Has he just been playing me? Is he in cahoots with Jillian?

Or is there another side to this story—a chapter in his book that I haven't read yet?

I close the Instagram app, feeling like the ground beneath me is crumbling.

But deep down, something doesn't add up.

The Adam I've been with doesn't match the man in those posts—the man Jillian is painting him to be.

I close my eyes and breathe. A part of me clings to the hope that there's more to the story than these damaging posts.

God, I'm so confused.

My phone buzzes again, jolting me from my thoughts.

It's a text from Adam, but not what I expect. There's an urgency in his words that I haven't seen before.

> Carlie, there's so much I need to explain. I know you're not into social, but I need you to watch my Instagram live in 10 minutes.

My heart nearly catapults from my chest.

An Instagram live? What is he planning to say?

My curiosity battles with my fear. I want to know what's going on, but I don't want to look like a fool again. I don't think my heart could take it.

I reply, anxiety and anticipation threading through each word.

I'll be watching. But we still need to talk afterward.

As I send the message, the reality of our situation sinks in.

Adam is about to publicly address the chaos, maybe even reveal his side of the story. And after that, we need to talk.

We both have things we need to get out in the open.

He responds.

I agree. We do.

I settle onto the couch, my gaze fixed on my phone. The world outside falls away as I wait for Adam's live video to start.

My stomach knots with hope and dread. This could be the moment that changes everything between us.

The seconds tick by, each one laden with expectation.

Then, my phone lights up with a notification.

Adam is live.

CHAPTER 31

Adam

I tap the 'Live' button on Instagram and my heart nearly gallops straight out of my chest.

The need to set the record straight—to lay out my truth for Carlie, and whoever else is watching—feels vital.

It's my lifeline to a future I want to have a chance at.

"Hey, everyone," I begin, forcing my voice to remain steady, despite feeling anything but. "There's been a lot of talk about me lately. Rumors about using someone special to kickstart my fitness business. But I'm here to lay out the truth."

A car honks loudly behind me, nearly making me jump out of my skin. I shake it off, trying to ignore the city noises, focusing on what needs to be said.

"Those who know me, know I value honesty and integrity—both in my personal life and at the gym. This situation blowing up on my feed—the bullshit being said —it's all been twisted into something it's not."

Taking a deep breath, I address the heart of the matter. "To those spreading and believing these rumors, *shame on you*. The woman you've seen with me is working hard on herself—*for herself*—just like I am with my potential business when, or if, I launch it. And right now, I have a non-compete clause I'm respecting from my previous employer. So, there *is* no Foxx Fitness. Not yet. Carlie and I—we're partners in this and rooting each other on. To the rest of you, we should be supporting each other, not tearing each other down at the first sight of blood."

I let the words sink in, hoping they resonate with my audience. Then, I focus on the most crucial part of my message. "Carlie, if you're watching, I need you to know that you mean more to me than a business strategy. Our time together has been incredible. Hell, it's more than that. You've become so important to me ... more than I ever expected."

My heart hammers in my chest as I continue. "I'm sorry for this drama—for the chaos. But please know, everything being said is nonsense. Because the truth is ..." I swallow hard, realizing I had no intention of saying this on Instagram of all places, but it needs to be said anyway. "I'm falling for you. *Hard.*"

When the words escape my lips, I release the breath I didn't realize I'd been holding so hard onto. "We need to talk—and I hope we can do that now. I'm outside your door, praying you'll let me in."

The comments are going nuts as I end the live session, but I can't bring myself to care or even read a single one. Instead, I lower my phone, and my entire soul feels exposed.

I've laid it all out there for Carlie, and now, it's time for the moment of truth.

I approach her door with my heart lodged in my throat and press the doorbell.

After a few excruciating moments, the door swings open, and there she stands, her expression a complex mix of surprise and guarded emotion as she says, "Adam, that was—"

Before she can finish, the door on the left swings open, and out hobbles Carlie's grandma. "Well, well, look who's back. We must be making quite the impression on you."

Despite wanting desperately to get Carlie alone, I chuckle. "Yeah, you could say that."

"You here to see Carlie, I assume? Or did you just miss my delightful company? Because my door is this one on the left." She winks at me.

Carlie shoots her grandma a brief, exasperated look before turning back to me, her eyes searching mine. "We need to talk."

I nod in agreement. "Yes, we do. I'm here to explain everything."

Carlie hesitates for a moment, then steps aside, motioning for me to enter.

As I walk past her, I catch a glimpse of her grandmother giving me an enthusiastic two thumbs up—a silent gesture of support that somehow eases a bit of the tension in my chest.

We walk upstairs and when I'm standing in Carlie's apartment, the tension is palpable.

So many emotions play across Carlie's face as she turns to look at me. I can tell my Instagram Live hit a nerve, but I'm not sure if it's good or bad.

"Watching you …" Carlie starts, her voice trailing off. She takes a deep breath, as if gathering her thoughts. "It was … *a lot.* Seeing you put everything out there, it's just —" A humorless laugh escapes her lips. "Leave it to Instagram to turn our love story into a reality TV show."

"Look, I know it's weird. I didn't know how else to get things across," I admit, crossing the space between us so I can hold her hands in mine.

"What I don't understand is … if you're …" She shakes her head, her green eyes full of pain, unlike anything I've seen before. "Why did you go to Jillian's?"

I blink back in surprise. "How'd—?"

"She posted it," Carlie responds matter-of-factly.

Of course, she fucking did.

I shake my head. "The rumors—all of this bullshit— it's *because* of Jillian. She started it all. I went there to put her on notice."

"That's not how she put it," Carlie says, her voice barely above a whisper as she drops my hands and hugs herself tightly.

"I'll bet." I huff a humorless laugh.

What a fucking bitch.

Carlie's eyes are glossy when her gaze connects with mine again. "You two were a thing?"

I take a breath, feeling a chilly shift in the air. I never

told her that I dated Jillian and maybe I should have done it before now.

"Yeah, we were. A long time ago," I admit, my gaze dropping to the floor. "But it ended badly. She cheated and I— Look, I never wanted any of that to spill over into ... *this*. Into us."

Carlie's eyes search mine, looking for something I can't quite decipher. "I didn't even know about all the Instagram drama until Lily called me an hour ago. It was like being hit by a truck I didn't see coming. Then, again when I realized—"

I run a hand through my hair, tugging at the strands. "Wait, you didn't know about the Instagram situation? Then why did you leave without saying goodbye? I woke up and you were just ... *gone*."

"Adam, I ..." Carlie hesitates, her voice wavering as she takes a step back. It's clear she's wrestling with something deep, something she's not sure she can share.

I reach out, my hand hovering in the space between us. "Carlie, whatever it is, you can tell me. After all of this bullshit, it's the least I can do."

She bites her lip, a storm of emotions crossing her face. Finally, she looks up at me, her expression reflecting a mixture of fear and resolve. "It's just ... *I got scared.*"

"Scared of what?" I prod gently, trying to bridge the distance between us. Hating how far apart we are right now.

With a half-hearted chuckle, she shrugs slightly. "I mean, facing my fears is not exactly my strong suit. I usually just write characters who are braver than me."

Her attempt at humor doesn't fully mask the genuine concern in her eyes, but it's so Carlie—using wit to deflect her vulnerability.

I shake my head. "Carlie, I swear to you, it's not like that. Everything I said on the Live, everything I feel for you—*it's real.*"

Reaching out, I run my knuckles across her cheekbone.

Her eyes close and she nods slowly, but I can tell there's still something she's holding back.

"There's more, isn't there?" I ask, searching her face for a clue.

Carlie takes a deep breath, looking as if she's about to be sick. But just as she's about to speak, her gaze drifts to the coffee table—to the envelope identical to the one I received from Nocté.

My heart skips a beat.

"That envelope ..." I start, my voice trailing off. A realization hits me like a freight train—a connection I hadn't allowed myself to really think about or believe. "Carlie, were you ... at Nocté?"

The question hangs in the air, heavy with implications.

If it was her ...

For a moment, neither of us speaks. Then, she nods slowly, her eyes not leaving mine.

"Yes, Adam, I was at Nocté. With *you.*"

A torrent of emotions washes over me—surprise, confusion, but most of all, an overwhelming sense of connection. The pieces of a puzzle I didn't even know I was solving fall into place.

This is why I was expelled from the Upper Tier.

She *is* the woman.

But how?

"Carlie, that night ... But you were so different ..."

Her expression shifts—a combination of vulnerability and relief washing over her face. "I was there, incognito, I guess. I needed to ... I don't know, escape for a while. Be someone else for the night. It was all role-play."

I take a step back, my mind racing to align this new information with everything I thought I knew.

Hell, I'd even wondered—looking for that birthmark on her clavicle.

Only, by the time I actually had the chance to see it, I'd completely let go of that fantasy.

A faint smile tugs at the corners of her mouth. "That night was just supposed to be a night of freedom. Something to get me away from all the complications of my real life. Being cheated on—it isn't fun."

"It's not," I agree, reaching out, and gently cupping her face in my hands. "Carlie, don't you see? That night, that connection, it was *real*. It wasn't just some random encounter. It was us, being drawn to each other, even when we didn't realize it. Those stupid, past experiences —they brought us together."

Her eyes are glistening with unshed tears as she leans into my touch.

"I know," she whispers. "I should have told you when

I realized. But it scared me, Adam. The intensity of it all. I was afraid of what it meant. What you'd think of me."

I brush a tear from her cheek with my thumb. "It means that we're meant to be, Carlie. That no matter how we try to fight it or deny it, we're drawn to each other. Our paths are intertwined."

Carlie's eyes sparkle with a mix of tears and mirth as she lets out a soft, incredulous laugh. "You're making it sound like fate," she says, her voice carrying a playful undertone.

"Isn't it?" I ask, my heart in my voice. "One night together at Nocté, only for us to find each other again on our own ... It's more than just coincidence."

She raises an eyebrow, a hint of her usual playful humor returning. "So, are we living in a rom-com novel now? I should start taking notes for my next book. Maybe I'll be able to get past my writer's block."

There's that humor of hers again.

The realization that Carlie and I have been connected in more ways than I knew hits me with the force of a tidal wave. Everything we've done—the ways we've been intimate.

"God, everything makes so much more sense now," I say, unable to hide the awe in my voice. "But I still don't understand. If you knew, why didn't you tell me?"

"I haven't known long. But I didn't know what to do," she admits. "I was afraid of how you'd react—of what it would mean for ... whatever this is between us. I mean, you said it yourself, I'm not the woman you spent the night with at Nocté. I was afraid you'd want her—*not me.*"

"No, that's where you're wrong." I step closer, closing the gap between us, and gently lifting her chin so she's looking at me. "Carlie, that woman you were that night is still a part of who you are. She's at the core of you—the woman you want to be. You just embraced her."

A small smile floats to her lips. "You think?"

"I *know*," I say, brushing her chin with my thumb. "Last night ... You blew my mind. Hell, I should have known, come to think of it."

"Why?" she asks breathlessly.

"Because there was only one other woman that made me feel the way you did last night. But as it turns out, it was the *same woman*," I huff a laugh. "Knowing this ... it doesn't change how I feel about you. If anything, it makes me feel closer to you."

A tear escapes her eye, and I brush it away with my thumb.

"We've both been hiding parts of ourselves, but it's time to stop. Let's be open with each other—no more secrets," I whisper.

Carlie nods, a small smile breaking through her tears. "No more secrets."

CHAPTER 32

Carlie

S itting on the small loveseat on the back deck of my apartment, I gaze out at the afternoon sky. Adam sits beside me, a fuzzy lap blanket thrown across us both.

There's a coolness in the air today, but there's also a calm that wasn't here before Adam's Instagram Live confession—and then revelation about our connection.

Even the birds seem happier.

His presence is a comforting constant in the whirlwind of emotions and revelations that have become my life. I can hardly believe how hauntingly similar to a romance novel my life has become.

It's almost laughable.

Adam takes my hand, his touch grounding me back to the present. "We've been through a helluva lot the past few weeks, haven't we?"

"That's putting it mildly. It feels more like a hurricane penned by a writer with a flair for melodrama," I quip, a smirk playing on my lips.

The side of his lips tilt upward. "Yeah, there's definitely some melodrama mixed in there."

"Adam …" I begin, turning to face him. I need to get this final piece off my chest. "For what it's worth, I really had no idea you were the man from Nocté when we first met. I didn't mean to lie—or take advantage of you."

His eyebrows shoot into his hairline. "You think you took advantage of me?"

"Didn't I?" I ask, my heartbeat thumping unevenly.

He shakes his head. "I mean, that's not the way I see it. We were both consenting adults, Carlie."

"Yeah, but I didn't tell you what I knew when I—" I shake my head. "I should have."

Adam nods in agreement. "Yeah, you should have."

I frown, wishing I could go back in time and have a do-over. "I'm sorry."

"It's okay. I forgive you." He nudges me with his shoulder, then laughs. "On the upside, we get three shots at our first time."

My eyebrows tug in and I shake my head. "What?"

His grin is enormous. "The first time was as strangers. The second time, we weren't on the same page. Next time, we start all over, knowing fully what we're getting ourselves into."

My heart nearly trips over itself.

There will be a third, first time.

I can't help but laugh. "Something to look forward to."

"Indeed," he agrees with a huge smirk. "When did you know? Or guess?"

Instantly, my mind flashes back to that first kiss—to the way he smelled and the electric current that rushed through me. It was a shock, to be sure.

"Our first official date," I admit, biting down on the side of my lip. "I mean, I didn't know *for sure*—but that's when I seriously wondered. There was something in the way you kissed—the way you smelled."

"When did you know for sure?" he presses, rubbing his warm palm over the top of my thigh.

His stormy gray eyes track my movement as I itch behind my right ear. "Last night."

"So, definitely not on the same page." He huffs a soft laugh. "Truth?"

My gaze flicks to his and I nod.

"Before your first session at St. Mary's, I was looking for you," he whispers, his gaze dropping to our laps.

"What do you mean?" My eyebrows tug in as I watch him struggle for words.

His tongue flicks at his lower lip as he continues, "Every time I saw a woman with red hair—I realized I was holding my breath, wishing ... Hell, I was *hoping* to run into the woman from Nocté—I was searching for *you*. Even though I knew I shouldn't. Even though it would mean being kicked out of the club."

"Why?" I ask, drawn into every word.

His eyebrows flicker as he sorts through his thoughts. "Because there was something in the way we connected that night. And I'm not just talking about the sex, either. Even though that was—" His sigh is utter contentment.

I can't help but grin, knowing that whatever I did—whatever *we* did—impacts him this way.

"When you walked into the gym that first time, Carlie I swear, my heart stopped. I think, maybe, a part of me knew," he whispers. "I was just too afraid to believe it."

I shake my head. "How could you possibly know? I had my hair up and I was a basket case. I was nothing like—"

I stop short, realizing I almost said *I was nothing like Zoey.*

Again, he chuckles under his breath. "You definitely weren't what I was expecting—but I kept finding myself searching..." he reaches out, brushing my hair over my shoulder and pulling back the neck of my shirt, *"for this."*

I inhale a sharp breath as he presses a kiss to my clavicle.

He'd been searching for my birthmark in the same way I was looking for his tattoo.

Part of me wants to shy away from his touch, but if there's one person I want to see all of me, it's him.

"I've always hated my birthmark. I try to keep it hidden as much as possible," I confess, watching him as he traces it.

He drops my shirt, staring deeply into my eyes. Questions are lingering in his but instead of putting words to any of them, he leans forward, brushing his lips to mine.

The kiss is slow, and sensual, and whisks all of my thoughts away with the summer breeze.

When he finally pulls back, I'm dizzy and breathless

and could totally be talked into round three with the right prompting.

"Don't ever hide from me. Not anymore," he whispers, his voice husky. "Got it?"

Silently, I nod, still feeling the lingering touch of his lips.

The intensity in his eyes anchors me to the moment —to the reality of how deeply we're connected.

Maybe he's right.

Maybe this is fate.

Because there's a vulnerability in his gaze—a raw honesty that makes everything else seem inconsequential.

I am *so* lucky.

Lucky Adam's the type of man who can forgive me for keeping the truth from him.

Lucky to be sitting here with him now.

Lucky to have found him at all.

Adam gently tugs a strand of my hair, his voice soft yet filled with emotion. "Carlie, since that night at Nocté, there's been this unspoken understanding between us. It's like we've been dancing around our past, afraid to step on each other's toes."

I let out a small laugh, despite the seriousness of his words. "More like I've been clumsily stepping *on* your toes."

He shakes his head, a smile touching his lips. "No, you've been finding your rhythm. And I've been amazed watching you."

The warmth in his words washes over me, filling me with a sense of belonging and purpose. He and I share a hurtful truth—we've both had exes break our hearts by sleeping with other people. It's how we were invited to Nocté in the first place. If anyone knows the kind of pain that causes, it's him.

I take a deep breath, hoping he understands what I need to tell him. "Adam, after being cheated on, I never thought I'd find my groove again. My ex—his words and actions cut deep and I've been hiding behind my fears, letting them dictate my steps for a long time."

"Carlie," Adam begins, but I press a finger to his lips.

"Let me finish," I whisper. When he nods, I continue, "But then ... there was you. That night at Nocté, you made me feel like the sexiest woman on the planet."

"That's because you are—"

I pin him with a *'get real'* look but press on. "Then, at the gym—both at St. Mary's and your place—you made me feel strong, capable, and beautiful. You've given me confidence I didn't realize I could have. I seriously don't know what I did to deserve this—*deserve you.*"

Adam's hand squeezes mine gently, reassuringly. "You didn't have to do anything to deserve this, Carlie. It's not about deserving. It's about two people finding each other at the right time. It's about connection, growth, and maybe a little bit of destiny thrown in." He winks at me.

I can't help but feel overwhelmed by his words, by the sincerity in his eyes. "There's that destiny thing again, huh? I used to think that was just a convenient plot device in romance novels. Now, I'm not so sure. But if this were a book, we'd be at the climactic final chapters, where the heroine realizes her own strength."

Adam chuckles, squeezing my hand gently. "And the hero realizes he's head over heels for the heroine?"

"Obviously," I say, rolling my eyes playfully.

Adam grins broadly, the sunlight reflecting in his eyes. "And what about the heroine? Is she smitten?"

"Oh, she's totally head over heels, too," I admit, my heart thumping loudly in my chest. "But there's something else she needs to do before she can fully embrace this new chapter."

Adam's expression turns curious. "What's that?"

I hesitate, gathering my thoughts. "She needs to confront her past. Face the demons that have haunted her, so she can truly move forward with the man of her dreams."

He narrows his eyes as I pause, feeling a sudden seriousness settle over me.

The truth is, I've been feeling like a character in someone else's story for too long. I've been pushed around and made to feel *less-than*.

No more.

Not from Michael. Not from Instagram.

And definitely not from Jillian.

Her narrative—the one where I'm the clumsy, hopeless sidekick ends now.

That's not who I am.

Not anymore.

Hell, maybe I never have been.

I look at Adam, my resolve strengthening. "I need to

confront Jillian myself. It's like I'm standing at the edge of my own plot twist, and it's time I take control of the storyline."

Adam's expression is a mix of admiration and concern. "Are you sure about this? It's not going to be easy. She's a master at twisting things."

I nod, determination coursing through me. "I know. But it's necessary or she'll just keep trying to break us up. I've let her, and others like her, define me and dictate what I get to have. But not anymore. This is me, Carlie, author of her own life, about to rewrite a wrong. It's kind of empowering, actually."

Adam wraps an arm around me, pulling me close. "Then I'm with you. Plot twists and all."

CHAPTER 33

Adam

This seems to be a new trend.

Confronting Jillian.

Driving to St. Mary's gym, I steal glances at Carlie sitting beside me. She's quiet, her gaze fixed on the passing cars. I can almost hear the jumble of thoughts in her head as the past and present collide and we approach our destination.

I think about the stories she's shared with me—the stark contrast between her sessions with me and those with Jillian. She once described Jillian as a 'militaristic drill sergeant.' That's a far cry from the approach I've always tried to take with her.

Hell, with everyone.

A part of me still can't even fathom what was going through Jillian's head when she acted that way. Sure, she'd always been more focused on appearances, but truthfully, that made her a good trainer. She could spot the places on a client that could be improved.

But she was never mean about it—at least, that I knew of.

Until Carlie.

Whether it's a solitary incident or an epidemic, I don't know.

All I know is that the woman beside me deserved better.

I've seen her struggle, but also grow. Her determination and resilience have blossomed with each session we've had together. It's a transformation that goes beyond physical strength, though.

It touches the very core of who she is.

"Hey," I say, breaking the silence and reaching out to take her hand in mine, "remember how far you've come since those first sessions at the gym? You've grown in ways Jillian could never understand."

She turns to me, a flicker of that fierce determination I've come to admire shining in her eyes. "I know, Adam. It's just ... facing her, it's like facing a ghost of who I used to think I was. It's weird. And terrifying. And ... oddly exhilarating."

"And you're going to show that ghost just how much you've changed," I assure her, squeezing her hand gently. "Jillian's part in your story ... it's over. Today, you close that chapter."

Carlie nods, a resolute expression settling over her features. "We *both* do."

"Definitely," I agree with a nod.

As we pull into the parking lot, the enormity of what we're about to do hits me. This isn't just any gym—it's a place where people come to heal and to improve themselves.

And that's exactly what Carlie has been doing—in more ways than one.

We get out of the car and walk towards the hospital entrance. The automatic doors slide open, ushering us into the familiar, sterile scent of the hospital—a blend of cleanliness and medicine that's oddly comforting. No matter how long I've been away, there will always be a part of me that feels like I'm coming home here.

Walking through the long corridors, we pass by busy nurses and doctors, patients moving slowly with their IV stands, and visitors carrying flowers and gifts. The soft buzz of conversations and the occasional beep of medical equipment create a backdrop to our own silent determination.

Carlie's steps are measured, her eyes taking in the surroundings. I can tell she's drawing strength from the resilience on display all around us. This place, a sanctuary of healing and hope, seems to embolden her.

Silently, we make our way to the gym—located in a wing of the hospital dedicated to physical therapy and wellness. As we pass through the threshold, the atmosphere changes.

The clinical ambiance of the hospital gives way to the energetic environment of the gym. The clanking of weights, the rhythmic hum of treadmills, and the muted thuds of medicine balls create a symphony of exertion and perseverance.

Pausing just inside the door, I notice Carlie's hands are shaking slightly.

I reach over and pull her into a hug. "Hey, you sure you're up for this?"

Carlie looks up at me, her green eyes flickering. "Yeah, I'm sure. It's something I need to do. It feels … *important*."

I nod, understanding her need for closure. "I'm here for you, every step of the way. You know that, right?"

She gives me a small, tentative smile. "I do. And having you here … it means everything to me."

Leaning over, I place a kiss on her temple and whisper, "So fucking brave."

Carlie pauses for a moment at the entrance, taking a deep breath.

As she stands taller, it becomes clear to me she's no longer the woman who shrinks away from confrontation. She's someone ready to stand her ground.

"Remember," I whisper to her as we pause just outside the main gym space, "no matter what happens in there, I'm proud of you."

Carlie nods, her gaze fixed on Jillian. "Thanks, Adam. That means a lot."

Again, I can't help but kiss her. My lips brush her forehead and she sighs into my touch.

We walk into the gym together, the familiar sounds and smells wrapping around us. I can feel the tension radiating from Carlie as her eyes zero in on Jillian across the room, her back turned to us, confidently instructing a client.

Carlie squares her shoulders and rolls her neck, a physical manifestation of her mental preparation. Her transformation from the tentative, self-doubting woman I first met to the confident, self-assured person she is at this moment is a palpable thing.

We're not just walking through a gym—we're walking into a moment of reckoning.

"Ready?" I ask softly.

She nods, releasing my hand to stand alone. This conversation—it's her battle to fight, but she knows I'm right there with her. A silent pillar of strength for her to lean on.

Jillian's smile is all carefully orchestrated personal trainer charm, but her eyes narrow when she sees the two of us. They zero in on Carlie's determined stance and a barely veiled sneer flickers to her face. Without even a moment's hesitation, she walks over to us.

"Carlie, Adam, what brings you here ... *together?*" she asks, her tone patronizing.

I can see in the shadows that flicker in her eyes, she wasn't expecting a united front.

Hell, she probably wasn't expecting *any* front.

She probably thought her BS would break us apart.

Carlie doesn't miss a beat, though. "I'm here to close a chapter, Jillian. One where the antagonist gets her comeuppance." Her voice is steady, her writer's mind turning this confrontation into a climactic scene.

I chuckle under my breath, sliding my hands into my pockets, and looking forward to however this thing plays out.

"What are you even on about?" Jillian, as expected, rolls her eyes. "Please, spare me your dramatics, Carlie, and talk like a normal person."

Carlie steps forward, undeterred. Her nostrils flare and her hands clench into fists at her side. "This isn't drama, Jillian. This is you, being called out on your web of lies. Like any poorly written villain, you underestimated the hero."

Jillian laughs, a sharp, derisive sound. "And let me guess, you think *you're* the hero in this story."

Carlie's eyes flash emerald. "Every story has its hero, Jillian. Sometimes they're hidden in the shadows, but they always emerge. And when they do, villains like *you* fall."

Irritation flickers across Jillian's face. She's not used to being spoken to like this. It's only a matter of time before she lashes out. I take a step closer to Carlie, ready for it.

"You're delusional," Jillian spits out. "This is real life, not a silly novel. God, you're such a loser. I can see why the two of you were drawn together. You definitely deserve each other's crazy. So, good luck with that."

Jillian's eyes flit to me and all I can do is huff a laugh. If she thinks that comeback is going to hurt either one of us, she's the delusional one.

Carlie's face hardens, her voice cutting through the gym's ambient noise. A couple of gym-goers stop their reps to gawk as she takes a step into Jillian's space and says, "Let's talk about real life, Jillian. Like how you treated me when you were my trainer. Remember all the ways you kept trying to make me feel small? Or the times you told me I was too hopeless to get fit? That was you trying to break me—to project your own insecurities onto me."

Jillian's smirk fades, replaced by a look of contempt. "You were a waste of my time, Carlie. Clumsy, incapable of ..."

Carlie interrupts her, her voice rising with conviction. "No, Jillian. I was a project you failed at because you were too consumed with your own jealousy. I didn't know about your history with Adam at the time—but *you* did. You saw a potential relationship happening between us and you tried to stifle it. But here I am, stronger, not because of you, but *in spite* of you. And that relationship you tried to kill off, it's a reality now."

Jillian scoffs, her voice dripping with sarcasm. "Oh, please. You're giving yourself too much credit. You're—"

Carlie cuts her off again, her tone unwavering. "Oh, and let's not forget how you spread those lies about Adam using me for his business, then concocted stories about him crawling back to you. That's the kind of plot twist you see in cheap thrillers, not in this *'real life'* you seem so fond of. Your heart isn't just black, Jillian—it's a void. A place where empathy and decency go to die."

Jillian's face turns a deep shade of red, her fury palpable. "You think standing here makes you something special? You're *nothing*, Carlie."

The tension in the gym is a physical thing, with bystanders stealing glances at the unfolding drama.

Carlie's voice, however, carries a note of finality as she

huffs a humorless laugh. "This is where your part in my story ends, Jillian. You're just another lesson along my journey. My only wish is no one else would ever have to deal with you. You're not fit to train anyone."

"I hate to break it to you, but I'm good at my job. Just because you couldn't trade your two left feet for ones that work, doesn't change that fact. So, if you even think about fucking me over—I'll *bury* you." Jillian's face is the epitome of rage as she spits out, "God, you're such a b—"

Her venomous words are cut short by a gasp from the crowd.

We all turn to see an older gentleman, distinguished and clearly important, his eyes fixed on Jillian with a mix of shock and disapproval. He's wearing a polo shirt with the gym's logo and "Board Member" embroidered beneath it.

Oh, shit. *Mr. Richards.*

Jillian's eyes widen in panic.

Mr. Richards steps forward, his voice stern. "Is this how you represent our gym, Jillian? By belittling our members and having a heated argument in front of everyone?"

Jillian stammers, trying to regain her composure, but her usual charm is failing her now. "I ... Mr. Richards, it's not what it looks like. I was just—"

"I've heard enough. Your behavior is unacceptable," he says, pointing to the door. "We'll discuss this in the conference room. *Now.*"

Jillian's face turns pale, her usual confidence evaporating. When she glances at us, her expression is a mixture of hatred and defeat.

Carlie lets out a jagged breath and turns to me with a triumphant sparkle in her eyes. "Looks like the villain's arc just ended."

I chuckle under my breath. That's one way of putting it.

Carlie steps back, letting Jillian and Mr. Richards pass. In the movement, she bumps into a gym-goer walking by with a chocolate protein shake in his hand.

The collision sends the shake flying right onto Jillian's back as she's ushered away by Mr. Richards. It sticks to her designer gym gear, looking like a bathroom disaster gone terribly wrong.

The gym erupts in a cacophony of gasps and stifled laughter. Carlie's eyes widen in horror—and then amusement.

"Well, I guess that's the messy climax this story deserved," she mutters under her breath.

Jillian whirls around, her shriek echoing through the gym. The sight of her, covered in chocolate protein shake, looking both furious and ridiculous, draws the attention of anyone who missed the earlier confrontation.

"This is outrageous!" she yells, pointing an accusatory finger at Carlie. "You did that on purpose."

"It was an accident." Carlie, for a moment, looks mortified. But then, she straightens up, meeting Jillian's fury with a calm defiance. "I'm sorry about the shake, Jillian, but maybe it's a metaphor. Sometimes life throws messy things at you. It's how you handle them that shows your true character."

Jillian's eyes dart around the gym as she realizes she's the center of a scene she can't control.

"You ... you did this on purpose!" she stammers again, trying to wipe the sticky mess off her clothes. When it doesn't work, she whirls on Carlie, giving her a shove.

The gym-goer who accidentally collided with Carlie steps in, pushing Jillian back before I can intervene. "Like the lady said, it was an accident, Jillian."

Jillian looks desperately at Mr. Richards, who's watching the scene with a grim expression. "Mr. Richards, I can explain—"

He holds up a hand, stopping her mid-sentence. "Enough, Jillian. This incident, along with your earlier behavior, is completely unbecoming of our gym's standards. Please, gather your things. You are suspended until the rest of the board can meet to discuss your future here."

Jillian gasps, stumbling after him as the gym slowly returns to its regular buzz of activity. Carlie watches her go with an expression of vindication clear across her face.

I lean closer to Carlie, whispering, "You okay?"

Sighing deeply, she turns to me and grins. "Every good story needs a dramatic ending, right?"

CHAPTER 34

Carlie

I'm still giggling as Adam and I traipse up the front steps to my apartment. The image of Jillian's mortified face is etched in my mind like a bad tattoo.

"That protein shake fiasco"—I muse aloud—"that was comedy gold."

"It definitely was." Adam grins, his eyes dancing with delight. "Her face matched your hair. I mean, who knew embarrassment was that shade of red?"

"Oh, I did." I chuckle. "But it's nice to have someone else sporting it instead of me."

As we reach the top step, there's Grandma Elsie, perched on a deck chair with a tabloid magazine across her lap.

"What's so funny over there, you two?" she asks, her eyes narrowing with the kind of curiosity that could outdo a cat.

"Just gym stuff, Grandma," I say, exchanging a glance with Adam that's brimming with unspoken hilarity.

Now, had we been filming, I'm fairly certain it would have been an instant hit on Instagram. Viral material, for sure.

Maybe then Adam's IG account would have something better to buzz about.

"Sure, gym stuff." Grandma arches a white eyebrow, and a smirk plays on her lips. "Why don't you two come in? I'm about to put the kettle on. I could use a little gossip to break up my day."

"Says the woman who was just reading Star Magazine," I tease, pointing at the tabloid.

She shrugs sheepishly.

Adam gives me a look—that *what do you think?* kind of look—and I shake my head subtly. There's more I need to face and I need to do it before I lose my nerve.

"We'll take a raincheck this time. I promise we'll do dinner soon," I offer with a smile.

Her eyes narrow and her smirk grows. "I get it. Off for some 'alone time'?" She winks so obviously it's like a neon sign. "I'll grab the earplugs then."

"Grandma—" I exclaim, my cheeks instantly burning.

There's embarrassment—and then there's *Grandma-level* embarrassment. Trust her to turn a simple 'no' into a nudge-nudge-wink-wink situation.

I mean, she's not entirely wrong, but still.

"What?" She chuckles sheepishly, clearly pleased with herself before she waves us off. "Go on, now. I'd hate to come between you and some hanky panky."

On that note, I spin on my heel, and reach for my

door. Adam and I escape up the stairs, my laughter now a mixture of amusement and sheer mortification.

"Your grandma is something else," he says, shaking his head.

"She's got a heart of gold but a mouth that could outmatch any sailor," I admit, unlocking my apartment door. "But hey, that's family for you."

"That it is. Brian is constantly and forever trying to find a way to push my buttons. If he can embarrass me doing it, all the better." He chuckles, shaking his head.

"We definitely need to spend more time with your brother," I say, running my hand along his arm and batting my eyelashes.

He just narrows his eyes and harrumphs. However, humor sparkles in his gray irises and I know a part of him would actually like the razzing.

Once inside, I close the door behind us, leaning against it for a moment. The laughter fades, replaced by a fluttering in my stomach.

This is it.

The moment of truth.

Facing Jillian was one thing, but for some reason, this feels harder.

Or maybe more significant.

"Want something to drink?" I ask, more to give my hands something to do than out of hospitality.

Adam shakes his head, his gaze gentle. "I'm good, thanks. Let's just sit and talk."

I nod, leading the way to my couch. Compared to his place, my house isn't anywhere near as sophisticated.

There are books stacked everywhere and there are piles of unfinished manuscripts printed and forgotten in various locations.

I really should clean up, come to think of it.

We sit down, and I'm acutely aware of the space between us, filled with unspoken questions and anticipation.

I tuck a strand of hair behind my ear, a nervous habit I've never been able to kick.

"Adam, there's something I've been wanting to tell you," I start, my voice barely above a whisper. "Something important."

He leans forward, elbows on his knees, as he gives me his full attention. "Okay, I'm all ears."

I take a deep breath, feeling like I'm about to step off a cliff. "It's about that night at the club," I say, my heart racing. "And, well, about me. The *full* me."

His brow furrows slightly, concern flickering in his eyes. "All right." He reaches out, pulling my hands to his. "Is everything okay? Are you okay?"

"Yeah, I'm fine," I respond, nodding a bit too vigorously. "I mean, I will be. It's just—what I'm about to tell you, I've never told anyone. Well, outside of my author friend group, anyway. So, it's kinda weird for me. " I pause, my heart a symphony of erratic beats. "That night at Nocté, I wasn't just pushing my boundaries or trying to move past what my ex did ... Though, that all played its role."

"I get that," he says, watching my every move.

"Well, that night, I was trying to embrace a part of

me that's always been hard for me to embody. It was liberating, scary, and ..." I trail off, searching for the right word.

Adam's grip on my hands tightens reassuringly, encouraging me to continue.

"It was *empowering*," I finally say, meeting his gaze. "I've always written about these strong, sexually confident women. That's my niche. But me, being like them? That was a fantasy. Until that night."

I hold his gaze, hoping that my words convey their meaning.

He nods, his expression a blend of intrigue and support. "Well, I'm shocked. There's more to Carlie than meets the eye. It's almost as if she's a dynamic woman."

I chuckle, his words lightening the tension in my stomach a bit. "Way more, apparently. Which is why I write under a pen name. It's how I express myself freely, without judgments or expectations. I wanted a safe space to explore. You know?"

"I get that, totally," he says, his thumb rubbing gently across the top of my hand and drawing my attention for a moment.

I smile, trying to pull some of his support into myself. "So, not even the Dirty B's—they're my book-club friends—they don't even know this. But I want *you* to know. I want you to know all of me."

He places his warm hand on my cheek. Then, slowly, he bends in, brushing his lips to mine. His kiss is slow and deliberate and takes my breath away.

When we pull apart, he says, "Carlie, whatever you're

about to share, know that it doesn't change how I see you. You're amazing, just as you are. And if you're not ready—"

I take in a deep, steadying breath, bolstered by his words. "Thank you, Adam. That means more than you know." I pause, finding the courage to reveal my secret. "My pen name is Zoey Cummings."

"Zoey Cummings? Wait a minute—I've heard of her."Adam's eyes widen slightly, a look of admiration and surprise mingling on his face. "Your books—they're ... *wow*."

I can't help but laugh, a mix of relief and amusement. "Yeah, *'wow'* is one way to put it. But writing as Zoey, it's been more than just a career. It's been a way for me to explore parts of myself that I've always kept hidden. Parts I was too scared to reveal to the people I surround myself with. So that night, I walked into Nocté with the decision to embody her and her confidence. I wasn't Carlie that night. That's why I was so—*different*."

He squeezes my hands gently, his gaze intense yet full of warmth. "I think it's incredible, Carlie. You've created this whole other world, this persona that's empowered so many. And now, you're embracing that part of yourself in real life."

"You don't think it's weird?" I ask, biting the side of my lip.

He snickers under his breath. "No, not at all. I think it's awesome."

I exhale, feeling a sense of liberation with each word I speak. "That night—it was the first time I truly felt like

Zoey. Because I went there not knowing who I'd end up with—*if anyone*—I was able to be confident, unafraid—in control. I did what I wanted with you without worrying about all the shit I'd normally let clog my mind. And I want to keep feeling that way. Not just in the shadows of a pen name, but in my everyday life. With *you*."

Adam pulls me closer, his voice soft yet firm. "I'm here for all of it, Carlie. For Zoey, for *you*, for every part of your journey. You don't have to hide any part of your-self with me. I find *all* of you sexy. The whole package."

His words wrap around me like a warm blanket, soothing the lingering fears and insecurities. In this moment, I feel seen and accepted in a way I never thought possible.

"We have a lot to explore, you and I," he whispers, his breath warm against my ear.

I smile, leaning into him. "Yes, we do. And I can't wait to start."

The room feels different now, charged with a new energy and understanding. With Adam's support, I feel ready to step into the light, to be more of the woman I am when I'm writing as Zoey Cummings. I want that empowerment not just on the pages of my books, but in the reality of my life.

After a moment of comfortable silence, a thought nags at me, pulling me back to a lingering mystery. My eyes drift to the envelope on the coffee table.

"Adam, there's something else that's been on my mind," I say, sitting up slightly.

He looks at me, curious. "What's up?"

I bite my lip, pondering how to phrase it. "Do you wonder why we got kicked out of Nocté? Like, did they know about us before *we* knew about us?"

He nods slowly, his expression turning thoughtful. "Yeah, I've thought about that, too. It's weird, right?"

I shrug, the mystery of it making my writerly brain go into overdrive. "It kinda feels like they found out. But how? It's not like we were obvious about it. I haven't gone back to Nocté since that night, either. Did ..." I clear my throat, uncomfortable about having to ask. "Have you?"

I hold my breath waiting for his reaction.

When he shakes his head, I exhale.

"No, there was a certain redhead who consumed my time," he says with a smirk.

I grin back at him, my brain still churning out ideas. "Well, then it doesn't make any sense. Unless ..." I trail off, thinking back to the conversation with Lily.

"Unless what?" Adam prompts, leaning in closer.

"Unless someone in our circle spilled," I muse. But there's a part of me that can't see Lily running off to London and tattling.

Maybe they follow Adam on Instagram and put two and two together there?

Adam takes my hand again, giving it a reassuring squeeze. "Well, whatever the reason, it doesn't change anything for us. But yeah, it's intriguing. Nocté's always been synonymous with mystery. Maybe that's part of its allure—the way they want to keep it."

I nod, my thoughts drifting to the elusive figure behind Nocté. "You know, whoever created Nocté, they're not just running a club. From an author's perspective, it's like they're orchestrating an elaborate game, one where the rules are known only to them. It's fascinating."

Adam cocks his head, considering. "I agree. There's something pretty awesome about that place. And to think—that's our origin story."

"Yeah," I say, a grin floating to my lips. "That'll be an interesting one to explain when people ask."

Adam nods, his eyes reflecting a hint of excitement. "We should probably play that one by ear. You know, read the room. Maybe we save the full truth for our close friends. But to everyone else, we met at St. Mary's. Both are technically true."

I lean back and chuckle. "A very good point."

His gaze holds mine, and in that moment, the air between us crackles with unspoken promise. The mystery of Nocté, the exhilaration of my revelations, our past experiences together—it all converges into a palpable tension, ripe with anticipation.

I lean closer, my voice dropping to a whisper. "Speaking of good points ..." I cringe internally at the terrible segue, but my hand finds his, our fingers intertwining. "There's one more adventure I'd like to embark on tonight."

His response is immediate—desire and understanding lighting up his eyes. "Carlie, I'm all in. Whatever you want, wherever this night takes us. I am. All. In."

The room, once filled with the weight of secrets and revelations, now pulses with a different energy—one of desire, intimacy, and the thrill of new beginnings.

Maybe Grandma will get use out of her earplugs after all.

"We've had two unforgettable encounters," I say, a playful challenge in my tone. "Think we can make the third time the charm?"

Adam's smile grows wider, a little hint of mischievousness despite the tender undertone. "With you? I have no doubt."

He stands, offering me his hand, and I take it, letting him pull me to my feet. As I step closer to him, my body tingles with an electric current that needs no words.

I lead him towards the bedroom, my heart thumping for a very different reason than when we first entered my apartment.

The mystery of Nocté and the outside world fades away, leaving only the here and now—a moment of discovery and hopefully, passion.

But most of all, uncharted territory waiting to be explored.

CHAPTER 35

Adam

Here I am, standing in front of Carlie, and oddly enough, it's like I'm truly seeing her for the first time. Her fiery red hair seems to glow in the soft light streaming through the window and each strand tells a story of the wild, passionate woman I've come to know.

Everything about her is breathtaking.

But today, there's something different in her eyes—a depth, or maybe a raw honesty that makes my heart race and my body react instantly.

There's a bit of that wild woman from Nocté shining through but it's mixed with the soft vulnerability I've come to know and love—and that's uniquely Carlie.

"I don't know what it is about you. I've never felt like this before," I confess, my voice barely above a whisper. The words feel heavy yet liberating, carrying all the unspoken emotions I've been holding back for a while now.

Carlie steps closer, her eyes finding mine. "Me too,

Adam. It's like all the masks are gone—all the games put to rest. I can't believe we're here, to be honest."

"Me either," I admit, standing on the threshold of Carlie's bedroom, my heart pounding like it's trying to break free.

A sly grin plays on her lips—it's the same dimpled grin that hooked me the first time I saw her—but tonight, there's a spark in her eyes that tells me this is going to be different.

"So, Mr. Mystery," Carlie teases, her voice a playful melody, "any thoughts on what we should do next?"

Her words are like a siren's call, and I can't help but move towards her. There's an electricity in the air, a current that seems to pull me in her direction.

Carlie is a force of nature, and right now, she's got me completely under her spell.

"I *was* thinking," I start, trying to match her wit, "but I got distracted by a certain redhead, wondering what *she* has in mind."

Carlie laughs, and the sound is like music. She steps closer, her hand reaching out to trace a line down my arm.

"Oh, I have a few ideas," she says, her voice dropping to a whisper that sends shivers down my spine.

This is new territory for us.

Carlie has always been playful, always been the one to crack a joke or lighten the mood. But today, there's an intensity to her playfulness, a determination that's both exhilarating and a little intimidating.

That night at Nocté, I had no reference, nothing to compare her to.

But now ...

She leans in, her breath warm against my ear. "Tonight, Adam, I want to show you just how much fun we can have when we're both on the same page."

And just like that, she's leading me to the bed, her movements confident and fluid.

I wonder if she even realizes it.

Every movement this woman makes sends my pulse racing as much as it sends blood to other extremities. My cock strains against my zipper and all I can think about is ...

How did I get this lucky?

After everything that happened with Jillian, I never thought I'd find this kind of intimacy—this kind of love. I thought I'd go to Nocté for a night of release, maybe a bit of intrigue, and that would be that.

Never in a million years did I anticipate falling ...

Carlie stops moving at the edge of her bed, her eyes holding mine for a moment before she stands on her tiptoes to press her lips to mine.

I sigh into her kiss, settling into the energy of this beautiful redhead and the amazing woman she is.

She runs her hands down the front of my chest, causing shivers to break out across my entire body. I don't know how her touch—even something as benign as that—can make me want her so badly.

All too quickly, she pulls away and the absence of her lips feels like a blow.

"Why are you—?" I begin, opening my eyes.

When they land on her, she's unbuttoning my shirt. Her hands tremble, but the look of determination on her face tells me she's fighting any sense of nerves.

She makes quick work of things and before I know it, my shirt is sliding to the floor. Then, her hands go to my belt, as she undoes it with slow, deliberate movements.

I hold my breath, feeling the brush of her fingertips against my skin and my brain reminds me of the other times she's touched me like this. Suddenly, I want more than anything to get out of these jeans.

However, when her fingers reach my button, I grab hold of her hands.

She glances up, surprised. "Do you not—?"

I chuckle softly. "Of course, I do. But I just want to be even."

She inhales sharply but nods. "Okay."

I bend in, placing my hands on the sides of her face so I can guide her mouth to mine. I need to feel how much she wants this.

She's tentative at first, but as I flick my tongue against her bottom lip, she parts for me with a groan. I sweep my tongue inside, tangling it with hers in a dance that feels both familiar and foreign.

The backs of her fingers press against my abs as she clings to the edge of my jeans like they're a lifeline. I take the opportunity to slide my hands under the hem of her shirt and tug it up her torso.

This time, there's no request for me to close my eyes

and thank god for that—because I have to see it again. I have to know it's real.

She's real.

As her shirt drops to the floor, I brush her hair back from her shoulder and inhale a quick breath because *fuck*.

She's so beautiful.

From the freckles that scatter across her creamy skin to her voluptuous breasts that almost spill over her lacy black bra—there is nothing about her that doesn't turn me on.

I feel her fingers tighten around my waistband as I press a kiss to her birthmark, then flick my tongue across it as I work my way from that place to the crook of her neck and up to her earlobe.

She bends her head backward and her eyes close as I kiss the edge of her jawline and find myself again at her gorgeous lips. Her breaths rise and fall quickly, making her chest heave and drawing my attention to her cleavage.

"You're so fucking hot," I say, unable to hold that thought back.

I smooth my hands over the edges of her breasts, needing to memorize the curves with my palms.

Suddenly, her fingers are undoing my jeans as I reach around to help her out of her bra. By the time it hits the floor, she's tugging me free from my constraints. Her hands wrap around the base of my cock and my eyes just about roll to the back of my head.

"Fuck," I mutter, as I thrust my hands through my

hair and try to stay calm. "I forgot how adept those hands of yours are."

She'd worked me in a very similar way the night at Nocté. I have no idea how many times she had me close to coming that night because I lost count. Totally on edge.

Carlie practically purrs with elation as she drops down before me—a goddess on her knees. "My hands are good, but my tongue is even better."

"Christ," I mutter, my eyes closing as my hands weave their way through her hair. I wrap my fist around it, pulling it into a messy ponytail, so I can get a good look at her in action.

She tugs my jeans and underwear to the floor and her fingertips trace the tattoo just above my cock.

For the first time, I realize that my tattoo must be for her what her birthmark has been for me. In a movement so quick, she presses a kiss against the tattoo. Then, her tongue flicks at it before moving on to the base of my erection.

It pulses involuntarily when her warm breath and the heat of her mouth presses against the tip. She wraps her hands around me, holding me firm as she pumps slowly.

Shit, it takes all of my control not to thrust into her as she flicks her tongue over the sensitive skin. The moisture pooling at the tip clings to her lips as she spreads them open and swallows me whole.

A sound between a growl and a moan escapes through my lips and I hold on tighter to Carlie's hair as she bobs up and down, humming softly as she does so.

The pressure starts to build at the base of my spine and I pull away, knowing she'll get me to come way before I'm ready to concede to that.

"Whoa," I breathe, trying to catch my bearings. "Time to switch."

A smirk plays at her lips and she says, "Afraid I'll get you to come with just my mouth?"

"There's no fear—only *knowing*. Now, get those damn yoga pants off," I demand, picking her up and tossing her to the bed.

She lets out a squeak in surprise but thankfully begins peeling them off of her legs as I kick my jeans off completely.

When we're both fully naked, I prowl forward, forcing her back until her head rests on the pillows. Then, I spread her legs before me like the feast I plan on indulging in.

Now it's her turn to let out a whimper as I press the pad of my middle finger to her clit and circle it slowly. She wiggles, cursing under her breath.

Without stopping the circular motion, I flick my tongue across her slit and she bucks outright. So, I reach out, pressing the palm of my free hand to her pelvis, locking her to the bed. Then, I sweep my tongue inside her, letting her juices flow over my tongue.

She tastes so good.

"Oh my god," she cries out, her words as breathless as I feel.

My dick throbs and I grind my hips into the bed, trying to relieve some of the pressure.

She is so fucking wet.

And it's so fucking hot.

I thrust a finger inside her, pumping it in and out as I lap and suck at her clit, trying to get her to squirm again. She works her hips up and down and I plunge another finger in, only to be rewarded by a gush of fluid that soaks my hand and fills my senses.

"What the hell?" she gasps, trying to bend upright. "I can't believe that just happened."

"So goddamn sexy," I say, needing to be inside her now. I gotta know how it feels.

Getting up on my hands and knees, I run my palms down the insides of her thighs amazed that this incredibly sexy woman is mine.

Mine.

Without the ability to maintain control, I thrust inside her feeling her juices slick and warm against me as I'm fully enveloped in her. She grips me hard, tightening around my cock but so slippery it takes everything in me not to get too excited.

"You know what I'd like to do to you," I say, trying to take my mind off of the way she feels pulsing around me.

"W-what?" she asks between shaky breaths.

"I want to see if I can get you to squirt like that every time," I say, thrusting in and out. My left hand palms her breast and I roll my hips, trying to get her to whimper again.

Her body quakes under mine and she moans loudly as I pinch her nipple. "Oh, fuck. I bet you could ... Keep doing that and I might again. Oh, shit—"

As if on cue, warmth surrounds me and the bed is soaked—I'm soaked. She's soaked.

"Fuck," I moan, reveling in the feeling of it. "So hot."

I love that I can do that to her. That I can turn her on that much.

I tip my hips, trying to hit her G-spot with my swollen head.

She arches her back and her breasts lift, needing my attention. I drop my mouth to one of her nipples, pulling it in and sucking on it.

Her gasp rings in my ears as I smile against her skin and suck again—harder this time. She gropes at my shoulders, her fingertips pressing into my skin as I continue moving in and out of her.

Sex has never felt like this.

It's never been an adventure—an exploration like this.

I can't imagine ever being with anyone else—not after this.

Not after *her.*

"Oh, god, yes," Carlie cries out as I tip again. "Like that—"

I do as she requests, rubbing myself against her as she seizes beneath me. Her body convulses and I can feel her orgasm as it rips through her. She clenches around me and I'm suddenly there, too. Falling right over that edge.

My balls tighten and a jolt of energy rushes up my spine—escaping through me as I spill everything that I am inside her.

Little electric shocks pulse through my shaft, as every

ounce of me stays seated to the hilt. I can't move—can't even *think* of moving right now.

Her fingers grope at my back and it takes all that I am not to collapse from the bliss overload.

"Holy shit. That was ..." Carlie mutters quietly, bliss evident in the tone of her words.

"*Incredible*," I finish for her.

"Incredible," she repeats, a huge smile breaking out across her face, showing off her dimples.

We lie there, basking in the afterglow, our breaths slowly synchronizing. I trace lazy circles on her skin, feeling a contentment I've never known.

The world outside this room, with its complications and chaos, seems miles away.

Just as I'm about to suggest we might need a round two, considering the energy we both still seem to have, there's a knock at the door. We freeze, our eyes locking in a mix of surprise and slight horror. The knock comes again, more insistent this time.

Carlie sits up, pulling the sheet up to cover herself, a flush of embarrassment crossing her cheeks. "Who on earth could that be?" she whispers, her voice a mix of amusement and apprehension.

I shrug, equally baffled, and watch as she slips out from under me, pulls on a robe, and tiptoes to the front door.

Then, I hear a muffled voice, unmistakably her grandmother's, but I can't hear what they're discussing.

Carlie's responses are hushed, tinged with a laughter she's trying to suppress. There's a brief exchange and then Carlie is back in the room, a hand covering her mouth to stifle her giggles.

"What did she want?" I ask, propping myself up on my elbows, now under the sheets.

Carlie closes the door gently and turns to me, her eyes dancing with suppressed laughter. "Grandma needed her reading glasses. She left them in the living room when she was reading my new manuscript." Her voice breaks into a chuckle. "And then, as if it was an afterthought, she added, 'And don't worry dear, I didn't hear some very loud moaning or headboard banging. But we might want to have the place inspected for ghosts.'"

I burst out laughing, the sound filling the room. It's the kind of laughter that comes from deep within, born out of a mix of relief and the sheer absurdity of the situation.

Carlie jumps back onto the bed, her robe slipping off her shoulders as she crawls towards me.

"Which basically means she heard everything," she whispers, brushing a hand across her forehead.

"Well, we weren't very quiet," I reply, pulling her into my arms.

"I know I wasn't, my god." She chuckles, scooting closer to me. "And we definitely need to change these sheets now. I can't believe you made me—" Again, her cheeks turn a bright red.

"I said it before and I'll say it again ... That was sexy as fuck," I say, brushing a strand of hair from her face.

She smiles sheepishly but relaxes into the crook of my arm. As we lay there, still entwined, the room once again fills with a comfortable silence. It's a perfect end to a day that's been anything but ordinary—one that's solidified everything I feel about this incredible woman in my arms.

I kiss the top of her head, a sense of completeness washing over me. "You know, your grandma's pretty cool."

Carlie looks up at me, her eyes sparkling. "She's one of a kind. Just like us."

As we settle down, wrapped in each other's arms, I think about how life has a funny way of throwing surprises at you—some in the form of unexpected encounters at a club, and others as a reminder from a grandmother that love, laughter, and a bit of embarrassment are all part of the journey.

This is our journey, Carlie's and mine. And I wouldn't change a single, absurd, beautiful part of it.

Epilogue

CARLIE - 18 MONTHS LATER

I'm standing behind a table stacked with copies of my debut rom-com, "One Night Stand-Off," a title that winks at how Adam and I first crossed paths.

It's my first book as Carlie Foxx, but the crowd here knows me better as Zoey Cummings, the steamy romance writer.

The big reveal was a gamble—like playing poker with your grandma and she's surprisingly good at bluffing. *True story.*

A fan, clutching her new book, beams at me. "I couldn't believe it when Zoey Cummings announced she's actually Carlie Foxx! And you're hilarious! This book had me laughing *and* swooning. I don't know how you do it."

I chuckle, signing her book. "Thanks. I thought it was time to show the world that I can write about more than just steamy scenes—though there's plenty of that, too. Just with a side of laughter."

After the last book is signed, my friends from the Dirty B's converge around me.

Tasia, with her usual cool composure, gives me a firm nod. "You've outdone yourself, Carlie. *One Night Stand-Off* is brilliant. Just look at how many people want to get a copy. It's incredible."

I beam back at her. "Hopefully, it's helped pull a few more people into Dirty Books, too."

"Oh, it definitely has," Tasia says with a chuckle.

Lily, ever the enthusiast, wraps me in a bear hug. "I knew you had it in you. It's like you've found your *true* voice."

Vivian chimes in, her eyes sparkling with mischief. "Speaking of voices, did anyone hear Quinn talking with the cute guy in the corner? I think there just might be a love connection happening over there." She wiggles her eyes suggestively.

Lily bends closer. "Don't tell Quinn, but London had a little something to do with that connection."

My eyes widen and I clap my hands. "Oh, that's so exciting. Quinn deserves some awesomeness in his life."

"That he does," Lily nods in agreement. "And lots of mind-blowing sex, too."

We all burst into laughter, the kind that comes from years of shared secrets and mishaps.

As we're laughing and chatting, I notice Vivian's gaze drifting over to Anna, who's discreetly—or maybe *not* so discreetly—peeking at her phone. I mean, it's not entirely unlike her, but the flush of her cheeks is.

"Anna, you're missing all the fun here," I tease, but

Anna just hums noncommittally, her eyes still fixed on her screen.

Vivian leans closer to Anna, peeking over her shoulder. "Is that a Joel Price video you're watching? I thought you hated that guy," she says, a teasing lilt in her voice.

Anna's cheeks turn a shade pinker as she quickly locks her phone.

"Yeah, he's an ass," she mumbles, but the hint of a smile on her lips tells a different story.

Lily quirks an eyebrow and exchanges a knowing glance with me.

Anna rolls her eyes, trying to deflect with her usual nonchalance. "Anyway, Carlie, your book is going to be a massive hit. You're a natural at romcom."

"Thanks, Anna. That means a lot." I laugh, letting the topic of Anna and her love-hate relationship with Joel slide for now.

Adam watches us with an affectionate smile from a few bookshelves over, his eyes meeting mine with that familiar warmth that still makes my heart flutter.

There are some days when I can't even fathom how lucky I am.

A couple of stragglers come up to my table wanting signatures. So, I spend a few minutes with each, talking about books and my process as an author.

As the bookstore clears out, Adam wraps an arm around my waist, his eyes shining with love and pride. "You ready to head out, Mrs. Foxx?"

I nod, feeling a rush of happiness. "Absolutely, Mr. Foxx. Thank you for being here."

"Of course, I'll be here. Supporting my sexy author wife is my number one priority," he says, his voice lowering into a seductive whisper.

I turn a knowing look toward him. "Number one priority, huh?"

A catlike grin creeps across his handsome face. "Okay, maybe my number *two* priority."

A shiver runs down my spine at the promise those words carry because I know exactly what he thinks his number one priority is.

And I can't wait to test out that theory later tonight.

I start packing up my things, sliding the leftover copies of *"One Night Stand-Off"* into a box. The bookstore, now quiet and calm, feels like the aftermath of a wonderful storm.

I glance over at Adam, who's already stacking chairs, his sleeves rolled up, revealing those sexy forearms that I just can't seem to get enough of.

"So, anyone up for round two at Adam's event?" I ask, turning to the Dirty B's. "There's a Chamber of Commerce thing at Foxx Fitness tonight. Should be fun, and you'll get to see Adam in his element."

Tasia raises an eyebrow. "A gym event? Sounds ... *energetic.*"

Lily claps her hands together. "I'm totally in. It's always a blast to see Adam showing off his gym. Plus, I've been meaning to check out the new yoga classes." She nudges me with her shoulder and I know she's insinuating the partner yoga Adam added to the programs as a reminder of our beginning.

Vivian nods enthusiastically. "Count me in. Maybe I'll find my next gym crush there," she says with a wink.

"Things still not great with Tyler?" I ask, folding the lid to the box over. She's been through four guys since I've known her and it looks like a fifth is likely.

She shrugs noncommittally.

I turn to Anna, who's just pocketed her phone. "How about you, Anna? Fancy some gym time?"

She hesitates for a moment, then quirks an eyebrow. "Do I look like someone who frequents gyms?"

"More like someone who points and laughs when someone hurts themselves," Vivian quips.

We all blink at Vivian.

I mean, she's not wrong.

I clear my throat. "Great, it's settled then," I say, excitement bubbling within me. "Let's head over to Foxx Fitness and show the Chamber of Commerce how the Dirty B's do it. Quinn, are you in?"

"Hmmm, what's that hon?" Quinn says from the middle of the store.

"Coming with us to celebrate Foxx Fitness's Chamber After Hours event?" I repeat.

He glances at the man standing next to him. He's taller than Quinn but built like an athlete. His dark hair and chiseled jaw are the works of any romance novel, if you ask me.

"I mean, maybe?" Quinn finally calls back.

"Well, I'm excited," Lily says, taking out her phone. "London says he's already there. I can't wait to have a look around."

Adam walks over, his smile wide and welcoming. "It's going to be a great night. And who knows, maybe you'll all end up joining a class or two."

Half of the group groans and the other half nods in enthusiastic agreement.

Over the past year, they've seen how much I've changed under Adam's care. Between his workout routines at the gym ... and his workout routines at home ... it's no wonder I've toned down to nearly my goal weight.

Tasia locks up and we all leave Dirty Books. The cool evening air is a refreshing change from the warmth of the bookstore. The walk to Foxx Fitness is short but filled with laughter and playful banter, the kind of camaraderie that comes from shared experiences and genuine affection.

As we approach Adam's new gym, the buzz of conversation and music reaches us. The lights inside glow invitingly, and I feel a surge of pride for my husband.

He's turned his dream into a reality, and it's thriving.

Just like I always knew it would.

As we walk into the building, the atmosphere is electric, buzzing with the energy of a packed house. The state-of-the-art facility gleams under the bright lights, and I can't help but feel a swell of pride in my chest as I look around. The gym is more than just a collection of equipment—it's a vibrant community hub. A place where fitness, fun, and motivation meld seamlessly.

And it's all thanks to the man at my side.

Adam takes the center stage, his voice booming over

the crowd. "Welcome, everyone, to Foxx Fitness! For those of you who are new here, let's set something straight right off the bat. We're not just a gym—we're a family. This is a place to embrace your fitness journey, absolutely. But we want you to also have fun, and find encouragement every step of the way."

His passion is infectious, and I watch as he captivates the audience, pointing out the various sections of the gym.

"We've got everything from high-intensity interval training to yoga classes designed to challenge and inspire you. And yes," he adds with a wink in my direction, "even partner yoga."

I grin back at him, my heart warming with the memory.

The Dirty B's disperse to explore the various spaces. Lily grabs hold of London's hand and heads straight for the yoga studio, her eyes lighting up at the sight of the tranquil, welcoming space.

Vivian, ever the flirt, eyes a group of toned trainers with a mischievous grin on her face.

Tasia, standing beside me, nods appreciatively. "He's done an incredible job here. Even I have to admit, it's kind of awesome."

I smile, watching Adam mingle and chat with guests. "He's found his calling, just like I found mine."

Quinn walks up, nodding towards a corner where a group is gathered around a high-tech treadmill. "Looks like the latest in fitness tech over there. Adam really went all out."

"Absolutely," I agree. "He wanted Foxx Fitness to be cutting-edge—but also a place where everyone, regardless of their fitness level, feels at home."

"Well, I think he's definitely accomplished that," Quinn says, his gaze drifting over to the guy he was talking with at Dirty Books.

I nudge him with my hip. "So ... What do you think of the guy?"

Quinn's grin broadens, but he shrugs. "We'll see. He's hot, though."

"That he is," I nod with a laugh.

As the evening progresses, the sense of community becomes more and more palpable. People are laughing, trying out equipment, and signing up for classes. The staff, enthusiastic and knowledgeable, are on hand to offer even more guidance and support.

Later, as the crowd begins to thin, Adam finds me, his eyes alight with excitement and a hint of exhaustion. "How'd I do?" he asks, wrapping his arms around me.

"You were amazing," I reply, standing on my tiptoes to plant a kiss on his cheek. "This place is amazing. You're going to change so many lives here."

He grins, pulling me close. "Only because I have you by my side. You inspire me every day, Carlie."

I reach up onto my toes and kiss his lips. "You're *my* inspiration."

"Do I need to bust out some Bette Midler or are you two going to stop with the cuteness overload," my grandmother says, coming up behind me.

I nearly let out a squeal of surprise.

She just snickers under her breath. "What? Didn't expect to find me here?"

"Not entirely, no," I admit, shaking my head.

"Well, even us old coots need to find a place to bend and snap, if you know what I mean." She winks at me, clearly happy she got to use the new term I taught her out in the wild.

"Yeah, but I think you mean snap, crackle, and pop," I fire back.

Adam covers up his laugh with the back of his hand. He's had to deal with me and Grandma for months now —he knows the game.

"Oh, good one, dearie. Good one," she says with pride in her eyes.

I catch Anna's eye and give her a knowing smile. She just shakes her head, but I can see a newfound lightness in her demeanor, a subtle change that speaks volumes.

Adam wraps his arms around me from behind, whispering, "Thank you for being here and for supporting me."

I lean back into him, feeling utterly content. "Always, Adam. Just like you're always there for me."

When the event comes to an end and it's time to head home, the Dirty B's, Adam, and I are the last to leave.

We step outside together, the night wrapping us in a serene embrace. I think about our friends, each on their own unique journey, and feel a wave of affection for them all.

And as Adam and I say our goodbyes and start walking home, hand in hand, I know that this is just the beginning of many more adventures to come. Adventures filled with love, laughter, and a little bit of gym sweat.

As we walk, I can't help but reflect on the journey that brought me here.

From Zoey Cummings to Carlie Foxx. From steamy romance to laugh-out-loud romcoms ... it's been quite the ride. And through it all, I've learned the most important lesson—embracing who you are is the true key to happiness.

"Dirty books, dirty workouts, it's all about getting a little dirty and a lot happy, right?" I say, nudging Adam playfully.

Adam laughs, his eyes twinkling under the starlit sky. "Exactly."

As we approach our home, the warm light from the windows spills out onto the street, inviting and comforting.

Inside, I know we'll find our own little slice of perfection, a world where love reigns supreme, and every day is an adventure. With Adam by my side, I'm ready for whatever comes next, ready to write the next chapter of our story.

And as we open the door, stepping into the warmth of our home, I smile to myself. The journey of Carlie Foxx, the romcom writer, and Carlie Foxx, the woman madly in love with her husband, is just getting started.

And I can't wait to see where it takes us.

Loving the One Night Stand Club? YAY!

Then don't miss out on Anna's upcoming book,
Dirty Developments!

It's all enemies-to-lovers, with tons of snarkastic goodness!

Get it now!

See ya there, Dirty B!

SHE CODED WALLS AROUND HER HEART— HE'S ABOUT TO HACK EVERY ONE.

Anna Chang has three rules: trust no one, never skip a coding sprint, and absolutely, under no circumstances, fall for your brother's best friend. Especially when that best friend is Joel Price—charismatic rockstar, smug heartbreaker, and the guy who under no circumstances can be trusted.

Now he's back. And worse? He's sleeping in her guest room.

With forced proximity, a family event from hell, and the entire Dirty B's book club egging them on, Anna's perfectly curated life is about to be debugged in the messiest, steamiest way possible.

Enemies-to-lovers? Check.

Brother's best friend? Unfortunately.

Still wants to kiss him? Absolutely not... probably.

Welcome to *Dirty Developments*—where the only thing more dangerous than catching feelings is letting them crash your firewall.

Available exclusively on my store October 13th, 2025!

Want to snag it elsewhere?

Hang tight for the February 9th, 2026 worldwide launch!

Carissa Knight writes steamy, emotional romcoms where second chances get messy, feelings get avoided (until they don't), and unresolved tension simmers for pages. Her books are built on tropes she loves deeply—especially second chances, forced proximity, and the occasional enemies-to-lovers situation that gets *way too personal*.

Though her romcom debut is recent, Carissa's no newbie to storytelling. Writing since 2010 as **Carissa Andrews**, she's an **international bestselling** and **award-winning author** of paranormal and urban fantasy. Now, under her romcom pen name, she's leaning into the chaos of love, heartbreak, and hot dumbasses who absolutely *do not* have their lives together.

Based in Minnesota, she writes for the readers who crave big emotions, found family, and characters who take way too long to admit they're in love.

Learn more at: romcomcarissa.com

 patreon.com/carissaknight

tiktok.com/@romcom_carissa

9 781953 304209